VAMPIRE HUNTER D

Other Vampire Hunter D books published by
Dark Horse Books and Digital Manga Publishing

VAMPIRE HUNTER D

VOLUME 8
MYSTERIOUS JOURNEY TO THE NORTH SEA
PART TWO

Written by

HIDEYUKI KIKUCHI

Illustrations by

YOSHITAKA AMANO

English translation by

KEVIN LEAHY

Dark Horse Books®
Milwaukie   Los Angeles

VAMPIRE HUNTER D 8:
MYSTERIOUS JOURNEY TO THE NORTH SEA PART TWO

Cover art by Yoshitaka Amano

English translation by Kevin Leahy

Book design by Heidi Fainza

Published by
Dark Horse Books
a division of Dark Horse Comics
10956 SE Main Street
Milwaukie, OR 97222
darkhorse.com

Digital Manga Publishing
1487 West 178th Street, Suite 300
Gardena, CA 90248
dmpbooks.com

Library of Congress Cataloging-in-Publication Data

Kikuchi, Hideyuki, 1949-
  [Hokkai mako. English]
  Mysterious journey to the North sea / written by Hideyuki Kikuchi ; illustrated by Yoshitaka Amano ; English translation by Kevin Leahy.
    p. cm. -- (Vampire Hunter D; v. 7)
  "Originally published in Japan in 1988 by Asahi Sonoroma Co."--Vol. 1, t.p. verso.
  ISBN-13: 978-1-59582-107-2 (v. 1)
  ISBN-10: 1-59582-107-4 (v. 1)
  I. Amano, Yoshitaka. II. Leahy, Kevin. III. Title.
  PL832.I37H6513 2007
  895.6'36--dc22
                        2006102529

ISBN-10: 1-59582-108-2
ISBN-13: 978-1-59582-108-9

First Dark Horse Books Edition: August 2007
10 9 8 7 6 5 4 3 2 1
Printed in the United States of America

VAMPIRE HUNTER D

Summer at Last

I

S and shot up, whipped up by something swinging around at an awful speed. Grains of it scattered in all directions like smoke. There were two massive explosions, and then a second later a human form could be seen on the shore where the black waves broke. It was Gyohki. Standing erect only briefly, he then bent his right knee. Just as he was about to hit the sand, he barely managed to catch himself. A streak of white ran right through his thigh—a needle of unfinished wood.

"You're unbelievable . . . ," Gyohki groaned. Dropping his eyes to his gory thigh, he then turned a look of both admiration and hatred toward the beautiful darkness before him. The darkness that harbored D.

D was just getting up, too. His longsword stretched elegantly from his right hand, as he'd just picked it up from where it'd fallen in the sand. It hadn't actually *fallen*—he'd intentionally dropped it. Just before Gyohki's explosive kick, with true split-second timing, he'd let go of his sword. Rather than getting Gyohki to drop off his blade, he'd dropped him along with his longsword. In order for his opponent to execute that lethal kick to its full efficacy, he needed to have perfect speed and power and to be well-balanced, and he'd been thrown off more than enough for D to block the kick aimed at his temple with his right elbow. Before Gyohki could connect with a second kick, D timed it so as to catch his foe's leg and jam a rough wooden needle deep into his attacker's thigh with his left hand.

Seeing the gorgeous silhouette leisurely closing in on him, the limping Gyohki leapt back. A second later he was waist-deep in the water.

"'He who fights and runs away . . .' It's a dated adage, but while there's life there's still hope. I believe I'll call it a day," he said in a tone free from regret. Preparing to dive, Gyohki then suddenly turned his eyes to where D stood at the shore. "You wanted to know who made me, didn't you? Baron Meinster gave me life, but I was perfected by *the other one*."

His body sank straight into the water. Soon splashing could be heard far in the distance, but that was the end of it. He must've swum out into the sea at a depth of seven thousand feet.

Perhaps certain that his foe was gone for good, D returned his longsword to its sheath and walked over toward Su-In. The circle of light from the illumination cord made her location clear in this murk—she was a bit further in than where he'd left her. Though he'd told her to stay there, it would've been hard to imagine a courageous character like Su-In just standing there awaiting her fate. Still, it was strange. If she were to go anywhere else, she most certainly should've gone to check on D, on whom her life depended. But she seemed to have done exactly the reverse and gone in the opposite direction.

D's pace quickened.

Su-In was standing in front of a huge tank they hadn't seen before. Unlike the others, this one was filled with a milky fluid, and it had but a single occupant: a young man who was completely naked. Black and blue marks could be seen on the side that faced her. At a glance it was apparent these weren't wounds that'd been intentionally inflicted on him, but rather had come about through some sudden event. The left side of his forehead was smashed open horribly, leaving a gaping wound you could see through if you looked hard enough. It was almost miraculous that his face had been so perfectly preserved, appearing just as youthful now as it had in life. His left shoulder was also twisted into a strange position—probably the result of a broken bone. No doubt these wounds were all the result of a fall from a considerable height. Judging by his face, he was a young villager. But who would've sealed up his remains more than a thousand years ago?

Not seeming to realize that D was watching her, Su-In kept her gaze trained on the pale, hazy figure. Before long, she muttered, "You fell, didn't you." The way she said the words, they seemed to simply spring into being without ever passing through her thought processes. "You fell—fell at the cape . . . stabbed . . . through the chest . . ."

D looked at the young man's chest. There was no wound there. Su-In had been talking about someone else.

"Let's go home," D told her.

They had more than enough time until her grandfather's funeral. But considering the way they'd come down, the thought of going back up made a casual term like "trip" seem horribly inadequate. Su-In's body trembled. But before she even had time to think about it, her flesh broke free of her will and she leaned back in D's arms.

Quickly taking the illumination cord, D looked at Su-In's blanched countenance, and then shifted his eyes to the contents of the tank. A corpse floating in a milky liquid and a fisherman's daughter—perhaps the young man's cold eyes could see the thread that joined these two very different lives. But that thread was soon frayed by a tiny groan.

Opening her eyes in the Hunter's powerful arms, Su-In realized the situation she was in and hurriedly tried to stand up. The hue in her eyes as she turned them away from D was ultimately conveyed by the pink that tinged her full cheeks.

"Trying to take advantage of me in a place like this—you should be ashamed!" she said, pushing D's hands away with much more force than was necessary. When she got to her feet again, she was already as steady as a rock. "If we're leaving, what are you gonna do about this place?" she asked as she looked around them. "This was Meinster's research lab, right? If you plan on trashing it, I'll help."

"There are probably traps."

"You've got a point there," the woman conceded.

"It's going to take a while to climb back out. Shall we go?"

"Are you sure it'll be okay?" Su-In asked nervously as she looked up into the darkness above.

Twenty minutes later, as the two of them were leaving the ruins of Meinster's castle, Su-In's gaze had become one of admiration as she stared at D.

After another hour, the pair was greeted by an unexpected sight as they returned home: more than twenty children. As was usual on the Frontier, their height and age, hair color and skin color ran the gamut, but when they saw Su-In and raced over to her, all of their faces glowed with the same expectation. Amid the cries of "Su-In! Su-In!" were some of "teacher," and this prompted D to stare at the sunburnt woman.

"Teacher—when is it?"

"When's school starting?"

Seeming perplexed by the youthful cries, Su-In knit her brow. "That's a good question. I'm sorry, but I don't know if I can do it this year."

Disappointment broke over the children like a wave.

"You see, my grandfather just died, and Wu-Lin's not around either," Su-In said, desperately trying to keep the gloom from her voice.

As the children continued to protest, the shouts of a man and woman who were obviously somebody's parents flew from the main house, saying, "Come on, now! What are you doing pestering Su-In at an awful time like this?" and, "We've got a funeral today!"

Before these rebukes, the children scattered like baby spiders.

Turning to face D, Su-In asked, "You think that's funny?" There was a bit of a challenge to her voice. Not receiving an answer, she continued, "During the summer, I run a school when I'm not out fishing. The kids around here want to know anything and everything. After all, at their age they've never seen anything but the gray sea and our week-long summer."

"Where's the schoolhouse?" asked the Hunter.

"Well, up until last year, we just pitched a tent in our backyard. But this year, they're gonna build a proper schoolhouse. As we rode along the coast, you saw the festival tower, right? It's right next to that. Once that's done, we'll be able to have school even in winter, and we've sent to the Capital for a teacher. The carpenters are working overtime to get it ready by the first day of summer. Looks like they're just gonna make it."

"And is the teacher coming?"

Shifting her eyes to the sea, Su-In replied, "Actually, Wu-Lin was supposed to talk to someone in Cronenberg about that."

Off in the distance, they could hear a child shouting, "Teacher!"

Saying that she had to go get ready, Su-In adjusted her grip on the spear gun and walked off toward the house.

After going in first, D watched the people busily scurrying around the house. "Is this everyone?" he asked.

"Yeah."

Ignoring the gazes of admiration and rapture that fell on him, D went back outside. He told Su-In, who stood by the door, "There's no one dangerous in there."

Lowering her voice, his employer said, "Of course not. They're all folks from the neighborhood. I'm begging you, don't start talking flaky."

"The puppets on the ferry could probably just as easily be disguised as your neighbors."

Tensing at D's words, Su-In said, "I know. We can't let our guard down, right?"

"You should help get ready for the funeral."

"I'm gonna do just that. I leave the rest up to you." With a trusting glance to that inhumanly handsome face, Su-In then went inside.

D circled around to the backyard. The grandfather's remains were going to be buried in one corner—Su-In had stated that would've made her grandfather a lot happier than being interred in the communal cemetery.

Out in the gauzy light of day, suddenly a thin melody and voices joined in song were heard from the verandah out back. The children from earlier were all gathered around a boy of about ten, who was playing a wooden flute.

To you, whom summer brought here,
I give a modest token of thanks.
The white flowers that blossom in the ice freeze all who touch them.
Until the waltz of summer ends,
You are one of us.
And when you go we'll pray for you,
O departing light of summer!

D stood in the languid daylight listening to the earnest, if somewhat off-key, voices of the singers. The shadow cast at his feet was beautiful, but fainter than anyone else's. Off in the distance, the crash of waves could be heard.

And just as it had begun, the singing halted without warning. The boy in the center of the group fiddled with the flute, a troubled look on his face. Putting it to his lips, he inflated his cheeks, but to no effect. Apparently either it was clogged or had a leak of some sort. All around him, the other children asked what was wrong and why it wouldn't play. They were all heartbroken—they'd been sincerely interested in singing. If they hadn't, they'd have long since gone and found something else to amuse themselves.

Their flutist looked ready to cry. His eyes scanned the surrounding area in search of help, coming to rest on the handsome figure. There was no telling just how he could've looked to a ten-year-old psyche. Pushing his way through the children packed around him, the boy ran over to D. Stopping three feet shy of the Hunter, he had both fear and expectation on his face as he looked up reverently.

Not saying a word, D looked down at the innocent face of the dark boy who didn't come up too far past his own waist. The young man's body sank slowly. Down to the same height as the boy.

"What's wrong?" the Vampire Hunter asked.

A tiny hand and the wooden flute it held were thrust out before his eyes.

Powerful yet slender fingers closed on the piece of wood as the Hunter took it from the boy. There were three finger holes, but a threadlike crack ran between the last two. Even patching it wouldn't be enough to get back the original tone of the instrument.

Looking around on the ground at his feet, D then quickly pulled a few wooden needles from the inside of his coat—two of them. Though they were less than an eighth of an inch thick, they were over eight inches long. The thumb of the hand that held the needle reached up for the end of it, and a well-shaped nail protruded ever so slightly from the end of the Hunter's finger. That nail moved in a tiny arc, and two inches of the needle fell to the ground, leaving a perfectly round cut on the end.

The boy's eyes went as wide as if he'd just watched a magic trick.

Adjusting his grip on the needle and taking off the opposite end as well, D then took the other needle and placed its point against one of the round cross-sections. Though he didn't seem to put any force behind it, the new needle slipped into the former needle without any resistance.

There were sounds of surprise all around him. At some point, the children from the verandah had crowded around the Hunter and the boy.

As far as the children could see, the two needles were of equal thickness. And yet the one that'd been pierced hadn't split or broken, and the one doing the piercing slid into the other without hesitation and came out the other side. As the tip came out the other end to the exact same length as the part he'd first sliced off, D pulled the two pieces of wood apart. Then he brought his right hand over to the needle he held in his left. The children caught the glint of a long, thin dagger there, which bore three finger holes with the blade in less than two seconds. Each hole was perfectly round.

Blowing into it once to get the sawdust out of it, D then put the flute to his lips. His cheeks indented ever so slightly, and a thin, mellifluous sound coursed from the instrument.

The multitude of tiny faces changed from looks of amazement to smiles.

Handing the new flute to the boy before him without a word, D stood back up. His eyes shifted to the verandah.

A holy man stood there. Ban'gyoh. Beaming all the while, he tapped at his freshly shaven head as he walked over. Clasping both hands behind his back, he said, "I declare, when a priest isn't reading his prayers, he's got nothing but time on his hands. I've been playing with the children since this morning. And what have you been doing? From what I saw earlier from the kitchen window, it seems you and Ms. Su-In came back on a boat . . . but you should take care. When a man and a woman recklessly let nature take its course, therein lies the way to lust and temptation."

Muttering a religious incantation in a pleasing tone, Ban'gyoh gazed at D reproachfully. But his heavily wrinkled face broke into a smile as he said, "Though from what it's been my pleasure to see, you have some fine points, too. Usually one as handsome as yourself is cold not only to women, but to everyone aside from himself.

Though your veins may be ice, the blood flowing through them seems to have become a bit redder. I have a suggestion for you. Now, I don't know if you're a bodyguard or a warrior or what, but why not abandon the way of the sword for good and look after the children here?" The holy man then laughed, "Oh, I'm just joking with you!"

As soon as he finished speaking, a lovely melody arose from around his feet. The boy had just blown into the flute. Though Ban'gyoh listened to it with his eyes shut, he soon gave a pensive nod. "I hate to say it, but the tone isn't very even," the priest mused. "Child, try playing this."

The young boy seemed perplexed by what the holy man then held under his nose. It was another wooden flute with tiny holes. Roughly two inches shorter than the one D had fashioned, it was also ten times as thick.

"No matter how skillfully constructed the flute may be, there are certain limitations in the instrument itself," said Ban'gyoh. "That one's a bit too tough for a child's throat and lungs. Come now, give it a try."

The child was very forthcoming. Pressing D's flute back against the Hunter's chest, he promptly took the new handiwork from Ban'gyoh and brought it to his mouth. The sound that filled the air was deeper and more composed than that from D's.

Ban'gyoh laughed proudly—behavior that hardly seemed fitting for a holy man.

Saying nothing, D stared at the flute in his hand, and then gazed at the one the boy had taken and the face of the holy man.

"Hmm. This simply won't do, sir," Ban'gyoh said, backing away with one hand raised. "It's not good to work so hard to cover for one's shortcomings with mere forcefulness. A good-looking man is not the be-all and end-all, you see. Here's a proposition for you—if you want children to favor you over some foolish old priest, you should hang up your sword and live here in their village for the next five years. I bet you'd make the finest mayor they've ever seen!"

Chuckling to himself, Ban'gyoh then walked back to the house. The children had retreated to the verandah.

Only D and the flute were left out in the stark light.

"For some reason or other, that priest's got it in for you," a hoarse voice grumbled from around his left hand as it hung by his side. "But for such an odd duck, he sure says some interesting things. So, how about it? Why don't you settle down here and become head fisherman or something? I'm sure you could get some animal protein out of that huge whale," the voice chortled. After a short pause, he added, "Hey, aren't you gonna tell me to shut up?"

D looked down at his left hand. The oddest expression lingered around his lips. "Head fisherman, eh? That might not be too bad," said the Hunter.

"Wait just a second," shot back a voice tinged with distress. "You wouldn't really . . ." The palm of the left hand was upturned, looking up at D. But soon, the voice let out a sigh—one of relief. "That's a load off my mind. I wouldn't care if you quit here. But wherever you go always ends up being the valley of the shadow of death. You'll keep traveling."

D said nothing.

As if to cut through the roar of the sea, the sound of a child's flute rang out.

II

It was early in the afternoon that the neighbors began to head home. As Su-In stood by the door thanking them, D watched her from the garden. The conversations of a number of the returning guests reached his ears. Dhampirs were said to have hearing three times as good as humans at night and twice as good by day, but apparently this young man's abilities far surpassed even those estimates.

Su-In's gonna be in for a rough time of it.

I wonder what the story is with Wu-Lin?

I hear she went to town, but what awful timing! She'd best hurry back, or Su-In's gonna have a hard time bearing up.

Yeah, they counted on their grandfather an awful lot. He might've had a bum leg, but he sure could do the hypnotism.

You can say that again. When my boy got attacked by a man-eating shark and the shock of it left him bedridden, you wouldn't believe my surprise when he made that child forget all about it in just five minutes.

Su-In's got some pretty mean tricks herself, although there's nothing to use them on out on the open sea.

That's okay. She does all right for herself. And it's downright scary how she throws a harpoon.

You know, I kinda get the feeling Wu-Lin's not coming back.

The other neighbor said nothing.

I wonder if Su-In hasn't really been left alone after all. My sister was like that when her husband and son went down with their ship. It was exactly the same. Not the tone of her voice or the look in her eye, but the whole atmosphere around her.

"What are you looking so down in the mouth about?" asked a cheery voice that was drawing closer.

As her grandfather's coffin was buried, Su-In hadn't showed any sign of being ready to burst into tears. The last shovelful of earth had covered him an hour ago. She'd had more than enough time to think about how she was going to make ends meet from tomorrow on.

"Your work should be done here until evening. I'm heading out to sea," Su-In said, gazing toward the surf with a faraway look in her eyes. The stern expression she wore was the same one she'd had that morning as she was washing her boat.

"You're going out now?"

"Summer's almost here," she replied. "I've got to make some money while I can."

"I'll go, too."

Turning a look of surprise toward his gorgeous face, Su-In said, "But you can't even . . ."

It was common knowledge that those descending from Noble blood would avoid running water. There were villages on the Frontier where the hundreds of houses were all surrounded by individual ditches. While it was understood at present that in order for such ditches to be effective they had to be wide and deep enough to drown an ordinary person, there was still no shortage of people who wasted their energy digging them around their house and waiting for rainy days. Out on the sea, the width and depth conditions would be more than met. However, for a dhampir like D—

"I won't have you taking any chances. I don't care how tough my enemies are, they'd never go after me out on the sea."

"One of them rode off into the sky on a cloud," D reminded her.

"Yeah, but . . ."

"I won't get in your way."

Locking her lips together tightly, Su-In glared at D and snorted out her nose. "Okay. But only if you stay to one side and don't do anything."

The wind at sea sliced at their cheeks. As they weathered gales that made it seem inconceivable that summer would arrive in two short days, Su-In's powerboat skipped nimbly across the waves. The sea ahead of them was divided into three distinct sections. Off to the left, a distant fleet of large motorboats gingerly moved in formation. They were catching migratory fish in the black nets that dangled in the water from the stern of the lead vessel. Directly ahead of them and a few miles away, a gigantic form was surrounded by a pack of small powerboats manned by skilled harpooners—and the focus of their massed assault must've been a tidal whale. The surface of the water was tinged with a light pink.

The prow turned to starboard.

"We're cutting in, so it could get a little rough. Be careful you don't fall overboard," Su-In said, her voice full of excitement.

Far ahead of the boat's prow floated a belt of white—a row of ice chunks. As the small boat moved ahead of them, it maneuvered more nimbly than any of the other vessels.

"Giant killer whales are drawn by the whale's blood. Besides the meat on them, their teeth, bones, and innards are all valuable—of course, they might come at the price of your life. Hey, don't tell me you wanna leave already," she joked. Su-In had a lot of pluck—a harsh environment like this wouldn't necessarily suit everyone. There were some women in Florence who would live their whole lives without ever going out to sea, but you could say Su-In was a fierce exception to the rule. This twenty-year-old woman had chosen the most rigorous of battlefields.

The boat rocked, and vermilion stained the water. The battle that'd already been joined was reaching its peak. The water was rough in this part of the sea, where almost a dozen power boats were moving around. The heads and tails of plump game fish came in and out of view as they streaked through the water and slammed against the ships' weak hulls.

"Watch yourself. These bastards can jump over fifteen feet."

Cutting the boat's engine as the vessel rocked from the waves striking it broadside, Su-In released a latch on the deck, scooped up five harpoons, and brought them to the starboard gunwale. Tipped with steel, each of the missiles was seven feet long and weighed over ten pounds. It must've been difficult just to hold onto them on the rocking boat. The rough trousers that covered Su-In from the waist down were so taut there wasn't a single wrinkle in them.

After setting four of the harpoons down, Su-In stood ready with the fifth. Hauling back with all her might with her right arm, she used her left hand to support the tip and take aim.

Someone somewhere shouted out her name, the cry echoing on for ages.

A black shape was approaching on the water's surface—a number of harpoons jutted from its top half. When the short, thick head closed to within six or seven feet of Su-In, her upper body leaned back. The shirt she was stuffed into bulged clearly with the shape of her biceps and the muscles on her back. Bracing herself absolutely perfectly, Su-In let the harpoon fly.

The steely missile lanced into the sea with such force you'd swear you could hear it sink into flesh, and an instant later the black shape that was approaching twisted wildly. Submerging its impaled head in the sea, it thrashed the water violently with its tail and dorsal fin. Ignoring the massive creature entering its death throes, Su-In got ready with a second harpoon.

"Not too bad, eh?" she called back over her shoulder to D as she shook her head.

The waves kissed her with spray.

"The crease where the head meets the torso is where you make the kill shot. Even most men can't hit it. Here comes another!"

Su-In's scream and the way she collapsed made it clear that her last remark hadn't been directed at the same beast that rammed them a second later. The woman barely managed to pull back her left arm—which dangled out over the gunwale—and use it to prop herself up as a massive black form made a vertical leap just in front of her.

It was certainly huge. And it just kept stretching longer and longer. The glistening wet belly that faced her was the only white thing on it. The tail was forked, and the body must've measured ten feet long and weighed at least sixteen hundred pounds. There was a malicious glint in the tiny eyes to either side of its compact head, and then a long, straight gash opened. Its mouth. It was the color of flames. In midair, the massive creature twisted into an inverted V shape. The turn had been intentional—it was coming back down headfirst.

Su-In was right under it—there wasn't enough time for her to change her position. And yet she managed to look up. Colored by fear and hopelessness, her eyes then reflected a streak of silver that slashed through the mouth ready to close down on her body.

A powerful tug on her collar hauled her out of the way as the massive form crashed down right in front of her, rocking the hull of the boat.

Realizing as she clung to the Hunter's powerful chest that the giant killer whale's head had been severed from its torso precisely along the line she'd described, Su-In got goose bumps. At the core of her being, she ached with a spark that was both feverishly hot and icy cold. On the deck a short distance from her, a sound like steel on steel rose from the head of a beast so thick she'd be lucky to get her arms around it. It was the sound of jagged teeth gnashing. She thought that must be the reason she felt the way she did.

"I suppose I acted out of place," D said, although he didn't sound all that apologetic.

"No," Su-In said, shaking her head from side to side. It surprised her that she could even say that much.

"Will one be enough?" D asked. His tone was so calm that she had to wonder where he stored all of his composure.

"Don't be ridiculous. We'll keep taking them till they're all gone." A certain will that even she herself didn't understand had been ignited, and Su-In pulled away from D.

"Hey there!" shouted a familiar voice that cut through the heavy seas.

While it was understandable that Su-In turned, the fact that D followed her example was highly unusual.

On the prow of the powerboat that ran in parallel to them about forty feet off their port bow, Dwight stood ready with a harpoon in one hand. "Imagine meeting you out here, stud," he called out. "I couldn't have asked for a better setting. I say we finish our duel from yesterday."

Turning to D, Su-In said, "What's he talking about?" She hadn't been informed of the altercation between him and Dwight.

"I owe him," D replied.

Puzzled, Su-In shifted her gaze back and forth between the two men.

"Like I told you before, I'm a fisherman. And out here on the sea, we'll do things my way. You don't have a problem with that, do you?" Dwight said, his right hand around a gleaming harpoon that was longer than Su-In's, and almost twice as thick.

From the bridge of the other boat, a young man who probably worked for Dwight was comparing him to D.

D nodded ever so slightly.

"Good enough. We'll each get one throw now. Whoever lands the bigger prize wins. So, give it your best shot," Dwight said, breaking into a grin. "Now, if you lose—well, then you hightail it out of Su-In's house. How does that strike you?"

In lieu of a reply, D took the harpoon from Su-In's hand.

"Hey, wait just a minute! Don't do anything stupid," Su-In angrily shouted at Dwight as she tried to wrest the harpoon from the Hunter. "I don't know what happened between you two, but this guy's working for me and I can't have you doing anything to him."

"This doesn't concern you. It's between him and me—man to man. Stay out of it."

"You big idiot!" the woman shouted indignantly, ready to give him a piece of her mind. But just then there was a terrible impact on the side of the boat. Without time to leave them with a scream, Su-In toppled over into the water like a log.

"Uh-oh, that's not good!" Dwight shouted, his comment relating to the black shape closing on the woman from behind. Distress rising in his face, his great tree root of a right arm hauled back his harpoon, and then whirled in an arc as he grunted.

Searing through the air, the missile's aim was unerring. Stabbing into the behemoth through its vital point at a thirty-degree angle, the tip came out by the jaw. A geyser of fresh blood shot from the creature's neck as it twisted its body and sank into the sea.

Quickly grabbing a second harpoon, Dwight managed to wring out the words, "How do you like that, hotshot? You might be able to knock me out, but up against one of these monsters you're not good for—"

And then he stopped. He'd just noticed that Su-In's harpoon had vanished from D's right hand. Su-In was clinging to the muscular arm the Hunter had over the side. Behind her, a black mass bobbed to the surface. The harpoon stuck through its neck was clearly Dwight's—a very satisfying hit.

"You blew it, stud," he sneered with one hand to his mouth. "See, Su-In. There's more to a seafaring man than just looks. You need skill on the waves. And I—"

The fisherman's voice died out again. Beside the beast he'd taken, another shape bobbed to the surface. Dwight's eyes went wide—it was a pair of giant killer whales! Seeing that the harpoon that joined them at the neck was one of Su-In's, he couldn't believe his eyes. Even when the strongest of brutes threw a harpoon with all his might, one of these beasts was the most he could ever hope to pierce. The rest would be a matter of accuracy. How skilled could this man be to have not only nailed two at once, but to have taken them both through the vital spot!

An attack by a new foe rocked Dwight's boat wildly. As the fisherman's hands hit the deck he looked at D, who'd replaced Su-In at the helm. Staring at the Hunter's handsome profile as he made a run for shore, something dangerously close to a smile spread across Dwight's face little by little.

Just then, the young man at the wheel of his boat screamed, "Wh-what the hell is this?!"

"What is it?" Dwight asked as he turned around.

A trembling hand pointed to the surface of the sea.

"Huh?!" the fearless roughneck exclaimed, but it came as no surprise that his body stiffened with shock when he looked in that direction. There was no problem with the three beasts he and the Hunter had slain, but now black lumps were bobbing to the surface in a bloody swirl with such force it pushed the trio of carcasses away. The other boats might've taken notice of this, as some of them had surrounded the swirl as well.

"What the hell is it?"

"Is that meat?!" someone cried out.

At the very same time, Dwight had also realized that's what it was. "It's meat," he said. "Killer whale meat. Someone's down there ripping one to pieces. Chopping up a damned giant killer whale!"

Oblivious to the cries of the fishermen, chunks of meat continued rising to the surface, but before long that came to an end. Even after the men saw that the bobbing pieces that filled their field of view had edges so clean they looked like they'd been sliced with a knife, not one of them was willing to point that fact out to the others. In the hearts of these men who lived and died on the seas, a certain legend from the past reverberated darkly. They knew perfectly well that legend was tied to their future.

III

Just as the western horizon bloomed with the color of fresh blood, a woman climbed out of bed in the town's sole inn. The time she'd spent there and the way she'd spent it remained on her naked skin as a pale, rosy glow that took her seductive beauty to a new level of temptation. It was "Samon of Remembrances."

"Going?" a thick, drowsy voice inquired from right beside her. The body lying back under the sheets contrasted starkly with Samon's own in terms of color and burliness. Like Samon, he was mentally and physically relaxed, but if the need arose his right hand would shoot like lightning for the sword that rested by his pillow.

"You don't have any further need for me, do you?" Samon replied, her answer coming as she put on her underthings. "I've already told you everything I know. And I let you have whatever you wanted in bed, too. Don't embarrass me any further."

"That's funny," he said, his hand shooting up suddenly to grab the woman's hair and yank back on it mercilessly.

Leaving a cry of surprise hanging in the air as she fell on her back, the woman found her face covered by another that was graceful and good-looking. Groans and sighs were exchanged, and then a second later Glen pulled away like he'd been shot from a gun. A thin stream of blood dribbled from his somewhat thick lips, causing vermilion flowers to blossom on the white sheets. Not even bothering to wipe at the part that'd been bitten open, Glen licked the blood from his own lips.

In the meantime, Samon had climbed off the bed.

"You do the damnedest things, don't you? That's the first time a woman's ever wounded me. And my own woman, at that," the warrior said, not sounding at all angry.

Samon replied dryly, "I'm not your woman. And I never will be, no matter how many times you may bed me."

"Then what's the story here?"

"I owe you. And until I pay you back, you can have your way."

"Oh, and when do you intend to pay me back?" asked the warrior.

"When I feel like it."

"And how will you pay me back?"

"I'll be the one to decide that, as well," Samon replied. Having finished dressing, she headed for the door.

"Let me just make one thing clear," Glen said as he sat up in bed. Serene as his tone was, it still had enough force to stop Samon in her tracks. "You and your compatriots are free to team up and take him on if you like, but only after I'm through with him. I'll be the one to cut him down. And then you and your friends can take what you want. Otherwise . . ."

"Otherwise what?" Samon said, her eyes glittering. They shone with obvious hostility.

"I'll kill the lot of you before I take him. Even you."

"Even me?" said Samon, her lips curling in a faint smile. "And would you mind if I told my colleagues this?"

"Do what you like. I wouldn't mind fighting the Hunter at my leisure after shooing all the bothersome flies, either."

Samon opened the door. "Do you have anything else to say?" she asked.

"When you and your gang decide to take action against him, come to me first."

It was an extremely odd request, but Samon nodded. And then, as if deriding him, she said, "Why don't you just challenge him first?"

"I don't feel like doing that yet."

"Oh, scared, are you?" Samon laughed.

"Is that what you think?" Glen replied, his voice low.

"No. So far as I can see, you're a man without fear. Take care that it doesn't cost you your life."

"Is that supposed to be a warning? You can bring all your friends here if you like," Glen said, his powerful voice rebounding off the back of the now-closed door.

Leaving the inn, Samon headed for the entrance to the village. The stars twinkled above her—the night sky was crystal clear. Only her warrior training kept the breath she exhaled from coming out in a white cloud. When she came to the protective palisade, Samon stopped in her tracks. Casting her tempting gaze above her, she said, "Come on out!"

A colossal tree stood by the side of the road, and one of its massive branches hung right over her head. It didn't have a single leaf on it, but a giant cocoon hung above her. Out popped a head. Then the left hand reached smoothly from the casing. No right hand appeared. "Noticed me, did you?" the inverted "Indiscernible Twin" said to her.

"My, but aren't you spry. Egbert's still moaning from his injuries," said Samon. Like her gaze, her voice was an ice-cold needle.

"He got it in the chest, me in the hand—if I had to say which of us was worse off, it'd have to be him. It always pays to learn to disconnect your nerves as early as possible."

"You've been following me, haven't you?"

"Yep," Twin confessed easily. In the starlight, Samon's eyes could clearly make out the slender, boyish face. "I was curious what you were up to. You were going out a lot."

"Orders from Shin, I suppose?"

"My own personal interest, actually," Twin said, cackling like a bird. "This is the first time we've seen each other's faces, but you're quite a fine-looking woman. It's a pity it's night, but then I suppose that suits us more, don't you think?"

"What do you want with me?"

"The guy in that room you were in—he's some sort of drifting warrior, isn't he? What's his connection to you?"

"I don't think I have to tell you that," said Samon.

"At the moment, you're one of our partners in crime. And we can't afford to have even one two-timer in the bunch."

Samon was silent, but her eyes bored right through the inverted figure.

Perhaps noticing as much, Twin cautioned her, "Don't try anything funny. Yesterday, we let everyone in on our secret plans. Since we've got so many injured, we decided not to attack for two or three days and rest up instead." His friendly tone died out there. "You wouldn't seriously . . . ," he began to say, but his sharp attitude only lasted a second.

Right before his eyes, what looked to be a female form had begun to take shape upside down, just was he was. As tension and bliss vied for a place on Twin's face, the expression that surfaced there was difficult to describe.

"The thought of me letting you in on my plans when you could never discover them even if you tried," she laughed haughtily. "From the very start I always intended to do this on my own. Anyone who gets in my way gets sent to the next life. The Vampire Hunter, the woman, or the rest of you."

As she said this, Samon slid her right hand into her skirt pocket. The woman before Twin's eyes put her right hand into her long skirt. As proof that the latter was a hallucination, her skirt didn't fly up in accordance with gravity, but stayed just as it would've been if she'd been standing upright. When Samon's right hand appeared again, there was a cold glint from it. A knife gleamed in the phantom woman's hand, too. It couldn't possibly be real. It was an illusion. However, it looked so solid that once it plunged into its target, blood that was all too real would surely gush from the wound. A heartbeat later, the blade that was about to bring death to Twin whipped around suddenly, slashing diagonally through the air. With a hard *clink!* a small stone then fell to the ground at Samon's feet.

"Hold it right there," said a hoarse voice from the other side of the gate.

"Shin—don't tell me you're a skirt-chaser, too?" Samon said, looking over her shoulder.

On the other side of the fence, a human figure as thin as a crane drifted out of the weighty darkness.

Inside, the warrior woman was terribly shaken. She believed she'd been amply careful to prevent being followed, yet two people had tailed her. The only reason she'd noticed Twin was because he'd let his guard down after achieving his aim of finding out where she always went.

"Who was that guy, anyway?"

"Were you looking in on us?" Samon asked. Her tone was hard. The pair hadn't set foot outside the room.

"I see, I hear, I smell, I touch. My eyes are everywhere, and my hands are numberless. I might be the breeze blowing under the door or the moonlight shining in through the window."

"So, what do you intend you do? I suppose you have some problem with this?"

"No. He can go ahead and do what he likes."

Samon knit her brow. She was having difficulty understanding what the interim leader was trying to say.

"It shouldn't come as any great surprise," Shin continued. "Tell him what we're going to do and make it as easy as you can for him. I don't suppose I have to tell you why."

"You mean we'll simply let him do our job?"

"That's right," he said, his voice echoing far and wide in the deep night. "I tangled with him on the ferry on the way over, and he should prove the perfect opponent for a certain Vampire Hunter. All he needs is a fighting chance, and he's sure to kill the Hunter." Laughing, Shin added, "And we're going to take it upon ourselves to make just such a chance for him."

Samon shook her head in disgust. "He won't like that. If he's going to do it, he'll do it alone—that's the sort of man he is."

"Is that what you love about him?" Shin inquired in a lewd tone. "If he's loath to accept any aid, we'll just see to it he doesn't know he's gotten any. Samon, you're to give him our information and keep us posted on his movements."

"Do you seriously think I could do such a thing?"

"Well, I really don't know. That's up to you—or up to him, actually. Glen was the name, wasn't it? You're a prisoner of his manly charms."

Whizzing through the air with blistering speed, a flash of silver linked Samon's hand to the figure.

A cry of pain rang out.

Quickly looking up at the branch above her to confirm that Twin remained under her spell, Samon then dashed toward the fence. Gathering her skirt slightly, she kicked off the ground. She easily cleared the ten-foot-high palisade, and as she came back down to earth a black figure lay on the ground just in front of her.

"Not as tough as you make yourself out to be," Samon laughed. But on taking a closer look, she froze. The figure she was so certain had been actual-size had become a wooden doll less than eight inches tall with a knife sticking out of it.

"You can't see me. And since you can't, your powers won't work on me," said Shin. His voice rang out from behind her—although it actually sounded more like he was whispering right into her ear. "It's not a bad deal. Whether you love him or hate him, the results are likely to prove equally satisfying. Or would you prefer to die as a traitor? If it comes to that, we'll kill him, too."

Unmoving, Samon seemed to have become part of the night. Shortly thereafter, when Twin had returned from the dreamy world of nostalgia and raced over still sleepy-eyed, a low and unsettling laugh slipped from the warrior woman. "Intriguing," Samon chuckled. "It's none of your business how I feel about him. But I'll tell you what I'd like to see—those two gorgeous men soaked in each other's blood."

Elsewhere, around the same time, the voice of the waves echoed around a tiny house overlooking the sea. As if listening to its every word, the gorgeous figure in the yard was motionless, becoming one with the darkness.

The door to the main house opened and lamplight danced on the verandah out back. Holding a long, thin bottle and two glasses in one hand, Su-In called out D's name. She wore an insulated half-coat of dark blue—it was the kind where the inner lining could be filled with hot water to keep it warm. If the lining was made of northern cod intestines, it would hold the heat all day long, but such coats tore quite easily and weren't really suited to rough work.

"Patrolling at this hour?" the woman asked. "Say, you care for a drink? I know it's chilly out, but I can fire up the stove, and the stars are so beautiful."

D climbed up onto the verandah. He might have intended to go to sleep, as his longsword hung from his left hand. He still had his coat on, which was thoroughly in keeping with his character.

Setting the bottle and glasses down on the round top of a little wooden table, Su-In settled back in a chair that was also crafted of wood. With one hand she switched on the oil heater by her feet. She held out a glass filled two-thirds with burgundy-colored liquid, and D accepted it. Not taking a chair, he leaned back against the railing instead.

"I've heard dhampirs don't drink, but I appreciate you humoring me. All you have to do is hold it. Just to set the mood," Su-In said.

Swallowing a mouthful, she turned her attention to D's longsword. The glass was in his left hand. His longsword was leaning against the railing.

"Always keep your right hand free—isn't that the warrior way? That's the way all the ones who came through the village were. That's a strange sword, though."

D didn't reply.

Not seeming to mind, Su-In continued, "I've never seen a blade curved like that before. Where was it made? You sure travel around, don't you? All alone . . ."

Her glass rose again, and her throat bobbed.

Suddenly letting his eyes drop from her drink, D said, "There's work again tomorrow."

Eyes going wide, Su-In set her glass down and exhaled violently. "Don't startle me like that," she exclaimed. "Why, the very thought of you caring about anyone else. Okay, even if you do worry about me, don't ever say it out loud. It'll ruin your image. Or could it be you're worried my getting drunk will make your job tougher?"

"That's right."

Su-In shut her eyes. Pulling the front of her fur-trimmed coat shut, she said, "The harsh truth. It really hits hard tonight, that's for sure. But I understand how it is. I can't get too dependent on you. After all, someday you'll be gone."

Her eyes turned upward, catching D. He was staring out toward the garden. Maybe he was watching the stars.

"It's okay, you don't have to worry," the woman told him. "Grampa's not gonna come back as some sort of monster. There're two more graves beside his, right? My mother's and father's. I'm sure they're all swapping jokes in the hereafter."

There was no reply from the Hunter.

Su-In continued gulping down the contents of her glass. "My mother and father died at sea," she said. "Got rammed by a monster of a giant killer whale before they could finish it off. Their bodies never came back up. So those graves are just markers. I bet Grampa can't even talk to them. But it's still better than Wu-Lin. Poor girl . . . I can't even make a grave for her," Su-In said, something gleaming in her eye.

It was something she personally had decided after talking to D. Everything would come out after those who sought the bead had been dealt with and the secrets of the bead had been solved—it would avoid causing any more complications. But Wu-Lin's funeral would have to wait until then.

Su-In gazed at D, a fierce light in her eyes. "You're gonna outlive me, right?" she said to him. "Chances are I could wind up just like Wu-Lin. If it comes to that, I'd like you to make me a grave. You'll probably be the last person to ever see me or my sister . . ."

The surface of the wine in D's glass didn't display even the tiniest ripple.

"You're going to hide," D said succinctly.

"Where?"

"I'm sure Dwight would be glad to give you some advice on that," D replied.

"Don't get the wrong idea about the two of us."

"They should know by now that I have the bead. The only use they'd have for you from here on out is as a hostage."

"You don't pull any punches, do you? But I don't wanna do that," Su-In said. "I'll be damned if I'm gonna run and hide. Especially not from the bastards that killed my sister. I know there's no way I could beat them in a fight, but I at least want them to know they don't scare me. What's more—"

D turned and gazed at Su-In.

"Thanks to you bagging three big ones for me, I can get by this summer without going out fishing. I've got a school to run."

Keeping silent for a bit, D finally said, "That's fine."

"Thanks for going along with my decision. It's always reassuring to have someone on your side."

"When does school start?" asked the Hunter.

"The day after tomorrow. Tomorrow's the schoolhouse's grand-opening ceremony."

"What do you teach?"

"Are you interested?" Su-In blinked her eyes. Her cheeks were a little flushed. "If we had a teacher like you, we'd be in serious trouble. Oh, the problems we'd have with students falling in love with you. I bet the grades would be the worst ever. Since you ask, I do math and social studies at the moment."

"By social studies, do you mean history?"

"No, geography. The kids are really looking forward to it. If you like, why don't you teach them something?"

D didn't say anything.

Sighing, Su-In set down her glass and stared at her own hand. "I can hold chalk," she said, "but a brush is pretty tricky with hands like these."

Big and thick as any man's, her hands were covered with calluses all the way to the fingertips. Hauling nets, throwing harpoons, washing boats—she'd been doing these things since childhood. After a whole decade of such work, any woman would earn toughened hands. Su-In took her index finger and tapped it against the table. Over and over, there was the sound of wood striking wood.

"You know, I wanted to be an artist," she said plainly.

"There aren't any pictures in your house, though."

"I burnt them all up, right after my parents' funeral was over. I think the only reason I'm here today is because I did that." She went on to explain that Wu-Lin had only been nine at the time, and her grandfather had already reached the point where everyday life was tough enough for him.

"I heard your grandfather helped people with hypnotism."

"Not that he could do much with it," Su-In countered quickly. "When folks work out on the wintry sea, there's not much you can accomplish just by looking in their eyes. All Grampa Han could do was ease their remaining pain some."

"That's enough," D replied. "It's better than just staying sad."

"I think so," Su-In said, power in her voice. "A few people forgot all about crying, thanks to Grampa. But after about six

months, they'd come back in tears and beg him to make them remember again. I don't know the exact reason why. But I get the feeling I understand. People can forget all kinds of sad things. But some things are just so sad, they have to be remembered . . ." Su-In's words died out there. "Why are you looking at me like that?" she asked.

"Did your grandfather always use his hypnotism?"

Su-In shook her head. "After *that* happened a few times, he just gave it up completely." An ambiguous expression flitted across her round face. A memory had come back to her. Most likely, Su-In herself didn't know whether it was good or bad. "Oh, that's right . . . ," she said dreamily. "There was this one time . . . about six months ago, I said to Grampa it'd been five years since he'd used his hypnotism . . . and he said that no, there'd been this one time about three years ago when he'd used it just once . . ."

"Who did he use it on?" D inquired.

"Just a second—I remember it clearly . . . I asked him that very same thing. That's right. But he never answered me. I always did wonder about that, though."

"Do you have any idea who it might've been?"

"No."

"You should get some sleep," D said as he pulled away from the handrail.

"You're really not gonna drink that, are you?" Su-In said somewhat bitterly, raising the other glass to her mouth. But it stopped short. With incredible willpower she returned the glass to the table. "I suppose you're right," she said to the Hunter. "I'll pass on that. A fisherman's one thing, but for a teacher to reek of booze wouldn't be good."

"You're right," D said, slowly stepping down from the verandah.

"D," Su-In called out to him in a low voice.

Not turning, D asked her what she wanted.

"Nothing. That's a good name you have."

"Good night."

Not saying another word, Su-In followed his back with her eyes as he walked away to the barn. Even after the figure of beauty had disappeared through the entrance and the door had shut, the woman didn't move for the longest time.

Demon Blades Abound

CHAPTER 2

I

A faint murkiness was still swirling through the early morn when a well-defined man with a fair complexion paid a call on Su-In's house.

The day started early in Frontier villages. There were boats to be scrubbed, fish to be dried, and water to be boiled for extracting iodine from the seaweed.

Wearing a cold weather coat over her pajamas, Su-In was out in the front yard doing her daily calisthenics, and her ears were greeted by the lively sounds of her neighbors going about their normal business. The clucking of chickens mixed with the pounding of hammers on boats that'd been pulled up into people's yards for repairs. Long gone were both the sadness and drunkenness of the night before. As her thoughts turned to the day's business and she grew serious, Su-In then heard another noise—a sad sound that seemed to knife through the waves. By the time the woman realized it was someone whistling, her eyes had already caught the young man in a cape who was coming through the gate onto her property.

"Excuse me . . . ," she started to say in a voice that was a mix of both familiarity and refusal, because she realized that this unforeseen visitor was the same swordsman from the ferry, and because on that previous occasion he'd seemed like another person—so eager for blood it had left her spine numb.

"Long time no see," Glen, the "seeker of knowledge," said in greeting from a distance of some fifteen feet. His tone was polite, and it came from a face that seemed as cold as the silver ceremonial masks they used in the Capital. "I take it you know what I'm here for," he continued. "Fetch him."

"And what would your business be again?" Su-In asked, all familiarity now gone from her voice.

"It's not with you. Is D in the barn?"

"He's still sleeping."

"Then you'd better go wake him." But no sooner had Glen spoken than his body spun around in a wide arc.

Next to the main house that rose behind Su-In, there stood a gorgeous figure. The scabbard he'd carried the night before was strapped to his back again. Motioning to Su-In to step back with one hand, D walked toward Glen with a calm gait. The Hunter stood there as if to shield Su-In. Ten feet lay between him and Glen—each of them would have to take a step closer to bring the other within reach of their blade.

"I love it," Glen moaned, sounding nearly moved to tears. The truth was, the depths of his soul were shaken by a sensation that was almost sexual. "You're ready to fight without even asking why . . . Just what I'd expect from the only man who ever scared me. That should speed up the proceedings."

His voice reached Su-In's ears as well. And she understood what he was talking about, but she still couldn't believe it. This man who challenged D was like a solid mass of violent intent given human form, and the Hunter came out to face him without even asking why—just what sort of people were they?

"Stop it!" Su-In shouted. Or at least she tried to—the words never did come out. The seafaring woman was completely paralyzed by Glen's bloodlust and the eerie aura that was now emanating from every inch of D. She thought if she got in their way, she'd be cut down. Maybe even by D. What stood before her now was a completely different creature from the man she knew.

"I bear you no ill will. You know why we're fighting, don't you?"

D didn't reply to Glen's query. As if he'd foreseen all of this, his eyes were barren of every possible emotion, but they were still dark and crystal clear.

"Just let me make one thing clear," Glen said coolly. "I'm not connected in any way to all those freaks that have been creeping around you. I'm here of my own free will."

Finally D's mouth moved as he said, "I know."

A faint smile skimmed across Glen's lips. As innocent as that of a child, it didn't seem likely it would grace this man's face at any time except the final seconds before a life-or-death gamble.

A tiny shadow slid across the faces of both men. It was cast by a bird in the sky. To Su-In, it felt like the sunlight had frozen—the sound of the waves solidified in midair.

Now. Although the next moves that took place came as no more than a blurry interplay of light and shadow to Su-In's eyes, someone with the appropriate level of skill might've seen it as follows. Glen made the first move. Though the blade that raced from the scabbard on his left hip set off a silvery rainbow in the morning sun as it made for D's waist, the arc of the sword that came off D's back just a fraction of a second later met the other weapon in midair, scattering gemlike sparks before both men shifted positions. Glen went to the right, D to the left. That much even Su-In saw.

"You're good," Glen said ecstatically as he and D both moved around in a nearly perfect circle. "But I'm just getting started."

There was no telling if D saw his opponent purse his lips slightly. A melody that, under other circumstances, would've won the heart of even the most cantankerous of musicians flowed out into the crisp morning air.

Glen's blade was held out straight, flat, and at eye level. The tip of it rose to the highest position. And, as if following his foe's invitation, D's longsword also rose over the Hunter's head.

"It's got sort of an odd name for a sword technique, but I've come to like it. It's called Lorelei," Glen said with iron confidence underlying every word, apparently quite certain that D had fallen under his spell.

It was said that long ago in a river in some ancient land Lorelei was a nixie who used her seductive song to lure countless sailors to where their ships would break on the rocks and she could drag them down to the watery depths. Though a whistle wasn't exactly a song, considering the astounding results it produced, it was entirely fitting that this unearthly technique had been given her name.

Those who heard the "Lorelei" whistle from Glen and saw his blade would be hypnotized in the blink of an eye, and like a child obediently following a parent or a disciple imitating the master's lead, they would perform exactly the same actions. Although the real point was, they always performed the movements just a little bit later than he did. A split second before the blade his opponent brought down with exquisite timing and every ounce of his foe's strength could make contact with Glen, the seeker of knowledge's steel would slice deep into the exact same spot on the opposing swordsman.

The reason Glen had been able to close in on Toto without the thief realizing it, and the way the two thugs that were puppets had imitated Glen's pose a heartbeat before he cut them down on the deck of the ferry—it all made sense. And now even the Vampire Hunter D was held captive by that nightmarish power.

"You scared me—worse yet, you're even better-looking than I am. That's unforgivable!" the swordsman cried, but the whine of his blade soon effaced his voice.

Although to Su-In's eyes it appeared as if both blades had exactly the same velocity as they fell with the force of a waterfall, there was a cry of astonishment, and then bright blood gushed from the left side of D's neck.

However, Su-In's turbulent gaze was turned toward Glen. With the deadly Lorelei technique on his side, the seeker of knowledge should've sliced through his sworn foe's neck a second earlier, but the young swordsman had one hand pressed to his right shoulder, and redness dripped from between his fingers.

It was incredible how much a person's face could change.

With an expression that would freeze the blood in most people's veins, Glen howled malevolently, "You son of a bitch!" The outburst was directed at someone behind Su-In.

As the woman turned to look despite herself, her eye caught a shadowy figure circling around behind the house.

"I'm beaten," Glen said to D, once again taking a stance with his blade flat at eye level. "I came here before they could get to you, but it looks like they must've gotten here first anyway. I'll be back."

"I don't mind," D replied, his left side already soaked in vermilion but his sword held ready over his right shoulder.

As Glen realized that his opponent wasn't necessarily agreeing to quit, fear raced into his expression for the first time. The whole point of the Lorelei technique was to cut into his foe a split second before the opponent could strike. A split second. If for any reason his timing was thrown off by even a fraction, he could wind up on the receiving end of the very same stroke from his opponent. With basically no time to spare, the attack literally involved the swordsman risking his own life. But that was precisely why it'd been worthwhile for this fearless seeker of knowledge to sweat blood to master this technique.

But just now, his technique had failed. Even hampered by the Lorelei spell, D had sliced into Glen's shoulder a split second faster than he could do the same to the Hunter. The only reason Glen had even been able to finish his attack was because the blow from D had been incredibly light and dull. Both of them were badly wounded—Glen knew he should pull out now. He thought D would want out as well. He hadn't yet realized the true nature of the gorgeous demon he faced. He didn't even have enough presence of mind to whistle again.

D was about to take a step forward, but brought his foot back down to crush the grass on the lawn as he halted. The sound of youthful voices and footfalls had risen from the road below. They were calling out for their teacher.

As the Hunter's ghastly aura wavered for the briefest instant, Glen leapt back a good six feet. Being just as seriously wounded as D was, he displayed an incredible constitution.

"I suppose I should thank these children. But let me make it clear I had nothing to do with the interloper who just interfered with our duel. And if I find him, I'll slice him to ribbons," Glen said, but he threw a hateful glance at the tiny figures coming in through the gate as he walked away impassively.

After the swordsman passed the children—who were rooted by the sight of him covered with blood—and was heading down the hill, Su-In finally spread her arms wide and called out, "Come here, kids!"

D was already circling around to the back of the main house. He intended to go after the mysterious intruder—his lowered blade was still in his right hand. The children couldn't see it. But perhaps if Su-In had concentrated on the weapon enough, she would've noticed the thin coating of semitransparent goo that clung to his sword from the tip to halfway down the blade. It was thanks to this substance that the shadowy figure had hurled at the last second that the Hunter's blow hadn't killed Glen instantly. Even D couldn't stop his sword a fraction of an inch from the target when he had his entire being focused on swinging it. And the fact that the substance could still be applied in that brief span showed ungodly skill on the part of the intruder.

The laughter of children streamed out into the sunlight. These little ones were fitting inhabitants for the world of light.

Once the children had left, Su-In went into the barn with one of the first-aid kits distributed by the village. D was seated on his saddle, holding some gauze to the wound on his neck. As his clothes were all black, the blood didn't stand out anywhere except where it stained his pale skin.

"How's your wound?" Su-In asked, her voice a bit high-pitched. Pushing aside a pile of life preservers, she knelt by D's side. Since the way D had walked off had been so composed, she hadn't thought his wound was very grave, but in the end it did bother her a bit. Listening absentmindedly to the children and answering them vacantly, she'd then told them what'd happened was simply a slight scuffle between friends and sent them on their way.

"It's nothing serious," came the soft reply.

"Good," Su-In said, her shoulders falling with relief. It was only a second later that she realized the hoarse tone had been somewhat like D's voice, but not exactly, and her eyes bulged.

"My throat must be acting up, too," D said.

The woman was also startled that he'd bother to explain. Perhaps because of her surprise she didn't think it particularly strange when he lowered the left hand he had held over his chest. She didn't even notice how dirt rather than fresh blood seemed ready to spill out from between his fingers.

"Let me have a look at it," said Su-In. "I'll patch you up."

"I'm fine."

"No, you're not. I know a lot more about wounds than you do. Except my specialty is more in dishing them out," Su-In said somewhat coercively. With that, she pulled away D's gauze and blinked.

All that remained on the firm and fearfully pale flesh of his neck was a faint line where the wound had been.

"That's unbelievable!"

"Did the children notice anything?" asked D. He was referring to the bright blood that'd stained the garden.

"Yeah. But I think I got them to believe me. I suppose since you and he were both so calm, the kids didn't know what to make of it."

"I suppose you should make a change of address after all," the Hunter suggested.

Su-In nodded. She'd certainly be a perfect target if she stayed there. Even with D around, there was bound to be an opening at some point. Her confidence from the night before had burned away like a fog in light of the ghastly battle she'd just witnessed. Worse yet, even D himself hadn't been able to find the person who'd thrown the gooey mass. But it was clear that freakish foes were close at hand.

"The enemy knows I have the bead. If they take you hostage, they'll be able to get what they want."

"I know. I'm not gonna make a stink about it. I should probably pass on school today, too."

D's eyes narrowed ever so slightly.

"That's why the kids were here. Didn't I tell you? Today they're having the opening ceremony for the school. The whole village will be there, from the mayor to the sheriff. You wouldn't think it to look at me, but I'm sort of the guest of honor."

"When does it start?" asked the Hunter.

"In thirty minutes."

"Then we can relocate you after the ceremony."

Su-In broke into a grin. Though her childlike smile resembled Glen's, the circumstances were completely different. That alone proved she was an honorable person. "Great!" she exclaimed. "Say, will you go with me?"

"I'll see you as far as the schoolhouse."

"There might be some strange characters inside," Su-In said, her smile growing broader. She'd seen how perplexed the remark left D.

A Vampire Hunter and a schoolhouse—there couldn't be any greater mismatch.

"I'm just kidding," she added. "Outside will be fine. There'll be a party, too."

There was a burst of hoarse laughter that was choked out with a cry.

With an expression that beggared description on her face, Su-In stared down by D's hip. His left hand was balled tightly. He must've been putting incredible force into it, because his knuckles were white and bulging.

"You seem to have a habit of talking in odd voices."

The Hunter said nothing.

"Do you have any ringing in your ears, or do you feel faint?"

"Don't worry about it."

"Tell me the truth, now," Su-In said soberly.

"I never lie," a hoarse voice replied.

"If it's hard being on your own, I can come talk to you at night."

"There's no need for that."

With his fist still balled tightly, D stood up. "You'd better get ready," he said. "I'm going to go get rid of the smell of this blood."

II

Their wagon arrived at the school grounds five minutes before the starting time. The smell of fresh white paint filled Su-In's nose, and her cheeks took a rosy hue. The roof, the columns, the windowpanes—every part of the building glistened in the morning sun. Set in the door of the small schoolhouse was a perfectly round emblem with a fish motif, while the simply carved letters read *Florence Elementary School*. Less than seven hundred square feet, the single-story schoolhouse was merely the start of something bigger.

Blinking time and again and firming her lips in a straight bar, Su-In stepped down from the wagon. Standing by the door up till this point, the mayor, sheriff, and smiling children all started toward her now.

With only one foot resting on the ground, Su-In took a deep breath. "That's strange" she remarked. "All the way here, I've smelt flowers. Even though it's winter."

"It's me," a hoarse voice said.

Su-In turned around, moved by sheer amazement.

Looking up at the sky and keeping his left hand clenched again for some reason, D replied morosely, "I used too much tincture on the bloodstains."

Gazing at his graceful profile absentmindedly for a short while, Su-In then finished getting out of the wagon. Even once she was down on the ground, she remained in a daze. There was a ring of people around her in no time.

"We've been waiting for you," the mayor said almost unintelligibly, his back permanently hunched under his morning coat. "This is the first school we've had in the village. We couldn't very well start without our most distinguished guest."

"I'm sorry. Now, what do I—"

Patting Su-In on the shoulder, the sheriff winked at her and said, "Not to worry. You only have to give a short address today. The kids are waiting inside. Right after you say your bit, the party starts. Granted, there's nothing stronger than soft drinks."

There was a chorus of "Teacher! Teacher!" and Su-In looked over at D as she was whisked into the schoolhouse.

Parking the vehicle to one side of the garden, D climbed down. The sunlight that leaked through the trees cast a faint shadow for him, and D began slowly walking around the garden.

After about ten minutes, a burst of applause echoed from the schoolhouse windows. Su-In's opening remarks had finished. At almost the same instant, the door opened.

"Stud, what are you doing skulking around out here?" someone asked the Hunter. It was Dwight. His morning coat was stretched to the bursting point in a desperate battle to contain his powerful body. Seeming a bit self-conscious about it, he tugged at his cuffs. "You'll freeze if you stay out here. Come on. Su-In will be safer with you inside, too."

"Indeed," said Ban'gyoh, his face suddenly appearing over the fisherman's shoulder. He was supposed to have headed off to another village right after the funeral was finished. "Being the only priest in town at the moment, this humble servant found himself invited to the festivities. If they have no qualms about a shabby holy man like me attending, I see no reason why they couldn't use someone working for Su-In. You should go see your employer in all her glory."

"Come on," Dwight said with a smile. "No one's gonna have a problem with anyone who can take out a pair of giant killer whales with one shot. Hell, we'll be glad to have you!"

Stopping for just a second, the tall and handsome form of the Hunter then quickly headed toward the door. The other two flanked him. The white floor creaked under his black boots.

Seeming somewhat awkward, Dwight nevertheless had his chest puffed out as he said, "This was all volunteer labor, you know. That part there was done by O'Reilly the grocer, as I recall. Just to let you in on a little secret—the boards have the names of the guys who put them up written on them. My name's on some of them, too."

"Oh, where are they?" asked Ban'gyoh.

"The bathroom floor," Dwight answered with a wry smile, but then he indicated the little door on the left. The classroom. The one on the right was the office and staff room. He already had a big grin on his face again.

Saying nothing, D walked over to the door and turned the knob. The door creaked louder than the floor had.

"You're an odd one," said a voice that only D heard as it came from the vicinity of the doorknob. "You could've crossed the floor and opened the door without making a sound. What's the story— you like to do things like ordinary folks every once in a while?"

D pushed the door open without saying a word. A fair number of little eyes concentrated on him from the orderly rows of desks and chairs, but they soon turned forward again.

There were fewer than twenty desks, and five of those were empty. Nonetheless, the mayor and parents were all along the walls and stuck between desks laden with large plates of sandwiches and snacks. Behind the adults, blue sky and the grove of trees could be seen through the windows.

Not seeming to mind the indescribable looks the parents gave him, D stood at the very rear of the classroom with his back to the wall. Dwight and Ban'gyoh came over to him.

Su-In was just stepping down from the lectern. In her place, the mayor stood before the group and declared, "Let the party begin!"

With that, the rigid atmosphere disappeared and people began to mingle. The desks were pushed together, and plates of food were passed around.

Su-In came over to D and said, "I'm so glad you came. I was going to go get you. But I thought you wouldn't go for the idea."

"Yeah, I know," said the fisherman.

"Thank you, Dwight."

As Su-In stared at him, this man of the sea bashfully returned her bow.

Poking his head out from behind the giant fisherman, Ban'gyoh pointed imploringly at his own grave face.

Su-In laughed despite herself. He certainly was an odd priest. "Thank you, too," she told him. The holy man gave a satisfied nod in return.

"All they've got is juice, but let's have a drink," Dwight said when he came back with a bottle. Not carrying a single glass, he proffered the whole bottle. And D accepted it.

"The grownups will get tired of this pretty quick. Let's go somewhere and get ourselves a real drink," the fisherman suggested. "You wouldn't have a problem with that, would you, Su-In?"

"I'm afraid we can't."

"Why not?" Dwight asked irritably, his gaze fixed on D. "Oh, I see. Well, you might be handsome enough to make folks weak in the knees, but you don't seem too hospitable. Certainly don't seem cut out to be a teacher."

"I wouldn't be so sure about that," the smirking Ban'gyoh countered. "He's quite an extraordinary man. As you saw, it's not like he has any particular dislike for children, nor do they have any for him. To the contrary—he's probably just the kind of man children would respond to. Because their eyes only see what truly matters."

"Just between you and me, why don't you stay here and get yourself a boat?" Dwight said to the Hunter without preamble, making Su-In's eyes go wide. That was exactly the same thing she'd been ready to propose to D the night before.

D was expressionless, almost as if he hadn't heard the remark at all.

"With your skill, you'd be the top fisherman in the village in no time. Hell, there ain't anyone that good in any of the villages around here. I swear, you'd be the best harpooner on the Frontier inside of six months. What do you say?"

Dwight's invitation didn't carry a speck of empty praise or social obligation. He was genuinely intent on getting D to join him and his friends. His ardor seemed to be sufficient, as even Su-In— who'd given up similar hopes the previous night—watched the black prince with a feverish gaze that seemed to devour him.

"I don't care how good you are, there's a limit to how long you can go on making a living as a bodyguard or a warrior. Once you get old, your muscles all tighten up and you can't move right. All the young pups coming up will drive you off, and the next thing you know, you'll be dying like a dog all alone out in the wasteland. Our town might not be big, but there are still houses here where you could settle down. There's land, too. Hell, give it a couple of weeks and you could make yourself a few friends. Now, I don't know what kind of situation you were born into or how you've lived your life, but it can't have been all that great. Isn't it about time you started giving some thought to your future?"

Having expressed himself with a fluid eloquence quite at odds with his outward appearance, Dwight watched D for some reaction with eyes that brimmed with expectation.

The answer came quickly, and it was brief: "I'm looking for someone."

Su-In's shoulders fell faster than anyone else's.

"Not a girl, I take it? You're not the type that'd do that," said Dwight, who also sounded quite weary. "I had a feeling it was gonna be something like that. Despite what I just said, I never thought for a minute you had the same sort of upbringing as the rest of us. I just thought it'd be worth taking a shot, on the off chance. Don't take it the wrong way."

"No one's ever asked me to become a fisherman before," D said as he looked at Dwight.

Somehow, it made the seafaring young man swell with pride.

Just then, a diminutive figure dashed over to D. It was the boy who'd chosen Ban'gyoh's flute over D's at Su-In's house.

"Say, mister—do you still have that flute you made me?" asked the boy.

"A flute?!" Su-In exclaimed as she and Dwight exchanged glances. More than the mention of the flute, it was the fact that he'd *made it* that left them dumbfounded. This young man—a construct of darkness and ice—had crafted a flute for a child.

Bending over, D pulled the instrument from an inner pocket of his coat and handed it to the boy.

"Wow! Thanks!" the boy exclaimed as he snatched it from the Hunter.

Without warning, the boy was then surrounded by envious cries of "Oh, you lucky dog!" and "No fair! You get all the good stuff!"

"What happened to the one the priest gave you?" D asked unexpectedly.

Staring sternly at the holy man's wrinkled face, the boy replied, "Oh, that old thing? It sounded real good, but it broke in no time."

"While he's still here in the village; ask him to make you another. I'm sure he'll give you a lot of them."

"Sure thing!"

Watching as the boy rid himself of his surly look and went over to Ban'gyoh dripping with affection, D then turned to Su-In. "Shall we go?" he suggested.

"Yeah."

"What, are you going already, Su-In? Don't tell me you're getting all cold on us, too," said Dwight. "This sucks."

"Sorry. I'll see you later." Walking over to the mayor and sheriff, who'd been watching her from a distance, Su-In said good-bye to them, then left the school accompanied by D.

"School starts tomorrow, doesn't it?"

"Do we have school tomorrow, teacher?"

Su-In didn't answer the questions that followed her. She couldn't. While her village was about to begin its sunny summer tomorrow, in the shadows a duel to the death of unrivaled ghastliness was playing out. She had chosen to throw herself into this whirling vortex, and the voices of these darling children were echoes from the land of light she couldn't approach now.

"Soon," Dwight reassured them.

When they exited the schoolhouse, the fisherman's nose suddenly caught something, and he turned and looked at Ban'gyoh. The aged priest was also wearing a strange expression on his face, and he took in great rasping breaths of air. "How odd," the holy man said.

"This is strange. For a while now, I've been thinking I smelled flowers."

"Not like a woman's perfume."

"I heard in the Capital they've come out with some for men recently. It'd have to be the grocer or the sheriff. I'm almost ashamed to call them men," said Dwight. "I'll have to knock whichever it is on his tail later."

"It's me," a hoarse voice announced proudly, but it then vanished with a muffled cry.

The aged priest and fisherman didn't seem to notice the latter noise as they stared at the person they thought was the source of the voice. Neither of them said anything.

Approaching the wagon without a word, D climbed into the coachman's perch first, then pulled Su-In up as well. Not even glancing at the two men who stood motionless at the entrance, he turned the wagon around and raced off.

After the vehicle had disappeared into the woods, Dwight and Ban'gyoh looked at each other and laughed until their sides ached.

III

The village's sole inn also had an outbuilding. Built more than a decade before the main structure, it barely served to keep out the rain and the sunlight now. The innkeeper had just been thinking about finally tearing it down when an old man who appeared to be some sort of traveling painter had come along and inquired if there was an especially cheap room available. Happy to be able to press the building into service one last time, the innkeeper agreed to let the artist stay there for half price. Although it'd been connected to the main building by a covered passageway, that corridor had collapsed in a heavy storm six months earlier, leaving the building a completely independent structure now. It was the ideal spot for someone of dubious character, as the innkeeper had been perfectly aware when he loaned the old man the place.

The far-removed sea could be heard through parts of the roof and walls of the jerry-built structure, while in his room, Professor Krolock applied something to the wound on his back to keep it from festering. The medicine's principal ingredient was iodine from the seaweed that could be found practically anywhere in a seaside town like this, and the mixture was quite effective. The location wasn't an easy one to reach, and due to his age the professor's body was far from flexible, so he put some of the dark blue ointment on the end of a paintbrush, and then slid it along the sword cut that ran in a straight line from his right shoulder down to just over his lumbar vertebrae. The flesh had swollen slightly—it was a shallow wound. Given the fact that he'd been sliced by the man known as Glen, his good fortune was almost miraculous.

Before long, the professor must have finished applying the medication, as he put the brush down on the cloth before him and screwed the lid tightly onto the medicine jar. As he seemed to recall something, his face—which some would find as kind as that of a doting patriarch—suddenly churned with a chilling evil.

"My movements haven't been hampered at all. And I know the location of the woman's home. I warrant I should take care of this before any strange interference crops up," the professor groaned. "Though all sorts of weird characters are flocking to the bead, they're only ignorant brutes, of course. They can kill people well enough, but they can't read a single chemical symbol. Pearls before swine! In this entire wide world, the only person who understands the incredible importance of the bead and can make use of it is me," the old artist muttered in a way that made him sound completely self-absorbed.

But then his voice was joined by another that said, "Well then, maybe you can enlighten me, too?"

"Who goes there?"

In his great shock, the professor leapt up from where he'd been sitting cross-legged on the bed, while right before him, an old man in a red cape descended from the ceiling. Standing by the side of the bed without making a sound was someone who only came up to the professor's chest now that the artist had straightened his back—someone no taller than of a boy of fourteen or fifteen. His face was hideous, the cadaverous hue of his skin dotted with age spots that looked like the maws of tiny caverns, and when he grinned, he exposed a row of yellowed teeth. He thrust the point of the dagger he held out before the professor's eyes. But no sooner had the aged artist seen it than it raced out with a gleaming trail, knocking aside the pillow the professor was reaching for and disabling the trigger of the gunpowder firearm hidden under it at the same time.

"Samon tells me you have some strange power, though I don't think you use that hog leg to work your tricks."

Perhaps the professor saw from the dexterity of the grinning old man that it would be useless to resist, because he then softly inquired, "Who are you?"

"We haven't met before. I'm 'Shin the Manipulator.' Ever heard of me?"

"Yes. I know you're a warrior that uses a strange power of your own. I'm Professor Krolock. Or rather, I'm a traveling artist too destitute to even afford proper lodging. But what may I do for you?"

"Don't play coy with me," Shin said, his eyes emitting a strange light. "You remember Samon, don't you? The woman you were up against just before you got that wound. I was tailing her and saw the whole thing. And since I followed you when you ran off, I found out where you were staying, too. What brings me here today is that it's occurred to me that, since you're after the bead too, you might actually know what it's for. True enough, I don't know any chemical symbols, nor do I fathom the riddle of that bead. But you're going to impart some of your wisdom to me. Don't argue with me about this."

"I'd have no problem with that," the professor said plainly. "But on one condition."

"What's that?"

"From a phrenological standpoint, you have a truly fascinating head, though it has piqued my interest as an artist even more. Kindly permit me to do a sketch of you. It won't take long."

The professor's proposal came because he suspected his opponent only knew that he faced someone who used an unusual spell of sorts. In fact, he was sure of it. Samon must've been the name of the seductive female warrior. When the professor first engaged her in the forest, he'd caught her completely off-guard, and while he'd let her see the thin animal hide he used in place of a canvas the second time, she had no way of knowing what'd been scrawled on it.

"If you'll indulge me in that request," Professor Krolock continued, "I'll be most happy to tell you everything I know. Chances are I possess the world's most detailed information on the subject."

"You think you're in any position to be bargaining?" Shin said, his vile lips forming an even more unsightly grin.

"Well, I suppose you'll kill me if I'm averse to telling you said information, will you? I'll offer some resistance, and even if you should manage to kill me, you'll never learn the secret of the bead then. To the uninformed, it's just a worthless lump."

"My compatriots and I are working for someone else. I'm sure he'll know what to do when we bring it back to him."

The professor smiled a bit at Shin's rebuttal. Although he seemed much more human than Shin, that only made his cruelty all the more disturbing to those who witnessed it. "In that case, why have you called on me?" asked the artist. "I believe I understand your mindset all too well. You don't truly intend to share the secrets of the bead with your lot, do you?"

A whitish line zipped to the base of the professor's throat. Before he could even draw a breath, a bit of vermilion seeped out onto the center of the blade, swelling like a leech into a long, thin blob of blood.

"I can make you talk if I have to," Shin growled. "I could kill you by inches. The only part of you I'd need to leave intact is your mouth, so you could tell me the secrets."

Even as the professor looked down at the naked blade that was pressed to his flesh again only a fraction of an inch from the last wound, he didn't have the least bit of agitation in his eyes. He then said, "Simply learning the secret of the bead won't help you at all. It's nothing more than a power source, in a manner of speaking. In order for it to be of any use, you must be able to skillfully manipulate what it gives off. And only I can do that."

The trembling of Shin's blade made his shock apparent. He realized the professor wasn't lying. "Okay," he said, "I'll grant you that one request. But once I do——"

"I know. However, once you've heard everything I have to say, you'll most likely wish to treat the wound you've dealt me as well."

And then Professor Krolock got off the bed and went over to the art supplies that were resting by his pillow. Less than ten minutes later, he tossed his pen back into a tube and stared down with satisfaction at the piece of vellum on his easel.

Shin didn't yet realize the significance of any of this. His dagger resting unpretentiously on his knee but his form still charged with deadly determination, he sat in a chair about six feet away as he modeled for the artist.

"Done," the professor said. Not to the real Shin, who sat before him, but to the likeness of him on the artist's bizarre canvas. "You may have some use for me, but I have no such use for you. Listen to me well. Leave this inn without saying a word, and find some lonely cliff from which to hurl yourself. And you're not to swim. See to it that you die. Select a locale where the tides are strong, so your corpse won't be discovered for some time."

"Understood," replied a voice that carried laughter. It didn't come from Shin, who was right in front of the professor, but rather from someone behind the artist.

But that wasn't the reason the professor gasped and rose from his chair. Rather, it was because the hideous old man who'd sat before him had unexpectedly vanished.

No, that wasn't entirely true. He was there. Well, *something* was there. The figure in the chair was now a detailed little doll.

Noticing this mysterious development, the professor was about to turn when a sharp pain struck him in the side of his neck.

"Trying to play smart with me?" Shin said, his words raining down cruelly on the professor as he huddled on the floor, his hand pressed to a wound that spilled bright blood. "I've seen what your trick is. But you can't see me. Now, what am I gonna do with you?"

As he said that, black blood shot from the professor's right shoulder like a mist and the old artist twisted in pain. Pressing the cold edge of his blade against the professor's cheek, Shin said from behind him, "Don't look at me. But never fear," he added, "I won't kill you yet. Though I don't feel much like letting you live anymore, either. Talk to me. At least you'll be able to extend your life a little that way. But I'm warning you—I'll know if you're lying."

"I see," the professor said in a tone of complete resignation. While both of them would be powerful freaks to the ordinary person, in a battle to the death, it was only natural that a professional warrior like Shin would have a decided advantage. "I'm in no great rush to die, either. Listen to me. This is how it is . . ."

The roar of the blazing oil stove was then joined by a low voice and the stench of blood. The voice droned on for quite some time. But before long, there was a cry that sounded almost pained. It belonged to the other man.

"Impossible . . . ," Shin rasped. "If what you say is true, I won't kill you . . . Rather, I *can't* kill you . . . But I can't let you out of my sight, either. Here you go!"

The professor's neck stung as if it'd just been burned, and the old man realized that as the other man had let out his cry, he'd also stuck some gummy little object to the artist.

Clearly made of rubber, said object was a tiny spider no larger than the tip of his little finger. Apparently reacting to the professor's body temperature the instant it stuck to him, its thin little body swelled up, limbs stretched from it, and it became what anyone would take for a genuine arachnid.

"That's one of my puppets," Shin told the professor, "and it's equipped with a poisonous sting. Not even you can see the back of your own neck. No matter where you go, I'll know your movements and hear your voice through that bug. Try anything funny, and one sting from it'll send you into the next world. For both our sakes, don't be indiscreet. At least—well, at least not until I've become a Noble."

The sun set. This was a special night, for tomorrow was summer. Though the wind blowing in from the sea froze the people's hearts, summer was on its way, and in order to greet it properly there were special preparations the townspeople had to complete. The final nail had been hammered into the elevated stage for the dance party just before sunset, and the performers who'd gathered had made all of the necessary arrangements for the following day earlier and retired to their wagons and tents. And the protective charms couldn't be forgotten—there were magical amulets from various regions that could be hung near windows or nailed to entrances. Bunches of straw and dried narcissus leaves folded into a triangle. Dried ears of corn with the heads of two thousand sem ants stuck in them, and highly detailed caricatures of Nobles carved onto bulls' horns.

Expectation for the white summer. Balmy breezes and the glistening green of fresh grass and flower buds ready to blossom.

And anxiety.

By their hearths, people struggled to remember the summer songs, and occasionally they looked to the sea with darkness in their eyes. Out in the dark water that was ever by their side and made their whole existence possible, there was a foreign object. But if it always came with the bright season, perhaps it was just part and parcel of summer.

With spears, hammers, and stakes in hand, the people of the northern coast walked the beach while watch fires illuminated the surf.

In his home of stone, the mayor of the village thought they might get through this first week without mishap, and assured himself that everything would be fine so long as there were fewer fatalities than last summer.

The sheriff was in his office, inspecting his weapons and trying not to dwell on the fact he might be the first one expected to square off against that thing. The last three years everything had gone off smoothly enough. He was sure he'd get by this year, too. And he had no doubt the shaved ice at the festival was going to be incredibly tasty.

Dwight kept telling his mother to shut up whenever she asked him when he was going to propose to Su-In, and he downed unrefined spirits, disheartened by the thought that he was doomed as long as that bodyguard was around.

And Su-In, having entered one of the dilapidated buildings in the Nobility's resort area and made the necessary preparations for her daily life, went to bed early that evening.

The face of a certain man appeared in her dreams, and realizing that it wasn't that of D, she awoke with a start just after midnight to find herself covered in sweat. As she mopped at her forehead, her eyes peered out into the darkness, where the man stood straight ahead of her. But he promptly vanished. It was just a dream, too.

Summer was coming, wasn't it? While it always seemed like there was a portion of its light that the villagers would never see, it would still be amply radiant when it arrived.

Around midnight, that same man stood in front of a certain house. Water dripped from every inch of him, leaving a damp black trail on the road behind him like an elongated shadow.

The man wiped away his own saliva with the back of his hand. Though a ferocious hunger assailed his whole body, he hadn't attacked anyone yet this year. He'd come ashore at a spot that wouldn't be known to any of the humans in the village. He wished to avoid trouble, his reason being that he'd found what he sought. Now he finally understood why he'd come ashore these past three years and what he'd been looking for when he'd done so. Another emotion, quite different from the intense hunger, was driving the man—a chilling sensation the man wouldn't ordinarily know, though just once in the past his body had been consumed by it.

Three days earlier, the man had been sleeping. But a certain intense force had awakened him, and in a certain place he'd seen someone. The place was on a long, long road, with a ceiling and walls that stretched on forever. The person was a girl in a truck. And the man had realized then the reason why he woke from his sleep when summer came.

Crossing a stone bridge that spanned a drainage channel full of steaming water, the man opened the gate and entered the property surrounding the tiny home. There was a light on in the main house. A shadow moved across it. The tall figure leaning against one of the pillars at the entrance had just moved.

As his body was blasted by a supernatural aura unlike any he'd ever felt before, the man tensed.

No, the man thought, a hateful memory rising like a tumor from somewhere deep in the recesses of his mind. *Once, long ago, we met. I sensed the exact same killing lust then. It was—in my castle . . .*

"I thought you might come. And here you are," D said from ten feet away.

"We met on the Nobles' road as I was on my way to the village. Who are you?" the young man asked, something apparently drawing his interest as well. Even in the dark of night his eyes were gorgeous, as cold and clear as ice. They suited the North Sea.

After a momentary silence, the man asked, "Where is she?"

"Who?" D asked in return, although it was strange that he even bothered to respond to someone he should've destroyed out of hand.

"I don't know."

"Who are you?" the Hunter asked again.

"I don't know."

"Where did you come from?"

"The sea," replied the man. "Someplace deep and cold."

"That's a fitting home for you. Go back."

"Stay out of my way," the man spat, tossing his cape behind him. Deep blue danced out in the moonlight—his garments were the color of the sea. "I have business here, and at long last, I've found the place. Where's the person who lives here? Where's the woman?"

The darkness between the two of them transformed. Most likely any ordinary person would've died in the grip of lunacy the instant they felt the aura that emanated from every inch of the man to completely envelop D. It was a ghastly miasma the likes of which even the Nobility could scarcely imagine. But then it suddenly vanished.

"You . . . ," the man groaned, the word sounding like a cry of agony.

"Now it's my turn to ask a question. Who are you?" said D. "I saw the portrait in the village's museum. The lord of Castle Meinster didn't have your face. But the curator of the museum told me another story. I'll see if you can confirm what she said. Don't you know *me*, Meinster?" D said, his eyes reflecting the image of the man.

And the man's pupils reflected D. His cloudy eyes called to mind those of a dead fish; they began to fill with a spark of recognition—and hatred.

"Yes, I believe I do," the man said. "Did you think I could forget? After I was not only hurled into that pit and had my own fortress destroyed, but then had the fruits of my precious research stolen from me . . . And it was *you* who did all that?!"

Not waiting for a reply, the man extended his right hand and pointed it at D's chest. A golden ring adorned his forefinger. The ultra-compact reactor within it took up only a fraction of an inch, but it could generate and focus as much energy as an earthquake measuring 8.0 on the Richter scale. A seven-million-degree beam of energy a millionth of a micron wide shot from an opening to lance through D's chest.

At least, it *should've* lanced through the Hunter. A perplexed look in his eye, the man stared down at his unresponsive device.

The pendant on D's chest gave off a blue light.

"I'm not saying," the Hunter replied, "and it will make no difference when you're dead."

The words came from above the man's head.

It didn't seem likely that anyone could dodge or parry D's sword when he brought it down right on top of them. The blade limned a gorgeous arc of death, and somewhere in its travels, there was a wild burst of sparks.

Just as he came back to earth, D leapt to the right. And as he leapt, his right hand flashed out. The thing that'd been racing toward

D's throat was stopped once again in a shower of pale sparks. And then something quite strange happened. The pole-like weapon that'd stretched to a length of at least seven feet to match the distance of D's leap then retracted smoothly into the man's hand so that only the stiletto point remained showing. No doubt it was some sort of weapon with a length that could be changed at will. Another sharp point protruded from the opposite end of the man's fist.

"Tell me something," the man said as he slowly closed the distance between them. "Why do I know how to use this weapon? Who am I?"

Surely it seemed a bizarre query; D had just called this man Meinster and he, in turn, had said he knew the Hunter. Summer had brought a bizarre visitor.

D ran.

The sharp black stiletto tip stretched from the man's hand. Though it moved with incredible speed, the Hunter's sword parried it with ungodly skill, and as the other man reeled from the terrific force of D's blow, the sword then made a sharp turn toward his right shoulder. But it slashed through thin air, and the sound of it only came later.

Somersaulting in midair, the figure in blue made a second leap just as he came back to earth. It carried him out past the gate.

"You're a fearsome fellow," the man said, never taking his eyes off D. "I suppose so long as you're around, I won't accomplish my ends. We shall meet again."

The shadowy figure spun around.

D took to the air, but by the time he arrived where the vampire had been, his foe had already crossed the street and reached the edge of the embankment.

On the beach, sentries had built watch fires. Noticing the fiend racing by without making a sound, one of the closest men cried, "Who the hell are you?!"

"Where do you think you're going?" shouted a second.

Both men dashed over to the figure, but instantly fell to the ground clutching their throats. The man in blue had torn them open with nothing more than his fingernails. Their tragic end had come with such speed that the rest of the men were frozen not by fear so much as sheer amazement.

This opening was all that the shadowy figure needed to throw himself into the waves that danced magically with the reflected flames of the watch fires. In a flash, the sea was whipped up into rough black peaks, and by the time the people had rubbed their eyes in disbelief, no trace remained of the figure.

Unsure exactly what had transpired and unable to even enter the sea themselves, the villagers could only gaze at the black crests of the waves until an eldritch aura hit them from behind, forcing them to turn in a daze. D stood there, blade still in hand. Although the people didn't notice it, this alone spoke volumes about exactly how dangerous the foe who'd just vanished actually was. Keeping his eyes on the rumbling surf for some time, D then sheathed his longsword.

"That character just now—it was *him*, wasn't it?" one of the men inquired fearfully.

"You were chasing him, weren't you? And you managed to run the fiend off?!" someone else said.

Little by little, murmurs of awe and respect arose.

"That's unbelievable," said one of the men. "Just incredible! Simply keeping that creep from killing you would've been an accomplishment in itself, but you actually chased him off!"

"You're working for Su-In, aren't you? You suppose you could help us out?"

But no sooner had someone spoken these words than a cry of "Hey, what's that?!" arose from the edge of the throng.

Everyone looked at the man who'd shouted—and then their eyes flew in the direction he was pointing.

About fifty or sixty feet from where the Noble had just submerged, something round was floating some twenty or thirty feet from shore. Only at the very edge of the circle of firelight could the people squint and make it out as the head of a beautiful woman.

Though the colors were tinged by the light of the flames, it was soon evident that she had gorgeous blond hair. And another thing—her eyes were red. As she glared at the people on the beach, her eyes were such an awful vermilion hue that their color would've been clear even if she'd been soaking in a sea of blood. Naturally, her body must've been underwater.

Was she a servant of the Nobility, or some sea monster? While her exact nature remained uncertain, something else became clear. Something was playing with the water behind her. Ordinary folks would've had trouble believing it, but it was a phenomenon with which those who lived on the sea were well acquainted. It was a tail—covered in scales, and splitting in two like that of a fish.

This woman couldn't possibly be one of those—

Her mouth twisted into a smile, but how many people there saw the canine teeth that jutted like fangs from her lips was anyone's guess. A second later, the woman's head sank into the water so quickly it seemed to just vanish. No one could manage to say anything intelligible.

The water rose, then parted. To give birth to a woman.

Although the sea was called the amniotic fluid that'd given life to all things, surely it couldn't have fostered many children as gorgeous as this one. The body that shot up into the air with tendrils of glittering water trailing behind it was the very epitome of beauty. Even the fish she held in her teeth only seemed to add to her loveliness. Swelling beneath the golden hair that hung down to her waist, her breasts were human enough. Her slim waist and the tempting curves of the hips below certainly caught the eyes of the men. Forking into two points at the end, her tail reflected the flames of their watch fires as if it were covered with a thousand tiny mirrors.

The waves shattered into pieces, and the woman disappeared into the sea headfirst.

D alone ventured to the shore. Gazing straight ahead, he quickly walked in up to his knees. There was a splash of water somewhere, and then there was no other sound to challenge the rumble of the surf.

Suddenly D felt a warmth on his cheeks. The air no longer had the same snap. The weather controller had ordered summer to call on the North Sea, and most likely it had also opened the door for strange visitors.

Behind the Hunter, cries of delight rose from the villagers.

Summer Festival

CHAPTER 3

I

Because it always arrived so abruptly, even those who eagerly awaited the summer found it hard to believe that it was actually there. As they listened to children who couldn't wait a moment longer shoving open doors and running outside, the people let the zephyr blow over them, warming them body and soul. At last, they were stepping into the light. But they were ever so cautious, as if it were all no more than a momentary dream they'd awake from the second they tried to step out into it.

However, if they listened closely enough, a melody that rang to the high heavens was coming from the forest, while the aroma of summer grasses and the smell of candy and wine wafted through the air. And finally they knew this season was more than just a dream and let its name rise to their lips. Summer. Only a week of it, but summer nonetheless. The days of feasting and merrymaking were about to begin.

It was that morning that the sheriff called on D—although it was actually Su-In he wanted.

"The lady of the house is supposed to be on the crime-prevention team for the festival," said the lawman. "But since Su-In's not here, there's not much else we can do. We've got no one else to substitute for her, either. Since you're in her employ, you think you could stand in for her?"

D agreed. Su-In had explained the situation to him—she'd even asked him to go if he could.

At nine o'clock Morning they arrived at the clearing on the edge of town. This was the heart of summertime. Magicians and acrobats were just some of the traveling performers who mingled with the crowd. Mobs of children formed around an assortment of vendors, and young men and women took part in jubilant line dances. But as D walked through the area, all commotion and cries ceased, and the feverish gaze of all crept over the Hunter. No cheers would ever go up at the sight of this young man. Everyone had the wind knocked out of them.

"Come now—step right up!" a lively voice called from the center of a square surrounded by trees on all sides. Wearing a silk hat and a morning coat over silver tights, it was clear at a glance the man was a traveling master of swordplay. A slender, straight blade dangled from his belt.

While warriors made a living renting out their swords and even their lives, this kind of performer only took on amateurs. In terms of ability, they were only about half as good as warriors, engaging in an entertaining pastime with little or no chance of physical harm.

But this man's weapon wasn't the sword on his hip. Removing his silk hat with a fluid motion, he thrust one hand into it. When it came out again, he held a pair of throwing knives between each finger, for a total of eight blades. Each was eight inches long including the hilt and only three-quarters of an inch wide. Both edges were dull, and the tips were blunted.

"Four in each hand, eight in all," the performer declared. "But rest assured, the tips and blades have been rendered harmless. Even if they should hit, they'll do no more than simply sting a bit. And anyone who can block all eight of my throws, or even dodge them, is guaranteed to receive a shiny gold Pegasus coin!"

That last statement proved highly effective, sending a stir through even the women and children who'd been listening spellbound. The Pegasus coin was the highest denomination in either the northern or southern Frontier. In a village like this, it would be enough for a family of five to live off of for six months.

Someone immediately called out in a breathless voice, "I'll do it!" Not only was the tone eager, but it brimmed with confidence, too.

There was a burst of applause. Like so many others, D turned to look at the speaker, although there were actually more women regarding the young Hunter than there were people looking at anyone else.

A young man of twenty-one or twenty-two stood across from the swordmaster—or rather, the knife thrower. Judging from the bulging muscles left exposed by his shorts and short-sleeved shirt and the way he carried himself, he seemed to have some experience with the fighting arts.

"Fine. Put your ten demis in the box right there then. I'll get you set up with a weapon. What do you favor?" the knife thrower asked, taking a half step backward and indicating the items behind him. A leather cylinder there contained everything from longswords, spears, and javelins to brass knuckles and gaff hooks. It looked like the whole lot must've weighed at least fifty pounds. Though all of the weapons were polished, the hilts were damaged and the blades were nicked, making it quite clear each had seen a great deal of use.

Dropping his copper coin into the designated box, the young man chose a javelin. The way his hands tightened around it like a pro and his feet settled into an easy stance were something to see.

"All set, are we?" the knife thrower asked.

"You bet!" the young man responded.

"Very well, then."

Holding his right arm across his chest, the performer made a gentle bow, and as soon as he straightened up again, a flash of silver streaked right to the young man's chest.

"Oh!" the crowd gasped, and at the very same time, there was a mellifluous *ching!* as the throwing knife careened off in the sunlight to return to the palm of the thrower's right hand.

"Well done!" the man in the silk hat cried out, his praise making the young man throw back his shoulders with self-importance. "Let's go on."

"You got it!"

Once again the silvery flash flew and was knocked away with the same sound. And again, the knife landed back in its owner's hand.

"Perfect! Let's continue."

"Sure thing."

The third time went exactly the same. Seeing how the deflected blade went back to the knife thrower's hand in exactly the same way every time, the spectators had stopped clapping. Everyone there had realized it had nothing to do with the young man's ability, but was entirely the knife thrower's doing. Like a puppet and its master.

"Throw it with everything you've got," the young man finally cried. He'd realized what was going on, too. And he didn't care to play the buffoon any longer.

"I'm sorry you feel that way," the knife thrower said with a grin. "I'm already doing my very best. But have it your way. I shall see what I can do to accommodate you."

"Great!" the young man replied. Gritting his teeth, he braced himself.

A flash of silver whirred at his throat. At the dull thud, the young man reeled backward, and three throwing knives fell from his throat to the ground.

Several seconds actually passed before a murmur of surprise rustled through the onlookers. The knives had literally flown faster than the eye could follow. While no one could actually see the knife itself, they'd all thought but a single blade had been thrown. Seeing how several people rushed forward and helped the young man up off his back, it didn't look like he was wounded, though he seemed to have been dealt quite a hard blow.

"Okay, who's next?" the knife thrower asked, but there were no takers.

Smiling wryly with the realization that he'd overdone it, he looked around with his elongated face, and then stopped cold on a new target. Directly ahead of him stood D.

"My goodness! Pardon me for saying so, sir, but you seem quite out of place in a village like this. Moreover, on a—"

The knife thrower's voice petered out. His face went pale. If nothing else, he could at least discern how powerful the man who stood before him was.

"I seem to have used an uncharacteristic bit of power that last time," the knife thrower continued. "It'll be quite some time before I'll have another contender. If you'd like to help me while away the time, you're welcome to try your hand free of charge."

No one in the crowd moved. There were no shouts, no applause. Everyone realized that if the handsome young man agreed to participate, this would be more than just a simple diversion to pass the time.

While his thoughts remained a mystery, D stepped forward. Of course, the knife thrower's invitation was no challenge to battle. And this young man wasn't the kind to take part in mere games. Yet he still advanced.

"I'm obliged to you for consenting so readily to assist me," the knife thrower said with a bow. "I suppose you'll be using your own weapon. If you manage to deflect my knives, I'll give you the gold coin. Very well, then."

They were fifteen feet apart. For someone as skilled as the knife thrower, that was essentially no distance at all.

"Have at you!"

D stood there without even drawing his blade. The scene seemed to be taking place in an entirely different season from their all-too-brief summer.

The single flash of silver scorching through the air was in fact four blades. But the spectators only realized that when a prismatic slash flowed out from the man in black's shoulder in what could only be described as an effortless sweep, and knocked them all to the ground.

Before anyone could even gasp with surprise, D dashed forward. As the pale knife thrower backed away, the remaining four blades in his left hand raced out. People saw a cross-shaped flash of light. The horizontal swipe batted away the throwing knives, while the vertical stroke caught the man as he tried to jump back, splitting him in half from his silk hat down to his jaw.

But the man who'd been instantly killed didn't fall to the ground. Something else fell instead. A doll in a silk hat and morning coat.

Shadowy figures leapt at D from all sides—the cook who'd been roasting chickens, the candy vendor, men who'd been playing chess by the sidewalk. And while their movements were human enough, their course of action was anything but.

The blades they brought down at the Hunter all met thin air. Before the men could launch a second attack, their torsos were bisected, turning them into tiny dolls that fell on the grass.

The tip of D's blade dipped ever so slightly—the blades of grass were being crushed to the ground. Only one person D knew had the power to control the gravity in a given area.

"So, we meet again, D!" Shin said, his voice rising with scornful laughter from somewhere in the area. "I'll have you know the sheriff who called on you was one of my puppets, too. But this time I'm not alone. I take it you're familiar with Egbert and his 'kingdom.'"

The tip of D's sword rose—then fell again. But no matter how much a dhampir's strength surpassed that of an ordinary man, this was bound to happen when the Hunter was subjected to five times the ordinary force of gravity. One on one, he'd beaten all the warriors' tricks. But going up against them in tandem would be another matter.

"Egbert's kingdom covers this whole section of the woods. Why, I suppose it's nearly a mile across. And everything in it is under his command. What's more, it's populated entirely by my puppets. Let's see you try and get out of this." Shin stopped there, but after a moment's pause he continued, saying, "But it seems you were wise to my puppets even before you tangled with the knife thrower. Care to explain why that was?"

D barely managed to hold his sword horizontally. But in a voice that didn't betray an iota of strain, he said, "I suppose I have Glen to thank for that."

On the ferry on the way over, Glen had taken one of Shin's arms. But if that wound had proved the puppet master's downfall, surely only this young man would've been up to the task of noticing it.

The Hunter sensed something surging forward. And it was more than just one person. Several ranks deep when they came together, they advanced on him from all sides. D had probably seen through their guise already. They were the same young people who'd been intent on dancing, mothers and children who'd licked their lips over watermelon, and men who'd been competing at the ring toss game. The people here in the woods— or, according to what Shin said, everyone for more than a half mile in all directions—were all puppets. And unlike D, they were immune to the effects of Egbert's kingdom.

Steely blades glittering in every hand, the mob surrounded D. Stark flashes of light were coupled with the sound of severed bone, and in no time at all a number of people in the foremost rank vanished.

"Keep going! He's only flesh and blood! He has to get tired eventually!"

With Shin's howl as their signal, the bizarre charge of the puppets continued, and then, when they'd been reduced to half their previous number, a voice cried out again.

"This is unbelievable—he's simply incredible," said Shin. "He must be under ten Gs out there. There's no use pressing him any further—you'll only be throwing your lives away," he told his minions. "Back! Fall back! We'll take him out from a distance."

The crowd backed away. Several people who'd remained to the rear held weapons that looked to be old-fashioned gunpowder rifles. But before they could raise them, much less fire, their heads were flying through the air—where they became doll heads. Faster than the group could retreat, D had advanced and raked his blade through the opposition. The only reason he'd remained rooted until now was to keep himself from being trapped by the chaotic movements of his foes.

"Oh my!" someone cried out in surprise, and there was movement perceptible in the woods off to the Hunter's right.

Without a moment's hesitation, without even looking, D hurled a needle of unfinished wood. Glistening briefly in the sunlight, the missile was swallowed by the forest, and then a cry of pain rang out.

The group of villagers that was about descend on D stopped moving.

D looked down at his feet. On the grass before him, countless dolls lay frozen in the same poses they'd held a split second before their transformation. At the same time, D realized he'd been released from the insane bonds of gravity.

"I'm impressed. But then, I should expect no less from the Vampire Hunter D," the Hunter heard Egbert say. But even with his highly perceptive hearing, D couldn't tell from where the voice originated. It sounded as if it was coming from both the heavens and the earth.

"Aren't you coming?" D asked calmly. If he were ever to invite someone to have a cup of tea with him, that was undoubtedly the same tone he'd use. To him, an invitation to tea or a challenge to the death were one in the same.

On careful inspection, the Hunter's shoulder was torn open and gushing blood, and his chest and back were covered with long, thin gashes. Given that he'd been taking on dozens of opponents at the same time and the gravity had been about ten times as strong as normal, it was something of a miracle he'd gotten off with so few wounds.

"I think I'll pass," Egbert replied simply. His tone was refreshed, and he sounded somehow greatly satisfied. "I was against the whole notion of teaming up from the get-go. After I was wounded throwing down with you before, I figured we might not have any choice but to gang up on you," he remarked. "But sure enough, it just doesn't set right with me. Next time, it'll be *mano a mano*. With King Egbert. See you later."

As soon as the man finished speaking, D walked off toward where he'd hurled the needle, not even pausing to catch his breath.

Drops of red spattered on the well-trampled grass. There was no longer any sign of the vendors or performers—all of them were now puppets that lay hidden in the grass. Even the fragrant woods had vanished, leaving D surrounded by gnarled beach shrubs. No doubt he'd been tricked into entering Egbert's "kingdom" while the sheriff was supposedly leading him to the real clearing. But any spell that could meddle with the sense of distance, direction, and time for someone like D was a fearsome power indeed.

Beyond the twisted bushes, a wrinkled old man lay on his back in a depression, his eyes glaring blankly at the heavens. A slender wooden needle ran into his windpipe and poked out through the nape of his neck. This must've been Shin's true form.

Perhaps D decided that if he left the corpse here to be discovered, it was bound to upset the summer festivities. Sword still clasped in his right hand, he bent down and grabbed the old man's armless shoulder with his left.

There was a thunderous roar to one side of the Hunter. As if blown away by the very sound itself, D's left hand snapped off at the wrist and flew more than ten feet away.

"Don't move," a voice shouted from behind another tree in the direction the roar had come from, but D had already turned.

Armed with a fire dragon rifle—a massive gun with a barrel bigger than a man's thumb—the figure who'd just appeared was the spitting image of the old man who lay dead on the ground.

"Looks like you fell for it," said the old man. "Not everything I manipulate necessarily seems to be alive. That right there's a puppet of a corpse."

Down at D's feet, the body of the old man had become a doll with a wooden needle stuck through it.

"To be perfectly honest, I thought it'd be enough just to take out your left hand today," the old man continued. "See, I heard from Egbert that it was a talking hand that got the better of his kingdom before. But now my greed's really kicked in. I don't care if you are the great Vampire Hunter D—at this range, there's no way you'll be able to stop a projectile. And if I get you right through the heart, you won't be getting up again. So unless that's what you fancy, you'll answer me. Where's the bead?"

D was silent. Thanks to his dhampir nature, the bleeding from his shoulder and all his other wounds had long since ceased, but a stream of red twisted like a serpent from where he'd lost his left hand, and he didn't seem to be doing anything to staunch the flow.

"Don't move your arm or even turn your head," the old man— Shin—said, licking his chops. Though he only had one arm to support the massive weapon, its muzzle didn't waver an inch. "Egbert also told me what happens when you get a taste of blood. You should've left when you figured I was dead, but you were stupid enough to show pity for me." Chuckling, he added, "That's probably why you're not smart enough to know what the bead does."

D's eyebrow rose. "And do *you* know what it does?" he asked.

Snorting as if trying to drive away some foul odor, Shin replied, "Someone else knew—an old fart that calls himself a professor or something. And true to his name, he sure did have some information for me. But what kind of fate is it to have to drink your own blood to win in battle? You really must lead a cursed existence! But that's not how it'll be for me. Instead of a lowly little half-breed like you, I'm going to be a true Noble. Now, where is the bead?" he asked. The words were bare of any sense of triumph, and rang with a tone of naked, wretched greed.

The steamy air and the aroma that surrounded them shook.

"Over there," D said, just making a small toss of his head to the ground to his right. "The talking hand has it."

Shin was speechless for a moment, but then his hideous old face twisted in delight and he nodded, saying, "Oh, I see. What safer hiding place could you ask for? Well, I'll be taking it then. Don't move." Laughing, he added, "On second thought, go ahead and do whatever the hell you like. I have no further use for you!"

Before Shin had even finished speaking, he pulled the trigger. With a sound like a small explosion, a lead slug weighing a sixth of an ounce shot through D's head. And at that moment, Shin probably knew what his own fate would be. A split second before pulling the trigger, he'd seen something. D's eyes were giving off a blood light.

While Shin's finger was desperately pulling the trigger, D was in motion. The gravity of Egbert's "kingdom" was no more, and he'd become a full-fledged Noble. Shin couldn't tell what move the Hunter was going to make next. The slug didn't even rip into the shrubs until after the rifle had been slashed in two by a blow that also carved Shin open from the left shoulder to the right lung and his body had thudded backward.

Out of reflex, D covered his nose and mouth. Shin had called him cursed for having to drink his own blood to win. But even the puppet master couldn't have imagined that the blood he'd spilled with a shot from his own gun would evaporate in the summer sun, forming a thick aroma that invaded D's nostrils and filled him with demonic power. Perhaps there was some truth to what Shin had said.

As D set eyes blazing with blood light on the real Shin, the Hunter's expression shifted ever so slightly. Suddenly, there was a puppet where the old man had been. And when D turned around, his left hand was nowhere to be seen on the ground.

II

Perhaps a thousand feet inland from the phantom woods that'd been the stage for D's deadly combat were the real woods. Not even the roar of the surf could be heard there. In its place, there was the humming and chirping of insects called out by the sultriness when the chill departed the night before like a dream. But their cries ceased unexpectedly, for an old man as thin as a rail had jumped in and roughly trampled their summer shrubs.

On the fallen trunk of a massive tree covered in emerald moss, another figure stood up. Having shed his trademark cloak, Professor Krolock stood there in a somewhat grimy shirt and trousers, both of which looked to be made of burlap. Seeing the one-armed old man who'd raced there, he asked, "Did you get it?" His haggard expression didn't change for a second.

"Yeah," the old man—Shin—said with a nod. "I've got it right here. Look at this!"

When the professor saw what the old man held, his face twisted in disgust.

Quickly, Shin added, "This is his left hand. The bead's inside it."

Anything could happen on the Frontier— nothing at all surprised its inhabitants.

"And just what did you intend to do next?" asked the professor.

At his query, Shin clutched the tattered limb to his chest, trembling. Try as he might, he simply couldn't contain his delight.

"That should be pretty obvious," the puppet master replied. "I'm gonna get out of town as fast as I can. I may have gotten the bead, but he's still alive. He's a scary one, and I have to count myself lucky to have the thing at all. The next time he sees me, I'm as good as dead. Those blood-red eyes of his—he didn't even see the real me, but it still felt like he was looking right down into the marrow of my bones." Chuckling, he added, "Of course, the next time we meet, I'll be so much better than him he won't be fit to lick my boots."

As the professor indifferently watched the grotesque tableau of Shin violently shaking the severed hand, he asked, "Have you actually verified that the bead is in there?"

The puppet master's countenance had been a picture of unwavering joy, but a sudden gust of agitation blew into his features. "No. But I—"

"Then your joy may prove somewhat premature."

"Impossible!" Shin shouted, holding the well-formed limb up to his eyes.

"You and I could return to the Capital, but if that hand doesn't hold the bead, it'll be utterly worthless to us. Why don't you check and make certain?"

The professor's words proved just persuasive enough to goad Shin into action. Waving the severed limb he held, the old man said to it, "Okay, answer me. Are you dead already, or do you still live?"

Although Shin—who'd reached the peak of his anger—didn't notice it, Professor Krolock surely looked to the heavens for deliverance.

All the chirping of the insects had died out. But what followed, almost like an apology, was a burst of indescribable laughter.

Realizing it was the hand that'd laughed, the astonished Shin flipped it over. He'd been looking at the back of it. Before his riveted eyes, the surface of the palm rippled, and something rose in it. A face. It had eyes. And a nose, too. It was even equipped with a mouth. This human visage clearly possessed a will of its own, yet its features were disturbing—as if it lacked what was most essential to a human being.

Chortling, the hand said, "Stop your fretting. I'm alive. And I've been that way for quite some time. I've lived a hundred times longer than you, I bet."

"Then I should be able to get right to the point," Shin said, his tone heavy with coercion and the blackest confidence. There was no trace at all of his earlier distress. "You're supposed to have a bead in your belly," he continued. "How about it?"

"Now that you mention it, I do remember swallowing something like that a good long time ago." With another chortle, it added, "What was it—about three thousand years ago?"

"Are you trying to mock me?!" Shin cried. Lowering his head to his chest, he thrust the point of a dagger before the tiny eyes. The weapon had been hidden in his chest pocket, and he'd drawn it with his teeth. "I'd like to see you try and hide your eyes and mouth again," he snarled. "Let's see if you can pull them in so far I can't gouge them right out of you."

"Why not carve the bead out of it while you're at it?" the professor suggested.

"Good idea!"

"Hold it! Just give me a second," the weird face said in a desperate effort to stop him. "I'm not sure exactly which of these things you want, but I'll try and find it now. Let me see . . ."

And then there was suddenly a distinct bulge in one of its cheeks.

"How about this?" the hand asked in a calm tone.

And then the impossible happened—

Spat from its mouth with an impressive whir, the dull silver bead shot right into Shin's eye before he could ever dodge it. Reeling backward as he let out a beastly howl, he intended to press his own hand to his eye, but instead wound up pressing the other hand to it. Prying the severed hand free again, he threw it away. But there was no bead left in the wound. Where his eye had been there was nothing but a bloody opening.

A burst of laughter echoed up from the ground. The severed hand was standing upright. Both eyes were open wide, and half of the bead jutted from its tiny mouth. How it could laugh with its mouth full was anyone's guess.

"Wait!" the professor screamed as he readied to pounce on the limb. The hand made no attempt to escape, but rather let the old artist easily get a firm grip on it with both of his own withered hands.

"You may have me," the hand laughed, "but that won't do you much good. At least, it won't help you get *this*!"

Though it was unclear exactly how it continued to talk while doing this, the hand spit the bead from its mouth. Limning a silvery arc, it flew toward the sea.

While the professor was distracted, a sharp pain shot through his hand, and he then shook loose the weird severed hand. It was only after diving into the bushes to search for the bead and coming out again empty-handed that he realized he'd been bitten. Seeing the tiny teeth marks around the base of his right thumb, the professor clucked his tongue disdainfully.

As a hue of hatred rapidly spread in Professor Krolock's eyes, he looked down at Shin, who was still writhing on the ground. "Indeed, it does seem your joy was a bit premature." As the professor spoke, he drew a knife from his belt and plunged it into Shin's neck up to the hilt.

"You son of a bitch . . . ," the old man said in a tone so mournful most would've preferred to cover their ears. He was looking up at the professor. Gouts of blood spilled from his mouth, yet still he spoke. "You idiot . . . You've still got my poison spider . . . on the back of your neck . . . I'll take you to hell with me!"

"You mean this thing?" asked the professor. Pulling the poison spider from the breast pocket of his coat, he waved it before Shin's eyes. "I couldn't see it myself, but I could catch a glimpse of it with something else. While you weren't around, I asked someone at the inn to set up a pair of mirrors for me. First I got one to reflect the nape of my neck, and then I held the other up in front of my face to reflect the first. After that, it was simply a matter of drawing a picture."

His energy apparently drained, Shin fell to the ground with a frightful rictus, while behind him a spider that'd become a small piece of rubber was discarded by the professor, who turned toward the sea with a ghastly expression hitherto unseen.

"I'll find you," Professor Krolock declared. "I'll do whatever it takes, but I shall find you. O little treasure, you alone can unlock the mystery of human and Noble blood. And you will be mine!"

And then, pressing down on one hand all the while, he began to walk once again toward where the bead had disappeared.

At the top of a cliff, the roar of the sea could be heard in the distance. If you turned off the Nobles' road onto the street leading into the village, this was the spot where the road ran quite close to the sea. Looking down from the brink of black rock, you'd be greeted by the fierce spray from waves crashing on the wild tangle of boulders below, and a school of monstrous fish a foot to a foot and a half in length could been seen through the water, massing with teeth bared as if waiting for some suicidal soul. The sight was enough to give some a strange impulse to suddenly throw themselves over the edge.

While the monstrous fish were carnivorous, they didn't always congregate below the cliff. Their behavior was a throwback to ancient times, when the Nobility had ruled the whole area and had thrown humans off the cliff either as an example to those who would defy them or merely for sport. The number thus dispatched had been so great and the practice had continued so long that it had become a sort of conditioned response in the fish. Even now, nearly ten centuries later, they would rise from the depths of the sea as if guided by instinct, swimming in circles and snapping their jagged teeth to beg for food whenever they sensed humans up on the cliff.

There were two people up there that might provide an afternoon snack. One was a she-beast dripping with allure, the other a statuesque seeker of knowledge—Samon and Glen. Probably they themselves didn't know whether it was mutual attraction or loathing that united them, yet their strange relationship continued.

At present, Samon's eyes sparkled with a dark enthusiasm, while the horrid shadows of defeat hung on Glen's face. Just a day earlier he'd challenged D, only to be defeated. Armed with the closely guarded "Lorelei" technique, he'd dealt a serious wound to his opponent, and he'd been fortunate enough to receive assistance from an unexpected intruder. But Glen knew better than anyone that without that aid, the blow he caught in return from D's blade would've been fatal, and his body burned with that knowledge and a deplorable sense of failure. His recognition of this fact gave way to an undirected rage that now escalated to the point where he wanted to shred the very bandages wrapped around his right shoulder and cut off his useless arm.

I just can't rise to that level, he told himself.

Sooner or later, a seeker of knowledge sees the end of the road—and that very phrase described the one fate he never wanted to find there.

As anger and despair tumbled across the swordsman's handsome face like colors in a kaleidoscope, Samon stared at him, her eyes brimming with an emotion that was neither fully contempt nor pity. She'd told Glen that it looked like her compatriots were going to try something first, prompting his visit to D. Glen had come out of the resulting duel less than triumphant. Mindful of the eyes of the villagers, she'd taken the injured man to the ruined temple and personally treated his wounds. This was the same hateful man who'd saved her from the professor's spell, taken her against her will, and continually belittled her. Therefore, when he'd challenged D at her insistence and he'd been left defeated, Samon had chuckled cruelly in her heart of hearts. The reason she'd patched him up was because, as long as he still lived, she could get him to rashly challenge the Hunter once more and make it that much easier for her compatriots to obtain the bead. And yet, as the sorceress stood on the cliffs gazing at the young swordsman, the same sort of pathos one might glimpse in someone looking at her beloved seemed to swirl in her eyes.

"Are you going to quit now?" Samon asked in a derisive tone. "That would be for the best," she added. "Your opponent is Vampire Hunter D—a swordsman unrivaled in the entire Frontier. That's not a level of skill a mere seeker of knowledge can hope to attain.

Throw away your foolish pride and leave town without further delay. And just forget any of this ever happened."

There was no way to describe her remarks save harsh and contemptuous, but it wasn't clear whether or not Glen even heard them as he looked out over the North Sea in silence, his sword in his right hand.

"I can't win, can I?" he said flatly, letting his words ride on the wind that blew by. "You're right—I certainly can't beat him. A little grub wriggling around on the ground can train all it likes, but it'll still never measure up to a greater dragon. But there *is* a way. I'm sure of it. There's a way for me to bring Vampire Hunter D to his knees."

Samon squinted her eyes—a sudden gale had struck her. When she opened them fully again, Glen was facing her.

He's gone mad, thought Samon. That was the only conclusion his expression allowed her to draw.

"There certainly is. Just one," the seeker of knowledge shouted, his whole body trembling. "When you went to get me some dinner, you also brought back news you'd heard. For once, I have to believe there is a God. Ah," he sighed, "to think that I was defeated, standing there on the brink of hopelessness when my savior should appear in such a form—"

All hint of color drained from Samon's expression. This fierce sorceress would leave the faces of even hardened combatants pale, but she backed away as her body filled with a mind-numbing primal fear.

"You can't be serious," she said, her lips trembling as she spat the words. "You wouldn't actually do *that* . . ."

"Yes, I'll become a Noble," the man declared resolutely, his eyes colored by a killing lust. "Although technically, I'd be one of their servants if a Noble bit me. Yes, little more than a fiend following the commands of the one who bit him, wandering the earth seeking the lifeblood of the same human race to which he once belonged. But none of that matters to me. Not if that's what it takes to surpass Vampire Hunter D." Laughing, he added, "Come to think of it, we could never ask for a clearer motive to do battle. A Hunter against a servant of the Nobility."

Samon was left stunned, literally rooted by his surpassing vindictiveness, and as Glen came before her, he reached out with his wounded right arm and grabbed her pale throat like an eagle clutching its prey. The woman tried to twist away, but he brought his face up to her light pink lips and said, "Starting this evening, I'll be going out every night. Looking for *him*, of course. You're going to ask around the village and try to find someplace he's likely to appear. We'll both be looking for him."

"But that's simply—Do you think I'd do that? Do you think I could?" Samon asked, her voice trembling. She was terrified by the tenacity of a man who could seriously order her to do such things. A blade of ice rode down her spine. It was actually quite sensual. Samon could feel her crotch growing damp.

"Do you have a problem with that?" Glen asked her. "If so, I'll throw you off this cliff right here and now. If you can't do anything but dress my wounds and roll in my bed, then the only thing you'll be good for is filling the bellies of the fish that gather down there."

Hand still locked on the woman's pale throat, Glen pulled her close. Samon didn't fight him. To the contrary, the temptress wrapped both hands around Glen's head and put her lips to his.

A long time passed.

As the string of saliva between them trembled with Samon's ragged breath, she stared at the man and practically panted, "I'll be glad to follow your commands. Up until the very day the Noble sinks his fangs into your throat," she laughed.

The woman's body was writhing with passion, but Glen knocked her down with a rough shove.

Letting the most lascivious of smiles rise to her lips, Samon said, "Well, I'll be going now. I have to meet with my colleagues and decide what our next move in this battle will be." Giggling, she added, "But I'll be back in your bed again tonight."

Once Samon had walked off, Glen turned to face the sea alone. And just after he did, the most astounding remark came from behind him.

"You just don't die, do you, pest?"

When Glen turned in a completely unhurried fashion, he was confronted by a muscle-bound giant standing fifteen feet away.

"My name is Egbert. I suppose Samon's told you about me."

As the man poked the iron staff in his direction, Glen smirked and said, "You've been there behind the rocks for some time now, haven't you? Yes, I have indeed heard your name. So, what's your business with me?"

"I want you out of town right now. Although, from what I just heard, I don't think you're likely to comply. So I'll have to feed you to the Nobles' fish the same way you were about to give them Samon."

Egbert's staff sank, and the tip of it touched the cliff, where it slowly began to etch a thick line in the stone. Glen didn't know yet what this action signified.

The tip of the cliff where Glen was standing was roughly twenty feet wide. After he'd completed drawing a line across the entire width, Egbert smiled and said, "Where you're standing—from this line on—is my kingdom. And now I'm about to smite an invader. I'll smite you in the name of King Egbert!"

Glancing at the iron staff the giant had braced for action once again, Glen sneered, "You think you're good enough to kill me? Fine. But I can't believe there's a warrior stupid enough to throw his life away because he's lost in the charms of some worthless slut. I don't have the use of my good arm," he added, "but I should still have everything I need to show you just how much better I really am. Come on."

Egbert's immutable, dignified countenance was ablaze with rage. After joining forces with Shin to attack D and failing miserably, he hadn't returned to the group's hideout, but had walked around the village instead. Gyohki and Twin had their own roles to see to, but

Samon hadn't been around since the previous night. As Egbert had convinced himself there was no point in heading back yet, the real purpose of his wandering had been to find the woman.

Of the five enforcers, Egbert seemed to have the most human blood coursing through his veins. As a result, he'd been drawn to Samon, whose nature was diametrically opposed to his own. Perhaps he hadn't expressed those feelings to her because he'd considered how many dissimilar points there were between Samon and himself, but when Egbert learned of Glen's existence from Shin—who'd followed the woman that first night she left their hiding place—his body burned with a terrible jealousy. Since Samon's compatriots understood that she had to throw herself at Glen in order to manipulate him, the giant hadn't voiced his personal opposition to the arrangement, but he swore to himself he would eventually settle matters with the swordsman. Finding just whom he sought there with Samon on the cliffs at the edge of town had left him almost demented with joy. And now that Shin had been slain and Samon had left, he was free to settle matters with this rival suitor completely unfettered.

"Hyah!" Egbert cried in a voice as sharp as tearing silk as he braced his lower half for battle, and then kicked off the ground.

Throwing a look of pity and contempt at the giant form as it made a pointlessly high leap into the air, Glen was then astonished as he tried to make a thrust with the sword in his left hand. His blade seemed to weigh five times as much, and it moved with a proportional sluggishness. When he barely parried the few dozen pounds of iron bar swinging down at him, it was not due to any miracle, but rather to sheer dexterity.

His sword shattered.

"Would you look at that," Egbert cried.

Dodging a horizontal swipe of the staff, Glen was forced back to the tip of the cliff. While his opponent's speed hadn't changed at all, the swordsman's was only a fifth of what it usually was. The instant Glen realized how truly dire the situation was, a powerful blow landed on his torso, sending him flying.

There was no rocky terrain below him. Without a sound, Glen the "seeker of knowledge" fell headfirst from a cliff nearly one hundred fifty feet high into the choppy sea full of monstrous fish.

III

Tousled by the cool breeze, Su-In's hair fell across her face, forcing her to repeatedly brush it out of the way with her fingers. The chill borne on the wind was due to the chunks of ice offshore. The weather controller's unfathomable logic also held sway out there, but when summer called on the village, it didn't extend out to the far reaches of the ocean. Cold air brought by the north wind grew tepid out over the sea, becoming a cool breeze that blew through the coastal town, normally unheard-of in summer. It was their summer wind.

Su-In was standing on a promontory. It was early afternoon—about the same time Egbert and Glen were engaged in their deadly conflict. The bluish green of the sea before her hurt her eyes. Although partway out it should've changed to a freezing ash gray, the sea that was visible from here was the color of summer, as if it'd been emblazoned with the blue of the sky and the green of the grass.

Pale ice floated out beyond the invisible line, while a little shy of it—about three-quarters of a mile from shore—a number of mid-sized power boats ripped the waves into white bits as they chased schools of fish. Based on their position, she thought they might be after rumble tuna.

She was at a spot about a twenty-minute walk from her hideout. It was called "Cape Nobility." She'd come here countless times as a child, and the initials she'd left remained scratched on the rocks and carved in the trunks of nearby trees.

As she'd looked out at the sea back then, she'd thought, *I'm going to live here!* But things were different now. She wondered instead, *Can I really live here?*

Fatigue rode heavily on her shoulders. Up till now, she'd had a way to deal with that. But over the last few days, Su-In had come to feel a strange sense of loss over how extremely important Wu-Lin and Grampa Han had been to her. She'd thought she had the confidence to live—the confidence to live entirely on her own, that is. But then her younger sister and grandfather had been taken from her. Su-In realized she wanted to go somewhere far away once the summer was over. She didn't think she could bear the next winter.

A certain face drifted into Su-In's mind, making her tremble in the warm air. The man she'd seen in the tunnel—he'd been in her dream last night, too. But she could swear she'd never seen his face before. And yet, something ineffably heavy and dark was closing around her heart.

Who was he? That was the biggest mystery, although she could accept that much. But another question welled up in her, and it brought terror with it: *What is he to me?*

Shaking her head, Su-In tried to call to mind a different face— the face of a young man who was far more handsome; colder, and harder. Though he hadn't told her a single thing about himself, she simply knew he'd traveled a path rougher and more horrid than anything she could ever imagine. And the mere thought of this lifted the weight off Su-In's chest and gave her a serene feeling.

However, the Hunter was bound to leave someday. That, above all else, was a certainty. Perhaps the whole reason she had him looking after the bead was because she didn't want him to leave. The truth of the matter was that Su-In was terribly afraid of the way her heart was behaving.

Her eyes were filled with an indistinct view of the sky and the sea, but they suddenly focused on a single point. One of the power boats towing nets out by the ice floes had suddenly listed to one side. And what the woman saw next left her speechless.

In the time it took her to unconsciously blink two or three times, the bow of the vessel was raised high in the air, the men on board were thrown into the dark water, and then the boat slid down into the sea so effortlessly it was unbelievable.

Noticing what was happening, one of the vessels accompanying the ill-fated boat cut free its own nets and swung about.

Su-In gasped.

In the sea off the ship's starboard fore, something black suddenly reached from the water. At this distance, it merely looked like a thin line, but Su-In pictured it as a crab's claw.

The captain of the boat that was racing to the rescue noticed it, too. He cut the wheel hard. The thing was less than six feet away. But the desperate life-or-death curve of his course only served to give whatever lurked in the sea the perfect angle to attack.

Su-In saw the limb that protruded from the sea pierce the bow of the boat. The vessel's own speed just served to make the claw seem all the more trenchant as it ripped its way down the hull like scissors slitting paper, and when the gash had gone halfway down the length of the boat, both the hull and its gaping wound sank into the sea. It took less than two seconds for the boat to list to the port side.

Having noticed the danger in the sea, another vessel began to flee. But before it'd gone thirty feet from the scene of the disaster, something happened. Although it didn't list and its speed didn't decrease at all, the distance between the boat's gunwales and the surface of the water was rapidly dwindling. As his vessel became a veritable submarine and sank beneath the waves, the captain threw himself into the water.

Unable to determine what was going on, another group of boats some way off started closing on the scene while Su-In shouted at them to stop, but they hauled the panting men from the freezing water and sped back toward the harbor without anything else transpiring. Nothing, that is, except for a certain pronouncement.

Although it didn't reach Su-In's ears, a heavy, dull voice that might well have issued from the king of all water demons echoed from the bottom of the sea, saying, "Know that any who venture out to fish shall meet the very same fate. The sea is now your enemy. If the thought of that fills you with dread, then do as I say. There is a girl in your village by the name of Su-In—you must take the bead she has and cast it into the sea any time within the next three days. Once you've done so, I shall once again return this sea to you."

The rescue boats returned to the village at full speed, and while the survivors were brought to the hospital, several other people hurried off to the mayor as quickly as possible to give him the urgent news. Insisting that the summer festival mustn't be disrupted, the mayor ordered the sheriff and members of the town council to assemble immediately for a committee meeting. The messenger sent to Su-In's house found D there, and when the young man appeared in a room in the town office like a black gale, the gloomy countenances were replaced with intermittent looks of rapture and horror.

Although D leaned back silently against one wall while the mayor first explained the current situation, then demanded some clarification about the bead and that it be turned over immediately, once the other man had finished speaking, the young man told them in an unhurried tone, "I don't have the bead."

"What in the—?!" the mayor said, the words dying in his mouth.

Everyone present exchanged glances. But no one was about to take D to task. They felt as if the threat from the deep suddenly stood right before their eyes.

"We have three days, don't we?" D said in the same steely tone as always. "During that time, either the bead has to be found or whatever's out in the sea has to be destroyed. That'll be fine with you, won't it?"

Once again the council members looked at each other, but all they could do was nod their agreement.

"Just what the blazes is that bead anyway?" the mayor said in a tone that made it clear this was the one question that couldn't go unasked.

"Even I don't know," D replied.

"Why did Su-In have it?"

"I don't know."

"What was that creature in the water?"

"I don't know."

"Where is Su-In?" one of the council members asked sharply.

"She said she had some shopping to do and was headed off to the village of Kraus. I don't know when she'll be back."

Kraus was the name of the port town where the ferry had landed.

"And another thing," the council member said doggedly. "As soon as you walked in here, it felt like all the air in the room had frozen. You're going to tell us just exactly what you are."

"You've got some nerve, saying that," Dwight interjected. As leader of the Youth Brigade, he was also part of the town council. "All I know is, he's a traveling bodyguard. Someday he'll be leaving our village. And isn't it the law of the Frontier that you never ask travelers about their past or where they're going?"

"This is hardly the time to be bringing that up, I think," the council member said to Dwight, thinking he'd found the perfect angle for his attack. "His answer to every single question boils down to 'I don't know.' Yet he has the gall to say all we have to do is defeat our enemy, like it'll be no problem. I'd sure like to hear just how we're supposed to do that. And even supposing the thing in the sea is taken care of, what guarantee do we have that a second or third threat won't surface as long as the bead and those connected to it remain in town? I'm worried about what'll happen next. Fine—we'll let him take care of the situation. But even if he squares everything away nice and neatly, I want you to remember that the matter of whether or not Su-In will be allowed to stay in the village will hinge on what kind of explanation we get when all is said and done."

"What do you mean, you heartless old pig?!" Dwight shouted, rising indignantly. "You lousy bastard! You think you have the right to say that about Su-In, or anyone in her family?!! When that wild son of yours got lost out in the middle of a blizzard and wandered off into the Nobles' resort, who was it that nearly froze to death out there finding him? Was it you? Was it any of you vultures sitting here around the table? Hell no, it was Su-In and Wu-Lin! And I hate to say it, but the last time you fixed up the house you still live in, just who was it that loaned you the funds you needed to renovate? Sorry, but was it the mayor? Was it the circuit bank? No, it was Su-In's grandfather!"

The council member averted his now-pale face. Logically speaking, what the man had said a moment earlier made sense. However, in a village like this where, aside from their one week of summer, they basically lived on sticks and twigs and slept in snowdrifts, a sense of obligation in interpersonal relationships had to take priority over pure rationality. The harshness of life on the Frontier wouldn't allow them to live any other way. If there was one thing people here detested more than a thief or a murderer, it was an ingrate.

"Yeah, but Dwight," another council member interjected, "there's some truth to what Tolso's saying. As long as we've got access to the sea, we can make a living. But even if everything gets taken care of now, what are we supposed to do if more of these strange characters come and pull the same thing a second or third time? I'm afraid that, in the end, Su-In's going to have to bear the responsibility for this. Bringing something as dangerous as a Noble into our one week of summer is a pretty serious offense."

"You bastard! Are you trying to tell me that this is the fault of someone living in the same village as the rest of us or something?" Dwight said, stepping away from his chair. His whole body shook with rage. "Great! That's just perfect!" the Youth Brigade representative shouted, waving his fist in front of the gloomy council member's face. "Well then, I'll bear the burden for my friend's crime. I take it you won't have any complaints if I get rid of that monster for you!"

"Now, that's not what we were saying at all!"

"Shut up! I don't wanna hear any more of your excuses!"

Dwight was just about to pounce on the other man when an arm in black stretched out in front of his chest. For a second, the expression the young fisherman wore made it look like he'd just been plunged into the heart of winter, but the man in black didn't even glance at him. Instead, he turned to the others, who were all swallowing hard.

"You mentioned the Nobility, didn't you?" D said like a beautiful shadow. "I heard it came from the sea. If I take care of this threat from the deep as well as the Noble, you're not to do anything else about Su-In or the bead. You needn't worry about a thing."

A buzz that fell shy of actual words filled the room. While the statement sounded preposterous, at the same time, everyone there sensed that this dashing young man might actually be able to make good on it.

"And how do you propose we destroy a Noble—particularly one that comes from the sea like no Noble should be able to do?" asked the sheriff. Fear and expectation intertwined in his voice.

"I'm a Vampire Hunter."

Now everyone's eyes went wide.

The mayor immediately said, "Well, now—in one sense, that's more than we could've ever hoped for. But I don't care how good a Vampire Hunter you are, what we're up against here is no ordinary Noble, you know!"

"I'm sure it won't be a problem," a dignified voice jeered through the open window. "He's a dhampir—so he's part Noble himself!"

Everyone's skin rippled with goose bumps. Even Dwight bugged his eyes, and he couldn't say a word.

Though D tossed his gaze toward the garden, the voice was heard no more, and all signs of anyone being out there had also vanished. The Hunter then quickly turned and told the group, "That's right." In an indifferent tone he stated, "All I ask is that you stay out of my way for three days," then exited with silent footsteps.

Everyone in the conference room was in a state of shock, and they slumped back in their chairs as if they'd lost consciousness. But before long, Dwight groaned in a troubled tone, "Oh, Su-In— what've you gotten yourself into?"

Shortly before D exited the meeting, the professor was leaving the vicinity of the town office at a rapid pace, walking down a narrow path that fed into the main street of the village as he said, "I believe that should suffice to restrict D's movements. All that remains is to locate the bead as swiftly as possible, but I don't know where it's gone—perhaps I should go back and scour that spot again?" he mused.

While searching for the bead, Professor Krolock had seen D hurrying toward the town office, so he'd followed the Hunter at a safe distance and reaped an unexpected bonus in the process. Though his cheeks looked ready to collapse from the sheer force of his grin, the professor did nothing to repress it as he hastened off toward the woods, where a waltz was playing.

Surreal Battles in the Icy Sea

CHAPTER 4

I

It was less than an hour after the trouble at the village office that D called on Su-In.

"Under no circumstances are you to leave," he told her. Su-In could sense that something was wrong, and asked the Hunter repeatedly to tell her what it was. After she mentioned that she'd witnessed the incident at sea, D explained the situation succinctly.

"So, who was the source of that voice?" Su-In asked, her eyes blazing with anger.

"I'm sure he'll show himself eventually. But for the time being, all you can do is stay right here."

"Okay. I'll do as you say. But how is the Noble connected to that thing in the water—you think it's something like that crab we saw?"

Making no reply, D asked her an odd question instead. "You said warriors had come to your village in the past, didn't you?"

Nodding, Su-In immediately replied, "Yes."

"Are you on good terms with the curator of the local museum?"

"Sure. She's a great person. And she's always been very good to me and Wu-Lin. In fact, she's the one who taught me everything I know about teaching school. Have you been to see her?"

"Yes. Yesterday," D said, gazing steadily at Su-In's face.

"What for?" she asked, a dubious expression shaking her girlish naiveté.

"At any rate, don't go outside." And saying this alone, D left.

After she'd watched the Hunter and his cyborg horse disappear in the distance, Su-In went back to the room and opened her book before she realized something.

D was in the dark. Perhaps due to some defensive system that still remained operational, a true darkness that not even a single ray of sunlight could pierce lingered above him. He could hear the waves. Coming and going, coming and going . . . He was at Meinster's castle—at the bottom of that colossal pit. But why had he gone back there?

Not even glancing at the wall of bizarre scientific equipment to one side, D began to walk along the shore. The chamber was vast. Although D could see by the light of a single star at night, even he couldn't see anything down here. Aside from the sound of the waves and the flow of the air, all he had to rely on were his own hyper-sharp senses as a dhampir. Or perhaps he'd already seen what he was looking for by the light of the illumination cord he'd carried last time.

Walking for another five minutes or so, he finally halted just shy of a stony quay. A square holding area had been carved out of the center of it, and a ten-foot-diameter sphere bobbed there with the breaking waves. A globe of flame spread from D's right hand. The light gave a pale blue tint to the edges of the sphere, revealing the seat fixed in the center of the craft and the bizarre machinery below. The panels surrounding the seat looked more like elegant cabinets patterned after bird wings than controls. The ring around the back half of the sphere must've been a stabilizer to control depth. Since no intake valves were visible, it was clear the craft didn't use water to submerge or to propel itself. This was one of the submersibles the Nobility had once used to "play" in the sea.

Going over to the quay, D touched the purple crystal that jutted from it. Without a sound, a steel gangway rose from the water, linking the spherical craft to the stone quay where D stood. Just as the sphere was locked in place, there was the sound of its motor turning over, and then part of the craft flipped upward. It was a doorway that allowed the Hunter to board as soon as he crossed the steel walkway.

D settled into the seat. The transparent door shut, and the seat turned forward automatically. Actually, the person seated in it could turn his gaze in any direction he liked and the omnidirectional operational system would follow the movement down to a thousandth of a millimeter. The seat then descended to the most ergonomic position, and the retractable control unit in front of it slid out at an angle adjusted to match that of the seat. A three-dimensional holograph of what appeared to be the submersible and its performance figures took shape in the air above the controls.

Shifting his eyes to the control unit, D inspected an unusual bulbous attachment that wasn't part of the standard equipment. It was a telepathic amplifier. Aside from the normal controls, this craft could also be operated by the will of its pilot. While it was common knowledge that the Nobility's superhuman abilities also included various telepathic powers, not even their advanced science had been able to incorporate such mental abilities into a machine. No one had, except for the ruler of this subterranean lair. Had it been Baron Meinster? Or *him?*

Gazing at the holograph for several seconds, D then threw a switch and shut off the display before turning on the telepathic amplifier. The walkway submerged, and the lines stabilizing the sphere came free. The main generator in the lower portion of the sphere set up a force field in front of the craft, and the sphere began gliding forward through the water with zero resistance. The scene to all sides was projected clearly onto window-like screens.

When the force field was set to the bottom of the sphere, the craft quickly began to dive. The depth reached seventy feet. Though the water was pitch black, the image on the screens was clear as midday. Readings from the craft's sonar were being enhanced and brightened by computers.

Advancing about seven hundred feet at a speed of roughly sixteen knots, the submersible closed on the black bedrock. There was a huge, perfectly round opening in the center of the floor—it must've been more than forty feet in diameter. That was the way out to the sea.

At the right edge of D's field of view, the depth, strength of the current, speed of the sphere, and other data appeared in rapid succession. The submersible entered a cave, and images in the craft clearly revealed the machinery set in the rocky walls. Wave generators, filtration systems, and saltwater synthesizers— everything one would need to make this subterranean sea as close as possible to the real sea, the crucible of life. Gyohki himself had been born here.

Rock walls that seemed to go on forever on all sides vanished unexpectedly. D was out in an incredibly vast area. He'd entered the sea. D turned the submersible toward where the ships had been attacked.

His foe was in these waters. According to eyewitness accounts, it was probably the same metal monstrosity that'd attacked him by the Nobles' resort. But what was it? Did D know, or didn't he? From the look on his handsome face as he watched the screens, there was no way to tell.

In roughly two minutes' time he reached his destination. The area was packed with schools of fish—it was a sight that'd make any fisherman's mouth water. The depth was thirteen hundred feet. It was another twenty-three hundred feet to the sea floor. D took her straight down to the bottom.

The comparatively smooth rocks were adorned by multicolored seaweed that swayed like submarine flowers. The riotous mix of hues made it look like a vast ocean garden on his sphere's screens. No doubt this place had been specially made by the Nobility for their pleasure outings. As proof, skulls could be seen half-hidden among the roots of the seaweed as it rocked with the current—almost as if the human remains feared the Nobility even now.

Colossal bones passed by. No doubt these were the remains of creatures that'd been spawned by the Nobility only to die in struggles against others of their kind.

D switched on the sensors. For three miles in any direction there was nothing save schools of fish. The larger shapes that occasionally appeared in the distance must've been giant killer whales.

The submersible continued to the north. Three power boats became visible between the rocks—each of them had its hull torn wide open. Not displaying the faintest interest in the wrecks, D had his submersible continue straight ahead.

The sight that lay before him was chilling. It looked like a vast, deep mortar that stretched on forever. As the slope descended smoothly, even the rocks and seaweed lost their colors, until the entire field of view went white. There was no more unsettling paleness in the world than this—the stark white of bleached bones. Though the conical depression was several miles in diameter, every last inch of it was completely blanketed by human skeletal remains. Surely these must be the remains of victims of a thousand years of the Nobility's "games" in the water, all swept here by the tides. The vacant sockets of countless scattered skulls were all turned toward D, and their mouths seemed to unanimously chant a curse on their cruel fate.

Following the slope of the depression, D slowly descended in the submersible. Ahead of the craft, the bleached bones were crushed by its force field and eddied all around it. The flesh of any ordinary person would've crawled at such a sight. Beneath the skulls that were raining down like balls, a black chasm yawned. The data informed him that its overall length was nearly a mile and a quarter and it was fifty feet across at the widest point. It was almost two miles deep. That was just about the limit of the submersible.

Points of light blinked on the sensor, becoming a three-dimensional image. Something was buried in the mud that lay at the bottom. A box. And it was shaped like a coffin. An abode of the dead, resting on the sea floor two miles underwater? No doubt the person D sought was its inhabitant.

The force field shifted under the sphere. The craft advanced at a speed of twenty-two knots. At the depth of eight thousand feet, the warning light went on. Disregarding it, the Hunter continued to descend.

The force field was positioned almost directly above a point on the sea floor that was slightly depressed. The whitish mud flew up.

At the bottom of the deep blue sea, a coffin rested peacefully. A bit larger than normal, it was ten feet long and seven feet wide. Sensors informed D that there were indications of machinery inside. But none of it was functioning now. Above it and around it, bleached bones that'd been disturbed from their sleep floated down like an unearthly snow.

D activated a remote manipulator that was mentioned in the performance data. A metallic arm stretched from the bottom of the sphere and removed the lid of the coffin. Sensors had already relayed the fact that the lid was made of steel.

Miraculously, the material that lined the box—satin, by the look of it—remained completely unscathed. The machinery that hemmed in an area large enough to protect a single sleeping person consisted of a variety of metabolic regulators and energy transformers. Judging from the propulsion unit nozzle set on the bottom of it, the coffin had most likely been intended as an emergency escape pod. As the situation demanded, the power for life support systems could be drawn from the seawater, and the coffin should've been able to protect its sleeping occupant for a millennium or two.

But the sensors provided D with a look at the force that'd rendered all the coffin's systems inoperable. The thick steel lid and box both had a straight horizontal slash through them right near the center. No doubt the energy that'd split the lid had served the same purpose as that which had given rise to this massive trench at the bottom of the sea.

The gold emblem on the lid consisted simply of the letter "M." It was Baron Meinster's.

When summer called, did he slip out of it and swim off to the village? The mud that was raining back down on it now said that no, he did not. Perhaps when he'd fled to the sea, someone had seen to it that tragedy befell him. And it had come more swiftly than anyone could've ever imagined.

Saying nothing, D sent the submersible climbing. It exited the chasm. A speck of light flickered on the left side of the display. And as soon as it did, a black form pounced on the craft, and something that looked like a leg impacted the view screen. For a second, the lights went out, and then the warning bell began to wail insanely.

II

Just as he crossed the boundary of summer, Dwight turned up the collar on his thermal jacket. It was terribly cold—and although he'd been accustomed to such temperatures until a day earlier, the cold was rapidly killing skin cells that'd just gotten used to warmer weather. About seven hundred feet ahead of him, there was already a string of ice chunks. Something colder than the wind hit his cheek, and at the very same moment his field of view was filled by what looked like a shower of white confetti. Only it wasn't paper— it was a genuine snowstorm. Ten minutes earlier, the summer sun had been shining down on the village as he pulled away in his power boat, but a mere six miles out to sea he was right smack in the middle of a winter storm.

"That's a hell of a change," Dwight grumbled, quickly swinging the bow of his boat around. Although he'd cruised over the line between the seasons while occupied with thoughts of Su-In, he wasn't exactly keen on the idea of plowing straight into the heart of winter to lure the menace out of the sea's depths.

Hold on, Su-In, he bellowed in his heart of hearts. *You've got yourself mixed up with sea monsters and dhampirs and all kinds of trouble, but I'm gonna set everything right. First, I'll take care of the monster and chase the pretty boy off. After that, I'll get the rest of them to recognize your character and all the good you've done. I can even replace the boats that got sunk out of my own savings. I don't know what the deal is with that friend of yours, but he's kind of won me over, too. I get the feeling I know how you felt when you hired him. It could be that driving him off is gonna be the most painful part of all.*

With darkened eyes that hardly suited such a broad-minded and frank-speaking young man, he gazed toward land.

It was just then that the water splashed off to his right. The loud smack that echoed was the sound of a sizable fish tail hitting the water.

Dwight moved with lightning speed. When he whipped around, he already had his spear gun braced against his shoulder. Although it held six shots, each weighed three times as much as the spears used by the average fisherman. This gun could punch through the skull of a seven-hundred-pound rumble tuna with just one shot. But as a result, the amount of gas pressure required and the weight of the weapon itself were beyond the bounds of common sense.

The sound of the splash faded away. It wasn't his imagination. And this wasn't where the schools of fish were. Could it be a lone fish that'd strayed from its school? Or was it something else?

Dwight cut the engine. The wind had gotten fairly strong in the afternoon, and the sea was rough. Miserable conditions for trying to locate fish.

"Come and get me," the man muttered, licking his lips. The will to fight became an energy that burned in his muscles—there wasn't an iota of fear in him. He was a fighter to the core. If he hadn't decided to make fishing his life's work, he might've been a warrior of some distinction out on the Frontier.

On the other hand, the thought of Su-In made his blood hot. They'd known each other since childhood, but in a tiny village like this, the same could be said for everyone around the same age. His memories of good-natured play with her were far outnumbered by instances when they'd squared off. If he hit her once, she'd given him two shots in return. When he'd teased her and said she was fat, she'd called him a Neanderthal and a whale boy. Strangely enough, that was probably what'd fostered his feelings for her. The girl was always looking straight ahead. After her parents died and they'd had the funeral, he couldn't ever remember hearing her reminisce about them. Su-In was always standing there on her own two thickset legs, solid as a rock. Still, there was a mighty gale blowing. And Dwight figured the time had now come for him to give her some support.

To his rear, there was a splash. Dwight turned around. Ripples were spreading between the crests of the waves.

"You'd better stop fucking with me," the fisherman spat.

"Hey," a sober male voice then called out from behind him.

As surprise and fighting spirit filled him, Dwight looked around three times. The well-formed face of a woman rested on top of the starboard gunwale. Her golden hair and alluringly pale skin were both glistening wet. For a second Dwight thought she might be a survivor of some shipwreck, but a certain incident quickly sprang to mind. The night before, his friends and the Vampire Hunter had seen a mermaid from the beach where the Noble had vanished. Was this it?! But the voice he'd just heard was that of a man . . .

"What are you staring at?" lips as red as a sunset clam spat in the same voice as before. "I don't know what brings you out here, but I'm glad you're here. I went out for a swim last night, but I've grown so weary of the taste of fish. I yearn for human flesh, like long ago."

Not one to be intimidated, Dwight asked, "You the one that sank those boats?" He quickly added, "Long ago? What the hell are you?!" His right index finger had the trigger of the deadly weapon pulled back as far as it would go.

"I don't believe I've seen you before, have I?" said the woman, or someone with a woman's face, at any rate. "Nearly a thousand years ago, I'd drag striplings like you down into the water and devour them. That was always a tasty treat." Laughing, she added, "I've restrained myself the last thirty or forty years, but as soon as I hit the sea here in my hometown, the taste of it came back to me."

"Save it for someone who cares!" Dwight barked back. "Are you a man or a woman, you bastard? I'm not much for killing women, but based on what you just said and the voice you said it in, I'm not about to stand idly by, either. So, were you the one demanding we give him the bead?"

"The bead?" said the woman with a man's voice. "You know about that, do you?"

"So, it was you after all! Get ready to meet your maker!"

Compressed air launched the missile at a speed of five hundred feet per second. Though the shot should've slain the woman, it only ended up taking off a bit of her golden hair before it sank into the sea, thanks to a big wave that'd hit unexpectedly and thrown Dwight's aim off.

"Damn it all!" the fisherman shouted as he reached for the starter button on the engine. But at just that moment, the boat rocked violently beneath his feet.

The sky whirled around—or at least it looked that way while Dwight plunged into the blue water with his coat and his gun, sending up a spray. Even as he fell, Dwight kept his eyes open—dragon fish and ryxan sharks usually attacked people the second they went in the water, tearing the flesh right off of them.

The woman's face was right in front of him, and her deep red mouth snapped open mercilessly. Even when he saw the rows of fangs that lined the crimson maw, Dwight wasn't surprised. The mouth of an armor shark was fifty times as big, and its jagged teeth were a hundred times the size of hers.

"You just blew it. Coming at me head-on was a big mistake," Dwight muttered as he shifted the spear gun to his right hand.

Grabbing his shoulders with both hands, the woman went for the base of the man's neck.

Shoving her head away with his left hand, the fisherman jammed the spear gun against her side. This time he didn't miss. A projectile that could go through three feet of tidal whale blubber and another eight inches of cranium pierced the soft female flesh, sailing off with a bloody trail to vanish into the depths of the sea.

The woman reeled backward. As she executed a somersault, Dwight launched a third spear at her torso. Her agonized movements twisted her body in ways unimaginable for an ordinary woman, but the third spear hit her just below the waist—right in her scale-covered abdomen—and sank halfway into her before stopping. As she continued to writhe, the woman stared steadily at Dwight. It was a look of such violence, such loathing.

Gripped by an unearthly horror, the normally fearless man of the sea kicked desperately through the water. His head smacked the hull of the boat. His failure to start the engine earlier had proved fortunate.

Tossing the spear gun into the boat, Dwight then climbed in, too. He hastily started the engine. Ahead of him, the deck of the boat burst upward, and a pale hand shot up through the hole along with the water. The hand then vanished. When he finished stopping up the hole with repair putty, another spot on the deck about a foot away was also breached.

Dwight knew he was in trouble. He wouldn't have enough time to make it back to land. Instead, he turned the bow of his boat toward the ice floes. It was too dangerous to stay out on the sea. He'd have to lure her up out of the water.

Setting the engines to full speed, Dwight headed back up to the bow to get his spear gun. Snowflakes blew against him. He'd just passed over the boundary again.

The surface of the sea swelled ahead of him. And the woman shot up from the water like a flower's petals bursting open, blood streaming out behind her. She looked positively demonic. Twisting in midair, she began a rapid descent.

Dwight's right hand still hadn't reached the spear gun.

What Su-In had forgotten was her textbooks. Even though she was dealing with children in her class, she still had to prepare the lessons. As soon as she recalled her oversight, it immediately started to drive her crazy.

D had told her everything he knew about the attacks she'd witnessed from the cape. She'd also heard that the major figures in the village had been informed about D's true nature. Chances were she wasn't going to be able to stay in the village much longer. But maybe that would be for the best. A northern village like this didn't have anything that would make her want to stay. And if she'd survived up there, she should be able to make a living anywhere.

D's elegant good looks filled her mind for a moment. That might be the way to live. Not that she'd be able to go with him, but maybe a life of one journey after another would suit her nicely. Hell, maybe she could go with him after all . . .

Su-In then recalled thinking that she might've seen D smile once. If she stayed with him, maybe someday she'd get to see that smile again. But all the woman's thoughts about that first taste of sweet happiness were consumed then by other tiny faces. *Teacher,* they were saying, *when does school start?*

Today, Su-In replied to them in her heart of hearts. She hadn't told them she was leaving yet. At the very least, she was still their teacher. The thought that she might never again stand at the lectern only served to strengthen her resolve.

"I suppose the least I can do is prepare a lesson for them," she muttered.

It was two hours after D had left that she headed off to her house. The air had a faint bluish tint to it, and it was brighter than usual. But Su-In was wrapped in a feeling of desolation. Empty for just one day, her home seemed as cold and distant as a stranger's abode. Wu-Lin and her grandfather were no longer there, after all. Su-In could hear the distant music of the festival as she went into the main house.

The textbooks were on a bookshelf in Su-In's bedroom, but now that she was here, there were a number of other things she wanted to get as well. Detergent, a spare light, fuel briquettes, another coat . . . She ran all over the house grabbing this and that, and before she knew it, the blue world outside was about to don its darkest shade. Gripped by a fear she couldn't quite understand, Su-In switched on the living room light and began stuffing her belongings into a bag.

Less than five minutes later she was done. Shutting off the light, she grabbed the door knob. Although she could turn it, the door wouldn't open.

What the hell?! she thought.

She put all her weight against it, but the door wouldn't budge an inch. It didn't feel like someone was pushing against it, or that the door had been locked. The entire door wouldn't move in the least, as if it'd been glued in place.

Then Su-In remembered a similar incident. Clutching her bag, she ran for the door to the kitchen. But just as she was about to go through it, a figure appeared from the right side to block her way. A gust of awful dread stroked the woman's plump cheeks.

"You . . . But you're . . . ," Su-In stammered, listening coolly to her own dazed words. "Grampa . . ."

"Su-In . . . ," the old man with the pallid face said, winking at her.

†

One blow from the attacker seemed to have blinded the submersible. The light-adjusted screens vanished, and the scene outside the windows was shrouded in a murky darkness. Fortunately, the holographic imaging system hadn't been damaged, and the Hunter learned quickly enough who his foe was. The three-dimensional image depicted the very same giant crab he'd encountered previously. Clinging to the top of the sphere, it was brandishing its claws.

No matter how resilient the glass of the sphere was, a blow from one of those steel limbs would be dangerous. The giant crab must've hidden between the rocks to conceal itself from the submersible's sensors. No doubt the crab had been closely monitoring D's movements.

Blows rained down on the craft in rapid succession. Although the sphere's force field could keep it anchored in one spot, it did nothing to make the craft any more damage-resistant. The lights went out, and a warning lamp came on. Another indicator reported that the generator was about to fail.

D shifted the force field to the top of the sphere. The crab was blown off. Blasted more than thirty feet through the water, the mechanical menace then recomposed itself. Folding all its limbs up, it sped back with incredible velocity. Apparently, the giant crab had highly efficient stabilizers and shock absorbers working on its behalf.

In accordance with the force field setting, the sphere continued to rise as D checked on the damage status of the craft. The Hunter felt a slight shudder. Something was wrong with the submersible's stabilizers. The force field projector was losing power, and if it failed completely, the craft would be left completely immobilized. But the gravest possible dilemma had also presented itself—the navigational power gauge was dropping by the second. Even before the Hunter had started this journey, it had been in the caution range. Now the power wouldn't last another five minutes.

D switched the force field to autopilot, and the force field then slammed into the middle of the crab at full power. The crab's legs twisted and its carapace creaked. But that was the extent of it. It was still coming after him.

The submersible didn't have either the weapons or the energy left for an undersea battle. Then the force field projector stopped. Any further fighting underwater would be impossible now. And the surface was still more than one hundred fifty feet away.

III

What wound up making the difference between life and death were the instincts of this seafaring man who'd lived out in the elements for so long. Before Dwight was even aware of it, his right hand had shifted to his belt instead, pulling out his gaff hook and swinging it at the grim reaper above him. The hook weighed nearly five pounds. With a *thunk!* it sank into the mermaid's waist.

A scream rang out, and a man's voice issued from the beautiful woman's lips. Due to the way Dwight twisted his body, the mermaid's descent was ruined, and she suddenly slammed down on the bow of the fisherman's boat. Dwight leapt over by the pilothouse and armed himself with one of the spare harpoons that were stored down on the gunwales.

The amalgam of woman and fish writhed on the deck. Stabbed in its human portion and still pierced by another harpoon in its lower half, it now had a thick gaff hook sunk in its midsection. No sight could've been more ghastly. However, even in her death throes, this beautiful woman had a face that was not of this world and eyes that were like nothing human. Her eyes were dyed deep red, and the fresh blood spilling from her mouth stained the fangs she gnashed incessantly. Fish tale squirming all the while, the woman glared at Dwight. That alone was enough to keep this man of the sea from hurling the harpoon he held at the ready.

The woman's hand seized the harpoon that pierced her waist. Wailing with pain, she tried to pull it free, but the barbs on the tip hooked into her flesh, stopping it. Agony warped her gorgeous countenance. Yet she kept on pulling. Even Dwight could hear the barbs ripping through her skin. With chunks of her own flesh still clinging to the harpoon, the woman threw it into the sea.

She moved to the gaff hook next. The hook came out easily enough. However, the woman didn't discard it. Clutching the five-pound piece of iron in one hand, she steadily crept toward the fisherman on her belly. With blood seeping from wounds in three separate spots, her whole body was smeared with vermilion. But even redder than that were her eyes, which smoldered with an awful hatred.

"I'm going to eat you . . . slowly," the mermaid said, her masculine voice choked with pain and curses. "But before I do, I'll rip you into a million pieces with this hook. Oh, how you're going to scream for me . . ."

"That's what you think," Dwight barely managed to reply. Despite the fact there was little power behind his words, he added, "Fuck you!" and hurled his harpoon with his remaining strength.

The woman's hand shot out in a horizontal blow, and there was a dull thud as the warped weapon dropped into the sea.

Covered in a fearful sweat, Dwight's face was suddenly blasted by snow. The woman was less than three feet from him. And there was still another fifteen feet to the ice floes. A hopeless distance.

Grinning, the woman bared her fangs.

Suddenly, the center of gravity shifted. In the sea just three feet off the starboard bow, a colossal sphere had bobbed to the surface, and the water it'd displaced had formed waves that struck the boat broadside. Although Dwight caught hold of the gunwale in an instant, the mermaid who'd been poised to strike was flung into the sea. Streams of blood trailed after her.

Somewhat bewildered as he watched a bloody cloud form in the sea, Dwight then quickly turned and stared at what had surfaced on the opposite side of his boat. Sounding stunned, he called out, "What in the—is that you, D?!"

It was a second later that the Hunter flew from the top of the sphere like a black wind, seeming to spread a pair of wings before landing on the deck of the boat. Not even glancing at Dwight, D gazed instead at the dwindling sphere.

"Hey!" Dwight called out to him, but then the fisherman's eyes bulged in their sockets. As if to push the spherical craft aside, a number of black, leg-like objects stretched from the sea.

That's the thing, Dwight realized instantly. *That's what sank the boats and tried to get us to hand over Su-In's bead.*

"We'll be onto the ice soon," D said sharply. "Make your preparations to get off. Here it comes."

"Got you!" Dwight shot back. Though there were a thousand questions he wanted to ask, he forgot them all, for he'd realized that the deadly battle he was involved in was not of this world. And in order to survive, he had no choice but to work with the gorgeous young man before him.

The blizzard erased the bizarre legs and claws. The ice floes were closer now. Skillfully manning the helm, Dwight brought his boat up against a flat section of the ice. D got off, and he followed soon after.

The wind and snow buffeted the fisherman's cheeks. As he knotted his hood beneath his jaw, he asked, "What are we gonna do?"

"How deep does it run around here?" D inquired. He was referring to the thickness of the ice.

"A good twenty-five feet at least. No monster's gonna follow us up through that!"

"Yes, it will."

"You can't be serious!"

"There wasn't any need for you to head out to sea, too," said D.

His softly spoken words irritated Dwight. "No one asked for your opinion," the fisherman shouted indignantly. "I came out here because it was the only thing I could think of to do. Did you believe

I was gonna just sit back and let you grab all the glory around here? If you're gonna give me a hard time, you can find another ride back to shore."

"Su-In would be pleased to know what you were doing, I'm sure."

"What?!" Dwight exclaimed.

"Keep your distance. It's me this thing is after."

And saying that, D spun around. Before him lay a desolate field of ice. The expanse was unusually flat.

"Hey! I ran into a weird sort of monster, too," Dwight called out.

His words stopped D in his tracks.

"A mermaid," the fisherman added. "She knew about the bead, too. Sure was a hell of a beauty, though it takes more than just looks to make a woman."

If Dwight could make such an introspective remark while the situation was still far from resolved, he'd already regained his typical boldness.

"I put two harpoons and a gaff hook into her, and it didn't even faze her," he continued. "When you popped up, she dropped back into the sea, but I get the feeling she's still hanging around here, just watching us for an opening. Heaven help me—I finally see why my dad's afraid of my mom!" Dwight said, though the groaning wind shredded his words.

Hit head-on by a particularly fierce wind, Dwight lost his balance and was driven back a few steps. "God damn it all . . . ," he snarled, trying to right himself again only to be driven back a few steps more.

It was a split second later that he learned it wasn't due to the wind.

The ice field between Dwight and D rose, and legs appeared after breaking through what had to be tons of ice. There were two of them, and the ends of the legs were spinning tremendously fast. While it came as little surprise that they couldn't break through the whole twenty-five feet of ice, the whirring drills worked on boring a larger hole, and surely the whole creature would appear once the remaining ice was thin enough to shatter.

The two men would've been stunned if that didn't take at least a few seconds more. Several more legs appeared, clicking as they twisted around to brace themselves firmly on the ice field with their claws. And then a black saucer that looked just like a crab stood before the pair, launching plenty of ice into the air in the process. The semitransparent dome in the middle of the thick body spun around to the front, and just as it halted, it split right down the middle.

An unsightly face quickly looked straight at D, and in an uninflected tone, the kingpin of Cronenberg—Gilligan—asked, "Surprised to see me?"

Su-In immediately guessed what was happening. Thanks to the harsh environment that'd raised her, she'd learned not to wallow in sentimentality. There was no way a dead person would be returning to life. Which meant this person before her had to be an impostor.

"Who the hell are you?!" she snapped.

Her grandfather's face grew distorted at her cry. The eyes, nose, and mouth all collapsed like melting rubber, and then a completely different face formed—a youthful one. Su-In had no way of knowing that face matched a man by the name of Twin.

"You're not very surprised, are you? What a disappointment," he said as he stretched his back, and he actually sounded quite crestfallen.

His clothes were still those of the grandfather. Su-In was just thinking how he was the same height and build as the old man when his proportions suddenly became those of a powerful young man. Taking a big step back, Su-In let go of her bag and braced the short spear she'd brought with her from her hideout. Aimed straight at the man's heart, the weapon didn't tremble in the least. She evinced the same skill as she did while fishing.

"Now, I'm not sure just what's going on," said the woman, "but you've gotta be one of the people after the bead—the same bunch that killed my grandfather and my sister. And the nerve of you, disguising yourself as Grampa Han. I'm warning you, I'm not gonna hold anything back!"

"I know, I know. Don't get so worked up about this," Twin said in a somber tone. One look at the spear Su-In leveled at him was probably enough to tell him both how skilled and how intent she really was. "I want to make it perfectly clear that I wasn't the one who killed your sister or your grandfather. Not that I have any problems with killing when I have to. Okay, just skip the pointless resistance and come with me."

"And what did you plan on doing with me?"

"We'll take you hostage and call him out," Twin replied. "The deal is, he gets you back safe and sound in exchange for the bead. That's the smartest way to play it, you know. The whole reason I stuck around here was to try and steal the bead, and to watch for an opening when I could kill him, but it just wasn't going to happen. He's too tough. There's not much I could do against someone like him all by myself. I even tried interfering when he was throwing down with that sword nut with the weird whistle trick, but it didn't do any good. Which meant I was left with nothing to do but the plan I just mentioned."

Twin let the tip of his left index finger slide down the head of the spear as he gazed intently at Su-In.

"Were you the one who tossed the back room, too?" asked the woman. "Just how have you managed to keep following me all this time?"

"I didn't follow you. See, I was here all along."

Su-In's expression shook with astonishment.

"I didn't disguise myself as your grandfather just now," said Twin. "They found his body in the sea, right? Well, that was me!"

"Well then—who was the guy D found disguised as my grandfather before?"

"My partner. Actually, to be honest, he's my brother. We were both born on the same day at the same time, so we don't know which of us is older. Since he was also posing as your grandfather, no one really suspected me. Of course, that Vampire Hunter had a sneaking suspicion. When he ran me through out in the barn, I was scared out of my wits!"

"If he stabbed you, why didn't you die?" asked Su-In.

"Because I'd turned myself into a corpse. Sure, you can stab a corpse all you like, but you can't kill it twice. If someone wants to kill me, they'll have to do it while I'm alive."

That must've been one of Twin's special warrior abilities. Transforming himself into a corpse so convincingly that even D couldn't see through his disguise and being planted in the ground, he'd only gone into action when necessary, then sank back into the soil when he was done. If his comings and goings hadn't been performed with positively inspired skill, there was no way he could've avoided detection by D.

"As I already said, Twin is a duo," the young man continued. "But aside from the two of us, no one in the world knows that. If it ever got out, we wouldn't be worth much as enforcers anymore. So, since you know now, I really can't let you live. Once you've served your purpose, I'll have to get rid of you."

Twin's hand reached for the end of the spear.

Su-In jabbed at him with all her might. All her anger over the deaths of her sister and grandfather was behind her thrust. Sliding between the man's fingers, the steel tip of the weapon struck him square in the heart. Twin's body shook, and then he seized the head of the weapon and pushed down on it. The business end of the spear was now behaving like a child's rubber blade, much to Su-In's surprise.

"See, this is what did it," Twin said as he spread his other hand for her to see. The semitransparent mucus that seeped out into his palm was the very same substance that'd dulled the edge of D's blade. "It's a type of fat our bodies excrete. Not that we can make as much as we like whenever we like or anything, but we have enough to protect ourselves from a sword or a spear, or to keep a window shut. So give up already," Twin said, but his last words came out in midair.

He probably didn't even realize what was happening until he'd flown clear across the living room and slammed into the very same door he'd sealed shut. He hadn't seen Su-In's skill on the ferry, where she'd dealt with one of Shin's puppets. But the way he twisted at the last minute and barely escaped hitting the door headfirst must've saved at least a bit of his warrior pride.

"Shit . . ."

As he got up from where he'd fallen to the floor with a face stark with anger, the tip of a whistling spear slammed into his throat and, warrior though his was, Twin vomited blood everywhere as he was knocked back against the door. Falling to the ground, his body then moved no more.

Although pain and regret drifted across her face for a brief instant, Su-In quickly regained her normal grit and pulled the short spear out of the man.

"I didn't want to kill anyone, but that was for Grampa and Wu-Lin. And you would've killed me, too. Don't idle now—move along to the next world. And be sure you don't wind up a servant of the Nobility."

Picking up her bag while still clutching the spear, Su-In headed once more for the kitchen door.

"Not yet."

More than the voice, it was the cool air stroking the back of her neck that had an impact on Su-In, making her turn.

Twin was standing there with his back to the door that led to the living room.

Su-In stammered, "How on earth could you . . ."

"Did you forget already that you can't kill a corpse? See, right before you stabbed me in the throat, I 'died.'"

The bag fell from Su-In's hand. Although she was trying her best to look natural, she had the short spear at the ready in front of her chest. But the instant Twin slid over to her without a sound, Su-In caught an intense blow in the solar plexus that rendered her unconscious.

"I've had enough of your screwing around. You wanna see what happens when a woman forgets her place? I'll slice your nose off to show you a thing or two," Twin muttered hoarsely, rubbing his throat all the while.

Squatting down by Su-In's side, he put the blade of his knife to the base of her well-formed nose. Although he had the face of a young man of cultured upbringing, as a warrior he was perfectly comfortable doing things that would make anyone else's flesh crawl.

Strength surged into Twin's fingers.

"You lopped my head off, but I survived. Oh, how it hurt then. It hurt so badly I wanted to die."

The snow flew fiercely, and the sound of the wind grew all the more sorrowful. But through the wind and the snow, Gilligan's bitter tone flowed out like a river of gloom.

"But I persevered," he said. "I kept going until I could get into this thing. You see, I did my homework for just such an unforeseen event. It didn't matter that you'd cut my head off—I wasn't about to just give up and die."

His sword already drawn, D gazed at Gilligan and at the black machinery that had become his new flesh. Then the Hunter suddenly said, "You're one of the 'Blood Seekers,' aren't you?"

"Oh, so you've heard of us, have you?" Gilligan said, and then he smiled silently. "Vampire Hunter D—you are no ordinary Hunter, nor even an ordinary dhampir. But why don't we see now which of us is closer to being a true Noble?"

Not responding, D brought his sword up perpendicular to his right shoulder—in the "figure eight" stance.

The Blood Seekers. In this world where the Nobility were the subject of fear and hatred, there was a cult that studied and worshiped their accursed blood—the very thing that made them so dreaded and reviled. All human beings face death one day, and the very thought of that eventuality can't help but turn a person's psyche to solid ice. And at that of all times, there's one thing that some people will unconsciously crave—the secret of the eternal blood of the Nobility.

The fanatics who sought that secret so they might share its power—taking part in all manner of cryptic rituals and even going so far as to let Nobles drink their blood—had been dubbed "Blood Seekers." To unravel the secrets of that blood, they would travel anywhere imaginable and learn everything they could about the Nobility—in ancient castles in desolate gorges, the sprawling remains of factories on lonely islands far out to sea, massive ruins that towered over the plains, and subterranean palaces where a wealth of information had been secretly cached.

Aside from his role as a kingpin in a Frontier town, Gilligan had another "role," and as a Blood Seeker, he had undoubtedly studied Noble manuscripts, gotten his hands on their products and mastered their technology, and even used his own body for experiments aimed at approaching the Noble condition. And it had borne results. The fact that D's blade had taken his head off yet he'd still remained alive was evidence of that. And the fact that he was running around in a piece of machinery incomprehensible to most humans was still further proof, which would mean that the secret of this "bead" he was risking his life to get had to have something to do with that, too . . .

"This time I won't let my guard down," Gilligan said with boundless confidence. "I've repaired the damage you did, painted on another coat of armor, and improved the engine circuits. It's twice as hard and twice as fast as last time. But if you'll tell me where the bead is—or rather, if you'll hand it over—I'll make your death a relatively painless one. We're out on the ice here—but go down forty feet and you're in the middle of the ocean. Your Noble blood will only work against you there. I, on the other hand, would have no problem."

The Nobility couldn't cross running water, nor could they swim. Secure in those ancient and immutable laws, Gilligan must've hidden himself deep in the sea and waited for D. When he'd challenged the Hunter on dry land, it'd merely been to get in a little practice with the machine. And he'd also foreseen that if he were to demand the bead, D would be sure to come out there.

"Hey!" the third person shouted, speaking for the first time. Dwight had both hands cupped around his mouth as he continued, shouting, "Just what the hell is this bead we keep hearing about anyway?"

Without even turning toward the other man, Gilligan said, "D, don't *you* want to know?"

Naturally, there was no reply. No doubt the only thought burning in D's brain at that moment was a plan to destroy the murderous black machine. No, that wasn't right. Beyond life and death, beyond anything and everything in the cosmos, this young man's thoughts were surely lacquered with a darkness no one in the world could fathom.

The figure of beauty advanced without a sound. When he'd closed to within six feet of the motionless giant crab, his pace remained exactly the same, but a silvery flash raced from sky to earth. It even sliced through the falling snowflakes. Giving off a beautiful sound, the blade rebounded from the giant crab. Dodging the legs that assailed him almost simultaneously with his own blow, D leapt back a good six feet.

"I suppose you see how useless it is now. Maybe you should try the same thing you did last time and drink some of your own blood to bring out your Noble nature, eh? By all means, allow me the pleasure of beating you as you *truly are*," said Gilligan. "Now, where is the bead?"

The sound of meshing gears totally shredded the normal sounds of the wind—it was the whine of the machine. Though its movements were less than fluid, it charged straight at D.

The tip of D's sword came down.

That move sent the crab circling around in the opposite direction. Its top half spun around. The launchers for its murderous wires were now pointed at D.

White smoke rose with a *Whoosh!* A cloud of loose snow. Although the curtain of white D's blade had thrown up from the ground was shredded an instant later, by the time its remnants had scattered in the wind, there was no sign of D on the ice field.

The crab was visibly shaken—apparently, it wasn't equipped with any scanning devices. The pilot's bubble spun around with dizzying speed, searching for the hidden D. Then it stopped.

The surface of the snow was flecked with red spots. Spaced a few yards apart and continuing across the ice floe toward the center, they were definitely drops of blood.

"You won't escape me," Gilligan cried from somewhere within the crab. "So long as you live, my dream will never come to fruition. No matter where you run, I'll find you and kill you."

And then the black mechanical monstrosity dashed off, its steps kicking up a cloud of snow that was almost beautiful. Even the great D couldn't hope to rival the speed of a machine like this.

Less than four hundred feet in, the bloody trail turned left. A snowy hill blocked the crab's field of view. Falling snow had collected over time on the irregular surface of the ice floes. D must've realized he'd be at a disadvantage fighting on the smooth field of ice. The bloodstains continued halfway up a slope of roughly fifty degrees.

Slowly the crab began to climb the frosty incline. Twice the snow gave way, but the machine deftly maintained its balance and climbed about twenty feet up the rise. At the top, there was no sign of D. The crab decided he must've concealed himself in the whitened banks. Jets of compressed air squealed in rapid succession, throwing up a cloud of snow. But the only scream was that of the wind.

The crab looked over the edge of the hill—the trail of blood continued there. Taking its own weight into consideration, it proceeded cautiously. If the snow and ice were to give way, it would prove problematic. Proceeding to what it'd apparently judged to be its limit, the machine had just stopped when there was a whirring sound as something wrapped around its leg. It was one of the wires the crab had launched earlier. By the time the machine realized the line had been thrown around it from behind and had turned around, a figure in black had already burst from the snow and had taken to the air like a mystic bird to close the distance between them. Though the machine tried to stop him with its other legs, they wouldn't move. Actually, a total of four of them had been entangled.

By the time the wire guns started going off, D was already in midair.

The glint of the Hunter's blade as he brought it down with one hand made Gilligan think of two things inside the machine's interior. *He'll never break through*, he first assured himself. But then he thought, *No! Not there!*

Yes, *there.*

D's blade sank into the machine, and it cracked open. Two days earlier, he'd struck the exact same spot up in the Nobles' resort. And in just the same manner, flames spouted from the iron crab. The automated repair system was spraying plastic sealant into the gap in an attempt to fill it.

Just as D landed, he brought his sword down on the four legs he'd immobilized. One of them was severed, and the crab's body tilted crazily to one side. Oil sprayed from the opening, staining the snow an inky black.

A claw attacked the Hunter. Ducking to avoid it, D then severed another of the crab's limbs.

The weight of the crab that it'd been supporting then shifted. Some of its legs sank into the snow, and beneath them there was an ear-shattering cacophony of destruction. Covered by the white torrents of snow and ice raining back down, the crab took less than two seconds to drive itself into the ground despite the fact that it weighed several tons.

The hem of his coat spreading out behind him like wings, D landed at the base of the mountain of ice that'd formed on the ground.

"What the hell is that thing doing?!" Dwight called out from behind him in a hoarse voice.

His answer came in the form of the engine sounds that started below the shards of ice. The glittering chunks shook, then collapsed without warning. Only the very tip of the pile remained above the surface when it finally stopped.

The crab must've dug a hole and escaped—just like it'd done when it'd first appeared from the twenty-five-foot-thick ice.

"Got away, did he?"

Not replying to Dwight's question, D sheathed his sword and turned to the fisherman. There was no tinge of tension or fear in the Hunter's handsome features, but Dwight shuddered as the wind-blasted expanse of snow and ice grew ever colder. Perhaps the only thing that was beyond life and death was beauty.

"I'll take care of him some other time," D said softly. "Until then, just sit back and keep watching. I think it'll probably be safe for the next few days, but you should still refrain from fishing."

"Okay," said Dwight. "None of this is anything like the sort of stuff that usually happens around here. Everyone's better off not knowing about it. At least while it's still summer."

Snowflakes stuck to the fisherman's face, then melted. As Dwight wiped them away with one hand, D faced the land. Back there, it was summer.

"It'll be over soon, won't it?" Dwight said in a distant tone. His eyes then dropped to D's left arm, and he remarked, "I just noticed something—what happened to your left hand?"

A Gem Stained Scarlet

CHAPTER 5

I

The second the hand closed around the base of his neck, Twin knew whose it had to be. Before the attacker's other hand could bring a weapon down on him, the young enforcer moved his right hand and jabbed at the foe behind him with his knife. It sliced thin air. And before Twin even had time to be surprised at not making contact with anything where his foe's body would naturally be, his throat was crushed and gouts of blood spilled from his nose and mouth.

He fell across Su-In's body as if shielding her, and didn't move another muscle.

"Didn't have enough time to turn yourself into a corpse," a voice muttered in the living room, although there was no one left to hear it, as one of the two people there was unconscious and the other had been reduced to a cadaver. "I got kind of caught up in the festive atmosphere and took my time coming back here, and what do I find? *He* isn't even here, but two people who shouldn't be are. For a little village like this, things sure develop quickly."

†

Feeling an oppressive weight on her back, Su-In opened her eyes. A bald head and wrinkled face had circled around in front of her with visible concern.

"Ban'gyoh . . . ," she finally managed to say. Her memory returned in a flash, and sitting up, she looked all around.

Seeing that she'd noticed Twin's corpse lying there, Ban'gyoh remarked, "He's been strangled. And I take it you didn't do it, did you? Which would mean . . ."

"So, you didn't do it either?" Su-In said, looking down at the body as she got to her feet. "Then I wonder who could've rescued me."

"I don't know. Who is this character, anyway? One of the people after the bead?"

"How did you know about that?" Su-In asked, a dubious look in her eyes.

Not at all flustered, the priest explained, "I was asked to lead a prayer for a bountiful catch today, and the house that I called on ended up being the home of one of the village's leading citizens. That's where I heard about the situation. Realizing how serious this was, I came over to see how you were making out, only to find you like this."

Su-In nodded. "A hell of a summer this has turned out to be."

"That it has," Ban'gyoh concurred. "But there's nothing to be gained by moping about it. Let's get rid of that body."

"We can't do that. We've gotta get it to the sheriff."

"It wouldn't do to stir things up any more during this precious summertime," Ban'gyoh said gravely. "From what I heard at that house, everyone from the mayor to the town council has decided to cover up the present trouble. The finer details can wait until after summer is over."

"That would be for the best," Su-In conceded. It was the right way to handle things. Right now, the week-long summer festival was the most important thing for the village, and it was no time to have everyone trying to solve Su-In's problems. "What'll we do with this body?"

"I suppose it'd be best to bury it in the backyard. He may've been a villain, but in death he sins no more. I'll give him the proper rites."

Thirty minutes later, Su-In went and put her shovel back in the barn while Ban'gyoh wrapped up the service before rejoining her.

"What'll you do next?" asked the holy man.

As they went back into the main house, Su-In explained her situation, then picked up her bag and returned to her truck.

"D must have the bead then, right?" Ban'gyoh said, wrapped in deliberation. Waving his hands to dismiss the subject, he then said, "I have an idea. What do you say to me seeing you safely back to your hiding place?"

"I'm sorry, but we're keeping it a secret from everyone. Even priests, I'm afraid."

"It grieves me to hear that."

"I'm sorry," Su-In said as she started the engine.

"I won't force the issue, then. Could you kindly give me a ride part of the way?" And with these words, Ban'gyoh climbed in beside her without even waiting for her reply. Su-In made no complaint—she was a resolute woman. They pulled out onto the street. Darkness played across the roar of the sea.

"Going right," said Su-In.

"Left for me," replied Ban'gyoh.

"Then this is where you get out."

"Yes, ma'am," the priest said as he jumped out of the front seat. His right hand was stuck in the breast of his cassock.

"Well, take care," Su-In said curtly, and then she turned the steering wheel to the right.

There was the sound of metal on metal.

The truck started to pull away. To the left. Although Ban'gyoh had gotten back into the seat beside her at some point, Su-In didn't even notice him. The vista that greeted her eyes must've been exactly the one she expected to see. Something glittered and shook in Ban'gyoh's right hand—a pair of gold rings that'd been separate a second ago, but were now interlocked.

"It must be fate that these served me with both you and your sister," he said in a voice so youthful it was inconceivable coming from someone with such an old and tattered appearance.

Ah, that voice and the golden rings in his hand—these were the trappings of none other than "Backwards Toto." The fact that Ban'gyoh was actually the Frontier-roaming master thief was a secret not even D had penetrated when they'd traveled together to the village.

"After hearing D had declared he was heading out to take care of the sea monster, I thought there was a possibility the girl had been left alone. And I see I was right on the money. I'll be able to question her at leisure and get the bead for myself. And what better hostage could I ask for?" Chortling in a low voice, Ban'gyoh/Toto stared straight ahead.

Though the truck had only gone about forty feet since turning left on the road, now the headlights picked out a black shape before them.

"D?!" Toto almost cried out in amazement, but he quickly noticed something. The figure wore no traveler's hat on his damp blond hair, and the road soaked up the water dripping from the hem of his blue cape. "The thing from the tunnel . . . ," he started to say, and then he chopped Su-In in the neck to knock her out and took her place behind the wheel. It was clear to him it was no coincidence this character had appeared before them twice.

Flooring the accelerator, Toto sped right at him with the truck. He wasn't thinking about killing the strange figure. His ultimate goal was simply to see to it they had every possible opportunity to escape.

The truck barreled toward the Noble like a charging bull and ran him down! Or at least that was the way it looked to Toto until the caped figure suddenly disappeared.

Ignoring Toto's grip, the steering wheel turned to the right. The thief didn't even have time to scream. Taking a sharp turn, the truck was off the road in no time, cutting across the embankment and plowing into the beach nose first. The vehicle came down with such force it flipped forward and landed on its roof.

Now upside-down in the driver's seat, the first thing Toto did was to check on Su-In's condition. The shock must've brought her around, because she was looking at him in a daze.

"We've got trouble. The Noble's shown up!" Toto said in Ban'gyoh's voice. He still wore the face of an old man, too.

A fearful shade flooded Su-In's countenance.

"And it's his fault we wound up like this," Ban'gyoh/Toto continued. "He put some damnable spell on us!"

Of course, the man had no way of knowing that as the Noble stepped aside a split second before impact, he'd also stuck the tip of his right foot under one wheel and twisted it, taking control of both that wheel and the steering mechanism.

"Where is he? At any rate, we've gotta get out of here fast!" Su-In said, her appraisal and actions both coming quickly. Shoving the door open, she crawled out. Toto followed right after her. Pulling a harpoon from a rack in the truck, Su-In remained behind the cover of the vehicle as her eyes darted all around her.

A cold wind stroked the woman's back. Turning, she found a figure in blue standing right there.

"But you're . . . ," she mumbled. Terrified as she was, she must've seen something in the Noble that inspired a feeling other than fear and loathing. "You . . . Who are you?"

Slowly shaking his head, the man replied, "I don't know . . ." His words were sucked under the roar of the surf.

"You're Baron Meinster, aren't you?"

Emotion stirred on the man's face.

"Mein . . . ster?" As the name trickled from his lips, it seemed like a question aimed at himself. A tinge of confusion flowed into his well-formed face, and in a heartbeat, a piercing light sparked in the depths of his eyes. "Meinster." This time he said it clearly. "Yes, that is correct. I have returned . . ."

The expression he aimed down at Su-In instantly became that of a cruel and arrogant fiend.

"I have returned!" he declared. "But why do I stand before a miserable creature like yourself?"

"Sorry to be such a disappointment," Su-In said sarcastically. She certainly didn't lack courage. And she hadn't even noticed the sound of people approaching from either side.

"Who goes there?" someone shouted.

"It's him!" another man cried. "It's the Noble!"

The beach was still under surveillance. These men had probably rushed over after seeing the truck have an accident.

The Noble—Meinster—turned around. And grinned. Two jagged fangs jutted from the corners of his thin lips.

"Hey, that's Su-In's truck!"

"Are you okay?!"

In response to their queries, Su-In replied, "I'm fine," as she got up. More than a dozen people had raced over to her. "Are you okay, Ban'gyoh? You'll be better off staying back there," Su-In called out as she stood ready with her harpoon.

All the men were armed as well.

A dozen against one—although those were hardly fair odds for a fight, the villagers gathered around Su-In were all chilled to the marrow. Baron Meinster, the legendary fiend, stood right before them. It wasn't easy to escape the psychological terror that'd been fostered in them over a millennium.

Suddenly Meinster went into action. Tugging at the harpoons held by the two men who stood to his right, Meinster took them away, tearing the men's arms off in the process.

"Dear lord!" one of them cried in terror.

Even their pain was forgotten as the men simply tried to get away, but before they could, the heads of both burst like watermelons—the result of one effortless swing of Meinster's right hand.

"Ki—kill 'im!" someone shouted, playing more to the men's fear than their courage.

From two different directions there was the sound of compressed air being released. Though battered by their own fear, these men of the sea were still true in their aim. In no time at all, Meinster's body was run through in a dozen places by iron harpoons. And there was definitely a black substance dribbling from his wounds to glisten in the moonlight.

A weird silence enveloped the darkness.

Rather than feeling delight at what they'd accomplished, the men seemed to think they'd just done something horribly wrong. They'd turned a Noble into a pincushion—and such a thing was almost inconceivable.

Meinster had his face turned to the ground. But then he smoothly looked up again.

Burning points of blood light froze the villagers in place.

"Well done," said Meinster. "You've done an excellent job of killing a Noble who's lived more than five millennia. But you cannot destroy me. You lowly worms will never have the power to accomplish that!"

The people saw his hands reach for the tip of a harpoon that pierced him. In a single action he tore it free and sent it howling through the air to impale the man who'd originally hurled it, as well as the person standing behind him. Even after they dropped to the ground, the rest of the crowd remained immobilized, and in due time they all fell victim to the harpoons they'd thrown.

Looking at Su-In as she stood there frozen in amazement, Meinster called out to her, "Woman! I've never seen you before—and yet, I have the strangest feeling I know you from somewhere. Do you have any such recollection?"

"No," Su-In declared bravely. Her tone was so dignified, she even surprised herself. "It's not my habit to have monsters as acquaintances."

"Is that so? Then I needn't show you any mercy. So here—"

When Meinster took a leisurely step forward, there wasn't as much as a drop of blood trickling from his body any longer. As his

hand slowly reached for the base of her throat, Su-In tried with all her might to knock it back. But the hand pulled away of its own accord.

Exhibiting a terribly human amount of uneasiness, Meinster looked at his hand and Su-In's face time and again.

Something stirred in Su-In's breast. Though a horrible fiend stood before her, she felt something that hovered somewhere between grief and nostalgia.

"Why . . . Why am I here?" Meinster asked her. Another face had taken shape behind the elegant visage of the Noble.

"Su-In?" the other face said.

"But you're—?!" Su-In cried, although she didn't even know what she was saying.

He knows me. Who could he be?

Perhaps due to the humid summer heat filling the air with the scent of the blood that'd spilled so profusely from the slain fishermen, the man's double-exposure set of features quickly became those of the one who called himself Meinster.

"You're a spirited woman," the Noble said. "Your blood may be lowly, but it should prove delectable enough. Now, show me your throat."

Once again the pale hand reached toward the chest of the paralyzed Su-In. The nails were perfectly manicured, and on the back of the hand was a single tuft of hair.

There was a clear, metallic *ching!*

And then what did the Noble do? He changed direction, and with the same leisurely gait he began to walk toward the beach.

"Now's our chance. Run for it!"

As Ban'gyoh's words echoed in her ear, Su-In voiced her agreement without a thought. "My bag," the woman then cried. She was still incredibly focused.

"It's right here," said Ban'gyoh, seeming very organized for a simple priest. But then, "Backwards Toto" would've been sure to take care of every detail.

Meinster only noticed the pair running for dear life toward the embankment when the coldness of the seawater that soaked him to the knees broke Toto's spell over him. The blazing blood light tinged not only his eyes, but his entire countenance, coloring him with hatred. For a Noble, nothing could be more humiliating than being duped by a human being.

However, Meinster didn't go after them, but instead calmly extended his right hand toward the figures that were melting into the darkness.

The pair was just climbing the embankment. A flash of blue light split the darkness, connecting Meinster's ring and Toto's right shoulder. Giving a small cry, Toto fell backward onto the beach.

"Ban'gyoh!" Su-In shouted. Vacillating for a second, she then jumped down too. She wasn't the sort of woman who could just leave an injured person there.

"I'm okay," Toto said in his false voice. "Don't worry about me. You'd better hurry up and go. He's coming!"

"You're the one that's hurt—you go! I'll buy you some time."

"Don't be ridiculous—hurry up and go now!" he said in a tone that almost shoved Su-In away as he picked himself up.

Meinster was coming toward them in no particular hurry. He'd passed the shoreline. Taking a few steps up the beach, he then turned.

Though Su-In and Toto couldn't see anything with their own eyes, they could hear a sound—the engine of a power boat.

Meinster alone saw it. He could make out the little boat chopping across the waves as it drew nearer, and the figure in black that stood at its prow. The night and the very darkness were cold and clear, as if they existed solely for that young man's purposes.

II

Once the vessel had closed to within fifteen feet of shore, D gave the order to stop in a low voice. As Dwight gripped the wheel, his eyes went wide. He'd just realized that the reason D had made him turn off their lights on the way back was because the Hunter had noticed the Noble on the beach—but in the darkness, and from a distance of more than six hundred feet. His latest command had come when they were fifteen feet from shore, just about to hit the beach.

So, I guess that's what it means to have Noble blood, he thought.

Leaping easily into the air, D landed on the sand right across from the Noble. Ten feet lay between them.

"So, we meet again," said the Noble.

"You really are Meinster, aren't you. I saw your coffin."

"My coffin?" the Noble said, his face twisting into a dubious expression.

"You don't know about it, do you?" asked D, though the way he said it made it seem like he'd expected just such a response. "At any rate, there's no place for you here. Go back to the darkness."

Dodging a flash of silver that whooshed through the air, the Noble sprang. Not back, but rather to the side. Into the sea.

D seemed to hesitate for an instant.

"As I expected, you have a problem with water, don't you?" the Noble laughed in a low voice. "Such is our fate. However, there have been those who've endeavored to change all of that. Like myself."

The Noble backed away, and the waves lapped around his waist.

"Aren't you coming?" he asked. "If your skills as a bodyguard are of use solely on dry land, I suppose you'll need to refund your fee. I shall come again. Only next time, it'll be from somewhere where no one will see me."

Before his foe had finished speaking, D stepped into the sea.

"Well done," the Noble laughed. "I will favor you with a fight now. You shall have a good taste of Baron Meinster's power before you are sent to your death."

From his right hand, a sharp black point flew at D.

Not bothering to lower the blade he used to parry the blow effortlessly, D closed the gap between them. From the upper right-hand side, he made a diagonal slash at the neck of the motionless Noble. The blade met no resistance—the Noble had sunk straight down into the depths. Changing his grip on the sword, the Hunter made a downward thrust, but it pierced only water.

"Take a good look around yourself," said a voice from underwater. Even with his ultra-keen senses, D couldn't discern from exactly where it had originated. Worse yet, there was something even D hadn't noticed up until now. The water that'd only been up to his waist had risen to his chest.

According to various legends that'd been propagated since ancient times, discovering a scientific basis for their own weaknesses was an endeavor that'd garnered every possible effort from the Nobility. To be precise, they sought to explain the destructive power of sunlight, their innate fear of the scent of garlic, and the way they burned from the touch of holy water—and some of the legends also mentioned running water.

Nobles couldn't swim, but water itself wasn't enough to destroy their immortal flesh. Even with lungs full of water, a Noble would have their heart kept beating by their accursed life force. The vampire wouldn't drown, but would rather fall into a sort of coma. However, even for a Noble, being left in such a defenseless state out on the Frontier was sure to prove fatal. If a water dragon were to chew one to bits, regeneration would be impossible. Worse yet was what would happen if humans should find the comatose vampire . . .

Because of this weakness, Nobles feared and cursed the water, and they hid themselves in mountain strongholds far from the shore. The Nobles who'd ruled this village were among the notable exceptions. And it seemed that of all of them, Meinster alone through his frantic efforts had achieved the results he desired and overcome this defect.

D felt the water around him leisurely forming a circle. While he realized it was due to Meinster's superhuman abilities, there was nothing the Hunter could do while his foe remained out of sight.

"Very well—here we go!" Meinster cried.

The normal movements of the sea were disrupted as a high wave assailed the Hunter from behind. A mass of water came down over D's head to swallow him. Or so it appeared for a second, and then he was leaping toward dry land with watery spray trailing behind him.

But look. Wasn't that fresh blood gushing from his abdomen like a stream? It was a wound from a short spear that'd shot up from underwater.

Attempting to stand up straight again, D thrust his blade into the sea to support his weight.

"That was actually aimed at your heart—but you're as good as I expected," the voice said again. "But not this time—"

When the last syllable came out with a faint tremble, a black shape zipped through the same spot where the Noble had disappeared. Its propeller churning water and sand, the boat was turned sideways to shield D from the waves, but its hull rolled almost immediately. Just before it did, Dwight jumped off.

"You okay?" the fisherman stammered, the color draining from his face as he rushed over.

"Get up there," D said with a toss of his chin toward land as he turned his eyes toward the sea's black surface. A dozen seconds passed. Breaking his stance, D returned to the beach.

Dwight was grimacing. He'd found the bodies of those who'd been slaughtered. But one look at D's abdomen left him pale, and he said, "Hey—you need a doctor!"

"It's not as bad as all that."

Grabbing the spear tip where it protruded from him, D pulled it forward. There was the sound of flesh tearing. Dwight alone grimaced, while the Hunter only crinkled his brow ever so slightly.

"I'll be damned if everyone around me's not some sort of freak," Dwight spat, his shock swinging a tad toward hatred. Turning to the sea, he said, "That bastard—he ran off!" His words carried the implication that slamming his whole boat into the Noble had proved effective.

D didn't reply. It would've taken more than that to make this foe forgo a chance to slay D. The way he'd sounded shaken with the last thing he'd said probably held the answer to that question. Some sort of change had taken place within the Noble—the last word he'd uttered had been in someone else's voice. "Su-In," he'd said.

D looked over at the embankment and said, "Su-In and Ban'gyoh were here."

"What?!" Dwight shouted as he jumped up. He turned toward the embankment with great haste. "They're not here now," he said. He seemed relieved, and the tension drained from his shoulders.

"She was headed the wrong way," D muttered.

Su-In would never go toward the village instead of her own house.

From quite some distance offshore, icy eyes watched as the two men went from the edge of the surf to the embankment.

With the demure laugh of a woman, a man's voice then said, "I've found his weakness! And the sea, of all places, is my home. I eagerly await our next meeting."

Samon entered the hut. It was a little building used for storing nets and fishing tackle. As the Nobles' road ran into the village, a narrow strip of shore continued along the edge of it. This was one of three such huts that stood by the edge of the beach.

Closing a wooden door with a broken lock, she heard a low voice from the floor of the fairly spacious room ask, "Did you see him?"

"No," Samon replied, shaking her head as she approached the shadowy figure who lay there. "How are you doing?"

"I don't have much longer."

Crinkling her brow at his self-deprecating tone, Samon pulled bandages and a jar of medicine from the paper bag she was clutching and set them down on the floor. "I'll change your dressings," she said.

"What's the point? Just leave them be." The voice was that of Glen.

Caught in Egbert's spell, the swordsman had fallen from the cliff to where the man-eating fish waited below, but he seemed to have barely escaped with his life. Barely—because while he'd said he didn't approve of what Samon was doing now, he didn't seem able to push her hands away as she reached for him, either.

"Try anything funny, and things could get ugly, you know," Glen told her. "It was one of your colleagues that did this to me."

"We'll settle with Egbert sooner or later," Samon said in an eerie tone as she unwrapped the discolored bandages around the man's upper body.

After parting company with Glen in the afternoon up on the cliff, she'd gone back to the hideout to wait for Shin and Egbert, but when neither of them came back, she'd paid a visit to Glen's room. Realizing that he hadn't been back, she was plagued by an ominous feeling as she searched the area around the cliffs where she'd left him, finally finding Glen laid out on the beach. She'd heard all about what'd transpired from the barely breathing swordsman.

What a sight he was. Not only did he have wounds from Egbert, but he'd also been attacked by the monstrous fish below the cliff. His body could be seen beneath the bandages, where his shoulders and chest were chewed up and bare bone was exposed. By the time Samon found him, he'd already lost nearly two-thirds of the blood in his body. After that, it was a miracle he was still alive at all. The only things that'd kept Glen going this long were Samon's careful nursing and the almost vindictive way he clung to life. Nonetheless, death was drawing ever closer.

" . . . see him . . . ?" Glen asked once again. He was slipping in and out of consciousness.

"I'll find him. You just have to hang on a little longer," Samon said. As she changed his dressings, her hands were heavy. Yellow pus seeped from his wounds.

The person she was promising to find was the Noble. Rumors were already spreading through the village that he had appeared the previous night. And only the man who came from the sea could grant Glen's two wishes—life without end, and the power of the Nobility. In her search for him, Samon had been walking the beaches.

Come to think of it, there couldn't be any more absurd hope than this. When would she find him? Even if she did encounter the Noble, how exactly was she supposed to make him grant Glen's wishes? Still, Samon was determined. She wasn't sure she could even get the Noble to listen to her, let alone convince him to do what she asked. And she didn't even know whether or not her own power could affect the Nobility. Yet she continued to look for the Noble on behalf of the tortured young seeker of knowledge before her.

This was the same hateful man who'd saved her, violated her, and then continued to seek her out for carnal pursuits as he would a common whore—and yet Samon, fearsome sorceress though she was, felt a fascination for Glen she couldn't explain, almost as if anything she could do for him would give her life meaning.

Glen was already half-dead. His body was nearly drained of blood, and the flame of life that sheer tenacity alone would not allow to go out was now guttering in the wind. When Samon looked at him, there was certainly a cruel and satisfied spark in her eyes. But despite that gleam, her actions weren't prompted by some desire to see Glen's suffering prolonged, but rather because the woman wanted him to live, and wanted to help keep him alive.

Suddenly, Glen turned around. Samon looked down at the floor. Was that really the face of the handsome young seeker of knowledge? Surely he must've hit something as he fell from the cliff, because the left side of his face was caved in, and his eye remained sealed beneath a swollen eyelid. His cruelly swollen upper lip revealed his teeth and gums, although half of the former were now missing, leaving him looking like some hideous old man. A chance meeting with him in the middle of the night would've undoubtedly made even a fairly bold man faint dead away, let alone a woman.

"Again . . . ," Glen groaned in a voice as thin as a thread. It was the tone of a dead man, and even Samon's keen hearing barely managed to catch it. "Go . . . look for him . . . again . . ."

Samon nodded. "Understood. I won't be long. Just hold on until I get back."

"Go . . . ," Glen said, the word slipping from him like a brief gasp before he turned his face toward the floor.

Checking to make sure he hadn't breathed his last, Samon then got back up and left the hut. If anyone had been there to see her as she did so, they would've been utterly paralyzed. A lurid aura welled from every inch of the woman.

Apparently unable to break her attachment to the swordsman, Samon headed off without hesitation toward the sea from which the Noble was rumored to come. Roughly twenty minutes had passed since D and the Noble's deadly battle on the beach had ended. Once Samon was in up to her waist, she drew her dagger. And what she did next would make anyone wonder what manner of woman she was. Putting the keen blade against her own pale neck, the beautiful warrior woman slashed through the carotid artery with one firm stroke. Something inky spread through the water.

"That should do it. If I die, he dies. The rest is up to fate . . ." Laughing, she added, "A life in hell with him will prove interesting."

And with that disturbing remark, the woman's pale figure slowly toppled over into the darkening water. Her now completely motionless body seemed to spread out and dissolve into the sea, while the trail of fresh blood that gushed from her swayed with the approaching waves like a length of cloth.

Glen heard the footsteps of approaching death. The footsteps of a shadowy figure.

His strength was pushed to the limit now as his consciousness threatened to fade away. With all his might, he tried to recall a certain face—the face of a young man far more handsome than himself. Doing so had been the only thing that'd allowed him to survive these last few hours. Hatred roused his consciousness, and curses brought his senses back to life. He couldn't lose. He couldn't let himself die without winning. If anyone was going to die, it would be his opponent in battle, as always.

The gorgeous features didn't appear before him. The footsteps of the shadowy figure didn't fade away in the distance. They were steadily approaching. And they stopped right by his ear.

Something cool touched Glen's neck, but he couldn't even feel the chill anymore.

This is the end, he thought.

Someone called out, "Glen."

By some miracle, this stimulated his cerebrum, setting his nerves trembling and giving him back his sight.

"Glen."

He opened his eyes. The face of a woman he recognized was looking down at him from above. For some reason, she had one hand pressed against the nape of her neck.

"You're . . ."

"You're going to get your wish," Samon said, her voice like frost as it rained down on his shattered beauty.

He was going to get his wish? Then she must've found the Noble. But how had she ever convinced him to come here? No, that wasn't it.

"Just as I was about to expire . . . I met *him*," said Samon. As she bent over Glen, her eyes were strangely red, and her skin was unusually pale. "I couldn't get him to bite you. But drinking my blood was another matter . . ."

Samon opened her mouth. Two teeth jutted from those pearly white rows like beastly fangs.

"And now," she said. "I can drink your blood . . ."

Glen's eyes sparkled. They shone not with fear or loathing, but with immeasurable delight.

What manner of man was this? And what manner of woman?

Before Samon's hands even touched him, Glen had pulled his own collar aside to expose his throat.

Fangs as white as snow sank into his pallid flesh.

III

Having been struck lightly on the cheek, Su-In woke up. A shudder ran down her spine. From an oddly high place, a monstrous visage was peering down at her. She soon realized it was only a picture. Suddenly, she knew where she had to be. It was a deserted temple on the southern fringe of the village. The monster on the ceiling was an illustration of a guardian of Hell she'd seen more times than she could count as a child. It was devouring people.

"Pretty disturbing picture, isn't it?" said a voice above her head.

Su-In tried to get up, but her body wouldn't move. Although she was completely consciousness, her nerves remained fast asleep.

"Sorry, but I had to dope you. This stuff doesn't have any side effects, but you're not gonna be able to move again until tomorrow night."

The face of a man she'd never seen before was looking down at her from above. He was smiling. And although Su-In knew she should hate him, she actually felt the waves of turbulence fading within herself.

"Are you Ban'gyoh?" Even the way she asked this was composed.

"You could say that. My real name is Toto. Nice to meet you. As you can see, I'm a complete gentleman. If you don't try anything funny, I'll deliver you home safe and sound."

"And a gentleman kicks a woman in the gut out of the blue while she's seeing to his wounds?! Don't make me laugh!"

That was precisely what he'd done in order to bring Su-In there from the embankment. The woman's voice held a tinge of rage.

Grinning sheepishly, Toto said, "In my line of work, you can't exactly lay all your cards on the table. You just accept that sometimes you have to get a little rough. Of course, I had a hell of a time after I knocked you out. You ever consider going on a diet?"

"No one asked for your opinion!" Su-In snarled, turning her eyes away indignantly. She then pondered her predicament and an escape route. This was the main building of the temple. Judging by the height and width of the ceiling and the illustrations on it, she was certain that's where she was. Off to the right side, there should be a row of statues sculpted to match the images on the ceiling. And at the end of that row was a door. From there, it was a straight shot to the front door.

"What did you plan on doing to me?" asked Su-In.

"Nothing. Relax. It's not you that I was after."

"It's the bead, isn't it?"

"Right you are," said the man. "Where is it?"

"You think I'd tell you even if I knew?" Su-In retorted, thrusting her tongue out at him.

"No, I figured you wouldn't. Which is why I'd have to get *him* to tell me."

"By 'him,' do you mean D?"

"Who else? See, I'll trade you for it. As soon as day breaks, I'll write up my demands and go deliver them."

Su-In let out a sigh. This was exactly the thing that concerned D when he took her to hide deep in the ruins. However, there wasn't anything she could do about it now. Moving only her eyes as she scanned her surroundings, Su-In noticed a bag sitting about a foot and a half from her head. The clasp was undone—he must've already gone through it. Noticing something else, Su-In said, "Excuse me."

"What is it? You hungry or something?"

"That's my bag, right?"

"Yep," Toto replied.

"And you've already rifled through the contents, haven't you?" said Su-In.

"You bet I have."

"How come you put everything back neatly?"

"Huh?" Toto exclaimed, knitting his brow.

"An ordinary thief would just dump everything out and check it that way. After all, it's a lot less trouble that way. And a thief with a bit more manners might pull things out one by one, but then they'd obviously just leave them there." With amusement in her eyes, Su-In gazed at the Frontier's greatest thief. "When you were dressed like a priest," she continued, "I didn't have the faintest idea you were one of the bad guys. You're not connected to the group D's fighting now, right?"

"No, not really."

"Did it look to you like that bag was really valuable to me?"

Toto didn't reply.

"What would you do if I told you I knew where the bead was?"

"Do you really know?"

"Are you seriously gonna take everything everyone tells you at face value? You have to be the dumbest thief ever."

"No doubt," Toto said with a grin. It was a manly smile, the kind that might've drawn a coquettish cry from most girls. It brimmed with self-confidence. Though Su-In didn't know it, "Backwards Toto" was one of the Frontier's most prominent thieves. "But dumb as I am," he added, "I like to think I read people pretty well. Now, I don't know whether or not you know where the bead is, but it's clear to me you'd die before you'd ever tell me. Which is why I've got no choice but to leave a note with my demands."

"Why don't you try torturing me to death?"

"As a rule, I don't like to waste time or energy. You know, torture's a pretty tiring business for the person doling it out, too." Toto paused, his expression becoming so frightening he looked like someone else entirely as he said, "If you keep needling me like that, though—"

Shrugging her shoulders, Su-In redirected her gaze to the bag. "Huh?!" she cried.

Toto turned, too. He'd noticed the look on Su-In's face. "What is it?" he asked.

"Nothing. It's just that what looked like a big rat came out from behind one of the pillars and ran off. Maybe I was just seeing things."

"I'm sure it's nothing. There's no danger here in this temple," Toto said. Yawning once, he laid down right where he was. "Get some rest already," he told the woman. "We don't want to be cutting into your beauty sleep."

"While you were disguised as a priest and had the run of my house, didn't you ever think of trying to grab me?"

"Don't even joke about that," Toto said, shaking his head fearfully. His expression was hardened by genuine horror. "I couldn't pull anything with a bodyguard like that around. If I'd even thought about it, he'd probably have seen right through me. I was honestly just trying to be friends with all of you."

It must've been a kind of mind control. An outstanding con man was supposed to be able to understand the people he was swindling and pretend to be on their side up until the very last second of the con, and Toto could do that far more easily and skillfully than anyone else. Up until the very end, the people he stole from never even suspected him.

"Then why don't you just leave things that way?" said Su-In, a sober expression on her face.

"Huh?"

"Just keep on being our friend. Or if you feel awkward being friends, then just be one of us. Make up some fake letter of introduction or something—I'm sure you're good at stuff like that—and get a job in the village office."

"Spare me," Toto said, sounding like he was ready to retch. And then he looked at Su-In with amazement on his face. Was she an imbecile or something?

"No one's ever suggested anything like that to you, have they?"

"Go to sleep already," he told her.

"Hey, don't dodge the issue."

"Shut up!"

"If you stay in your present line of work, what are you supposed to do when you get old?" asked Su-In. "I can't help wondering if you've got enough money socked away somewhere."

"Don't worry yourself about it, you damned dope," Toto replied. His voice held anger—and agitation. The words of this sea woman had carried a strange weight. You might even call them persuasive.

"So, you know something about the bead?" she asked.

Toto said nothing.

"You mean to tell me you're going after it without knowing anything about it at all?"

"I've got a feeling about it."

"You met my sister, didn't you?"

Toto fell silent at this sudden change of topic.

"It's all right. I don't think you're working for the one who killed her or anything. But I want to ask you about something. Tell me how my sister was when you saw her. When she left the village, I never would've dreamed I'd never see her again."

For a while, Toto remained silent.

Without warning, his right hand stabbed into the darkness. Su-In managed to catch a glimpse of the silver flash that shot from it. There was a bizarre squeal, and then it was completely silent.

"What was that all about?"

"I took care of your rat," Toto replied, still facing the other way. And then he agreed to tell the woman what she wished to hear.

Su-In's eyes were twinkling, as if she were a little girl listening to a fairy tale coaxed from her stubborn but kindly father.

†

"Has Samon come back?" Egbert asked. More than the volume of his voice, it was the urgency of it that made the other figures in the murky chamber stiffen.

"What are you doing back so soon?" Twin could be heard to say from behind a white lace curtain riddled by the moonlight.

"How about Gyohki?"

"I'm here," replied a voice from the door to an adjoining room. "At present, I'm nursing my wounds. I was nearly killed, you see."

"Shin's been taken out."

"What?!" he exclaimed, his reaction brought on by Twin's words. Gyohki fell silent.

Today, Egbert had spent his time searching for Shin—it was a day earlier that he'd witnessed D killing him. However, when he'd returned to the scene that evening in hopes of at least retrieving his colleague's corpse, what he found there was nothing more than a doll that resembled a dead body. He was stunned. If that corpse was just another puppet, Shin should've long since rejoined the rest of them, whether he'd defeated D or not. But since Shin hadn't done so, they had no choice but to suspect that he'd taken the bead and run off. It was this very night that the man's corpse had been discovered off in the distant woods—only an hour earlier.

"A fitting end for a traitor—but who did the deed?" Gyohki asked in a weighty tone.

"I don't know. But I did find this next to his body."

What fell to the floor without a sound was a tiny rubber doll in the shape of a spider.

"Okay, this is just my interpretation, but I think Shin was using this thing to threaten someone. And whoever it was killed him when he tried to run off with the bead. Who do you suppose would do that?"

"Someone who knows the secret of the bead," Twin muttered. "That's what I think, too."

At Gyohki's words, Egbert's shadowy form gave a nod at the center of the room and said, "You remember what Gilligan told us? It's Professor Krolock!"

"Him?!" Twin cried at the top of his lungs. "Well, they say Professor Krolock's a walking warehouse of information. I guess it wouldn't be all that strange for him to know about the bead."

"Where is he?"

"At an inn, I'd imagine. He's probably being a lot more brazen than you'd expect."

"Why's he here? You think Gilligan sent him up here? If that's the case, he should at least stop by and pay his respects."

"An old man put some strange spell on Samon, too," said Gyohki.

"That's right," Egbert concurred. "And I'd bet you anything that was him. With a power like that, he'd be able to get Shin's poison spider off, and maybe even kill the old puppet master."

"Does he have the bead?" Twin asked in an intense tone.

"I don't know. But I don't think he could've taken it after that."

"Is it still inside the Vampire Hunter's hand, then?" Gyohki practically moaned. "Very well. Leave him to me."

"You have a plan?"

"Actually, I saw something interesting this evening," Gyohki replied.

"Which was?"

"I wouldn't want to spoil the surprise. Once we have the bead, we can finish him at our leisure. The rest of you will have to give me a hand."

"Fine with me," Twin replied loudly, sounding quite satisfied. "But I think there's one more person who should be here to help us reach a consensus."

"Samon's still not back yet?" Egbert asked in a somewhat disappointed tone. "Well, I guess that's okay. She won't be making any more of those odd little trips out, at any rate. So, Gyohki— how exactly is this gonna go?"

As the giant leaned forward, the main door suddenly creaked open and a gorgeous woman in a white dress came in.

"Speak of the devil," Twin said in a tone dripping with sarcasm.

"Oh? And what were you saying about me?" asked Samon. With silent footsteps she walked to the center of the room and stood right in front of Egbert.

"Just this—" the giant began to say, and although the impression he got from the familiar face of the lovely woman was somehow different from before, he went on to explain what had been discussed at the meeting that day.

Once she'd heard everything, Samon said, "I see," and nodded meaningfully. "It was definitely Professor Krolock that made a mockery of me. Not that I know where he is. At any rate, Gyohki, exactly when and how did you intend to do away with D?"

"Tomorrow—in someplace he's not too comfortable."

"I heard D's a dhampir," the woman said. "So he wouldn't be comfortable—in the water."

"Exactly."

"And yet you think he'll just stroll out into someplace like that? He's not stupid, you know. Even if he did, how would you finish him off? At any rate, from what Twin says, it seems he's hidden the woman somewhere. Do you have some way to lure him out?"

Apparently, the rest of the group didn't know about the other Twin or what had happened to him.

"I know," said Gyohki. "We can't simply invite him to step into Egbert's kingdom. But he'll have no choice but to come, you see."

"How?" Twin asked in a tone of boundless curiosity.

"I have something lined up. Come tomorrow, you'll see," said Gyohki, putting on airs to the very end.

"But more importantly—Samon, what's your boyfriend up to?"

Although Samon made an indescribable expression there in the murky darkness at Twin's question, it faded quickly enough, and she replied disappointedly, "He's not around."

"Not around?"

"I haven't seen hide nor hair of him since noontime. I wonder if maybe he didn't go off somewhere . . ."

"You've been dumped?" Egbert asked, his face turned to one side.

"Perhaps," Samon said without argument as she turned and walked toward a door in the back of the room. "I'm tired. I'm going to turn in early."

"Whatever you do, don't waste your time looking for the man who ran out on you," said Gyohki. "Tomorrow's going to be a busy day. You'll have to find out where Professor Krolock is and bring him back here. We'll dispose of D."

"Since when do you give the orders?" asked Samon.

"Oh, do you have a problem with that?"

"No—it doesn't matter to me either way," the woman replied. "At least, not now."

"Looks to me like you're taking this dumping business pretty hard."

"Say what you will. Good night," said Samon. And then her silhouette, which suddenly seemed all the more alluring, slipped through the doorway and vanished into the darkness.

And this is what happened an hour later.

Sensing someone sneaking over to the old-fashioned bed where he slept, Egbert awoke. Had he not been a warrior, Egbert never would've heard the footsteps of the person coming closer, then bending over by the side of his head. As he turned to face the intruder, he asked, "What do you want?"

Upon seeing the person who'd just pulled back by the light of the moon, Egbert blinked despite himself.

"You're not a very perceptive man, are you, Egbert?" Samon said reproachfully, having already regained her composure. "When a woman creeps into a man's bedroom, he should keep his questions to himself and just accept her kisses."

"What are you up to, Samon?" Egbert asked, his voice carrying more than its share of expectation.

As he sat up in bed, Samon approached him seductively. Egbert had already noticed that the warrior woman wore nothing but a flimsy negligee. Her gossamer gown melted in the moonlight, tracing in black a form so voluptuous it took his breath away. But Egbert's eyes could also make out her full breasts, her pale pink nipples, and all the tempting contours of her crotch and derriere.

"So, am I supposed to take the place of your boyfriend who ran off? Well, I don't have a problem with that," Egbert chuckled. But his voice was a bit indistinct.

"I knew how you felt about me."

Standing by the side of the bed, Samon said no more, but reached for the front of the negligee with her hand. The fabric slid down her like a fog, catching on her breasts for a moment, and then quickly landing in a pile on the floor.

"I'm terribly hungry, you see," the woman confessed. "I want you. So just hold your tongue and take me."

No sooner had Samon made that request of him than she straddled Egbert's groin and wrapped her pale, silky arms around the man's strapping neck.

"Hey," Egbert said, but before he could stop her, his lips were covered with something that tugged at them like a leech, yet delivered the sweetest sensation imaginable. A hot tongue slid into Egbert's mouth, and he didn't hesitate to suck on it.

Having given him an appreciable taste of her lips and tongue, Samon pulled her face away from his. While her features were twisted with lust, her eyes alone held a cold spark that seemed to mock the man.

Egbert's hand brushed one of her breasts. "Your tits are like ice," he said.

"But they burn all the more with my feelings," Samon replied, pressing her lips to his once more.

Egbert was entranced.

From the first time he'd seen the woman's face, the stouthearted warrior had been drawn by her surpassing sensuality. Perhaps

Samon realized as much, because even on the way to the village, her words and deeds had further stimulated him to such a degree she almost seemed to be provoking him. Twin had probably teased Egbert because he'd noticed that as well. Egbert had loved Samon so much that he'd killed the young seeker of knowledge who'd been her lover—not that he thought that would make Samon his. He'd gone after Glen because the man seemed to be a warped individual intent on tearing Samon apart both mentally and physically. The way things had been going, the giant probably never would've confessed his own feelings to her in the end. But now Samon had pushed everything else aside to fulfill the feelings his eyes had always betrayed.

Egbert's integrity oozed away like mud. But who could really blame him? His powerful arms wrapped around her lithe torso, and his parched lips sucked at the woman's moist, full ones so hard it seemed he'd twist them right off.

Turning her face away as if to escape him, Samon then bit down on the man's earlobe.

"You're incredible. I love you, Egbert," she said, her feverish tone and moist puffs of breath slowly sliding down to the nape of his neck, then stopping. "I love you best, after him."

Samon's mouth snapped open viciously. A pair of fangs glittered there like solidified moonlight.

"Samon, what happened to you?!" Egbert shouted in amazement.

Just as Samon's despicable lips were about to clamp onto the man's throat, she began to gag and choke. A scream spilling from her, Samon clutched at her own throat.

"When did you decide to serve the Nobility?" Egbert said as he brought one hand up to his unscathed throat. His voice brimmed with sadness. "And is that why you forgot all about my power? This whole room is Egbert's kingdom! Of course, this is the first time I've actually had garlic mixed in the atmosphere. That was just a step I'd taken to guard against D and the Noble. I never would've thought you'd wind up one first, though."

"You bastard!" Samon cursed as she fell to the floor. "Damn you to hell, Egbert!"

"I really did care for you. I suppose the least I can do is release you from the curse of the Nobility myself." Taking up the iron staff that leaned against the side of his bed, Egbert stood behind the writhing Samon. Raising the weapon high over his head, he cried, "Die, Samon. Rest in peace."

As he turned his face down to the contorted Samon with that holy pronouncement, he met her gaze. A blazing pair of crimson eyes. In that instant, sparks of the very same hue exploded in Egbert's brain.

His staff slid down. When it had fallen to waist level, Egbert shook his head fiercely, and then raised his weapon once again. He had both eyes shut.

"Could you really kill me, Egbert?" Samon managed to utter in a hoarse voice. The stink of garlic still eddied in the night air. The mere act of speaking was pure torture for her. "Were you lying when you said you cared for me? If you weren't, you'd allow me to follow the path I choose, no matter how far it means I may fall. That's what I did. All for him—"

Even in the midst of agony, Samon still sounded proud.

"I need you," the woman said. "I need you if I'm to help grant his wish. We mustn't let Gyohki and the others go after D. The Hunter's life belongs to my man."

Were these not words of chilling love?

As the woman told Egbert how she'd given her own blood to a Noble and become his servant in order to save the dying Glen, her words certainly hit home. Though his iron staff was still poised in the air, he sounded quite moved as he said, "Oh, how I envied him—he's still alive then, is he?"

"I kept him alive. Though I had to subject myself to this curse to do so."

"What'll you do if I give you what you want?" the giant asked her.

Despite all the pain Samon was in, her eyes glittered. Just then, the smell of the accursed plant abruptly vanished from the air.

"I shall love you," she replied. "Just as I do him. In any way you please."

For a second, a hue of distress that beggared description drifted into Egbert's face. However, he quickly made his decision.

"I've always thought it might be nice to be a Noble!"

The naked female form arose, brushing by the tip of the iron staff as it slowly sank to the floor.

Fighting in the Darkness

CHAPTER 6

I

The villagers knew that summer had come—it had risen from beyond the sea in the form of a man in blue. And knowing what his arrival entailed, there wasn't really much to be surprised about. Though two girls and a young man had vanished the night before, even that couldn't be allowed to disrupt their summer. A number of family members and other relatives had searched in the woods and ruined lodges with the Youth Brigade and Vigilance Committee so as not to disturb the festival, but their actions hadn't borne results, and the stakes and javelins they carried shimmered mockingly in the white heat and threw ugly shadows on the blue flowers that covered the ground.

Magic tricks and carbonated drinks, candy and snow cones. Summer still remained in full swing.

Early in the morning, Toto left Su-In behind and exited the ruined temple. He was off to deliver the ransom note he'd written the night before to D.

The watery sunlight made the young leaves sparkle. As the thief swayed on the back of a cyborg horse and looked at the flowers in the grassy fields, his face brimmed with a pure appreciation that was unimaginable given his line of work. After about forty minutes, he came to the part of the woods where the festival was being held. Not surprisingly, everyone was still asleep. The entrances to the performers' trailers and flexible housing units were all shut tight.

"I hope I can get this taken care of quickly and join in the fun," Toto muttered, but then he suddenly pulled back on his reins.

Roughly thirty feet away, a figure that appeared to be female was standing in the shade of a grove of trees. After further scrutiny, it turned out to be a girl of twelve or thirteen who wore a lemon yellow dress. Pulling back her long black tresses, she tied them with a ribbon the same color as her dress. From the look of her, she had to be one of the traveling performers. But what made Toto's eyes open as wide as they could possibly go was neither the girl's features nor her overdeveloped bust line. In one hand, she disinterestedly toyed with something shiny. Bouncing it in her palm, she let it fall on the back of her hand, then let it walk, one by one, down all five fingers. Without a doubt, it was the very bead he sought.

More than questions of why some girl he'd never seen before should be playing with it, more than anything, it was shock and jubilation that filled Toto's heart. There'd be no need to go to D now—all of his hard work was about to pay off right here. He could gain the girl's confidence—or slug her if that became necessary—and simply take the bead from her.

Toto didn't actually know what the bead was worth—that was why he hadn't answered Su-In the night before when she asked him about it. The only reason he was going to such lengths to try and get the bead was that his instincts as a thief told him it actually had tremendous value. The constant problems that'd been springing up ever since he first met Wu-Lin back at that inn only served to reinforce that feeling. And the people that were involved here were so incredible, he'd never run into their like in his long career as a thief, and didn't think he was likely to do so ever again, either.

Toto's spirit had been stoked. There was a fortune to be made here, too. But more than that, he felt his reputation as a thief depended on his beating out all the others and getting the bead first.

I'll do it. I'll give it my best shot, he told himself.

But while Toto had decided his course of action, the reality of the situation was a bit harsher. D was always around the bead. From what Toto could see, the Hunter was tougher than any of the others—just unbelievably powerful. As proof, the thief hadn't been able to do a thing even while his skillful disguise got him into Su-In's house. If that's all there'd been to it, he still might've managed something, but as he patiently studied D's behavior, a strange feeling came over him. The Hunter's beauty was of the kind that would only occur once out of all the boundless possibilities, but an untamed shadow and an undefined sadness hung heavily on his features. At some point, Toto was shocked to discover that he'd started following D around along with all of the women. Toto had left the house both because he sensed his disguise might be seen through eventually and because of this strange psychological state. After that, he'd considered various things and plotted at length before finally deciding to kidnap Su-In.

But now all that's finished, Toto thought, licking his lips.

When he went to wheel his horse around in the girl's direction, her vivid splash of color vanished between the trees without warning.

There's someone in there, Toto decided instantly, and he got off his horse. Crouching down, he raced off in the same direction that the girl had gone. The way he could make the sound of his footsteps and every other hint of his presence vanish was pure artistry. Even an insect resting on a leaf wouldn't notice this man racing by less than four inches away.

He heard a voice. Standing behind a thick tree trunk, Toto poked half of his face out to watch.

The girl was facing a well-groomed middle-aged man with a mustache. Surprisingly enough, the pair was more than thirty feet away from Toto. This wasn't a forest in the deathly still of night. It was a boisterous summer morn, with birds singing and insects chirping in the grass and bushes and trees. His frighteningly good hearing was one of the things that'd helped earn Toto his reputation as the greatest thief on the Frontier.

Seeing that the bead was no longer in the girl's hand, Toto felt relieved.

"Now, don't forget what we agreed on," the girl said pedantically. "Cash in advance."

The man held out his hand. From it, something shiny spilled into the girl's palm. Gold coins, no doubt.

"You'll get the rest when the job is done," he told her.

"Okay."

"Before we get started, could I have a demonstration of your ability, just to be sure?"

"Oh, aren't you the cautious one. Be my guest."

The girl closed her eyes, and the man roughly pressed his right hand to her round forehead. And then—

What a sight it was. In no time at all, the girl's face became that of someone else. And that wasn't all. Her height and build also changed, and in the span of two breaths, the person who stood there was—

"Su-In," Toto said despite himself, though he was ordinarily a master of concealment.

Yes, she was Su-In.

Did that mean the girl was a traveling performer who could change into anyone the man told her to? Not exactly. Toto had already noticed there were some minor differences between this transformed Su-In and the real thing, because the girl had never actually *seen* Su-In. And yet the only reason she'd been able to mimic the woman with more than ninety percent accuracy had to be because her information on Su-In had come from the bearded middle-aged man—Gyohki. The image he had of Su-In was transmitted from his brain to the girl, where she then began transforming at a cellular level. Needless to say, that image had been transferred through the hand he'd touched to the girl's forehead. In a manner of speaking, the girl was a metamorph whose shape could be determined by external forces.

"Remarkable," said the man. "On closer inspection, there are some differences, but from a distance this should suffice. Now, would you say something for me?"

"I won't be in any danger, will I?" said the girl.

Toto was amazed to hear she sounded exactly like Su-In. If she had a photograph of whomever she was trying to duplicate, she could've impersonated that person for the rest of her life without anyone around her ever noticing.

Toto grew tense. The man with the mustache wasn't your average person.

"Relax," said the man. "Do I look like someone who'd lie to you?"

"Yes," replied the girl—or Su-In—with a nod.

The pair soon got on a cyborg horse that was tethered there and rode off to the west, while another horse and rider followed after them at a distance of sixty feet.

D lay inside the barn. A blanket was spread on the ground, and his upper body rested against the wooden box of life jackets while his legs were stretched out. His longsword was cradled on his left shoulder. He was sleeping.

Descending from both humans and Nobles, dhampirs could operate by either day or night, though for the most part they chose to sleep during the day. The reason for this wasn't so much that they often worked in a field where they had to do battle with demons by night, but rather because the Noble disposition of their blood prevailed over their human tendencies.

The night before, D had gone to both their hiding place and here after Su-In was abducted, and he'd found the remains of one of the Twins buried out back. Though it was unclear what he thought when he saw the handprint that remained on the man's neck, the Hunter stopped his search then and went into the barn to sleep.

To look at his handsome countenance, no one would've ever thought he still drew breath, but the fact that his features didn't retain the slightest stress from all of his deadly battles of late was truly shocking. Pain and even death itself were unwilling to mar the young man's beauty.

His eyes opened. They were already completely focused.

Without making a sound, he got up. The light filtering in through gaps in the wooden door turned the dust he stirred into dancing flecks of gold. Shifting his sword to his back, D left the barn. Looking at the steep road that continued down to the beach, he then went straight over to the main house. His left arm hung naturally by his side.

An iron arrow was stuck in the door. Around the center of it was wound a piece of white paper—obviously a letter. Raising his left arm, D smiled wryly before using his right hand to pull out the arrow. Holding the edge of the paper with his teeth, he skillfully untied the string that held it in place, discarded the arrow, and uncurled the letter.

I have the woman. If you want her back, bring the bead to "The Black Lagoon" on the western edge of town at precisely 1:00 Afternoon. This all depends on you.

It was from Gyohki. His plan had been set in motion.

Staring down at the end of his left arm, D said, "Worthless little bugger," with a straight face.

That worthless little bugger was writhing on the floor as the first light started creeping in. Of course, the limb hadn't really started moving until Toto had left; up until then, it'd played dead.

Su-In had noticed it, too. Still under the effects of the drug she'd been given, she couldn't move her body, though she could still think, and her eyes, ears, and mouth were all working fine. At first, she'd thought it was a rat that looked like it'd been impaled on something had come back to life. But as the light swelled with the dawn, she realized she'd been mistaken.

Pinned to the floor by a foot-long iron stake, the thing writhing as madly as a rat looked like it was someone's left hand, of all things! A fear that surpassed description filled Su-In's chest with ice, but then she suddenly understood. When D had come to see her, he'd kept his left hand stuck in his coat pocket the whole time. Though she hadn't thought to ask him about it, she had to wonder—did that left hand belong to him? But even if it was—

"Hey!" someone suddenly called out to her.

It took a while for her to realize the voice came from the hand. Stranger yet, she could recall hearing the same voice before.

"Hey, Su-In! Can you hear me?"

"Was that you? You're some kind of talking hand?!" Su-In exclaimed. At some point, her fear had evaporated, and now she just found it funny. She certainly had plenty of pluck.

"You got something against talking hands?"

"Not at all," the woman replied. "It's just—you're D's hand, aren't you?"

"Well, I'm thinking about trading up one of these days."

"I knew it. What are you doing here?"

"That's a hell of a question to be asking," said the hand. "Do you have any idea how much you owe me, you little ingrate? It should be pretty obvious I'm here because I was worried about you. I'm quite conscientious, you know. I try to keep my landlord's position in mind."

"You've been following me?" asked Su-In. "Since when?"

"Well, I was the one who saved you when that butcher disguised as your granddaddy was about to shave your nose off."

"So, it was you that killed him then?"

"Hey, I didn't *kill* him. I *saved* you."

"Okay," said the woman. "What did you do after that?"

"I was in your bag the whole time. Down on the beach, I was ready to catch a ride on the priest's back, but he was good enough to bring the bag along when you folks made a run for it."

"Oh, then that rat I saw last night was really you—"

"Well," the hand said, "I got out of the bag before he went through it. But he's a hell of a shot for a lousy burglar. It'll take quite a bit of work to get me free now. Give me some help here."

"It's no use. I got a shot of something and now I can't move."

"You worthless little bugger," the hand spat, using the same words as its master while it twisted wildly.

Running through the hand from the base of the middle finger to almost the center of its palm, the stake was sunk a good four inches into the hardwood floor and wouldn't budge in the slightest.

"Damn," the hand continued. "Haven't had anything to eat but wind lately, so I can't get my strength up. If I only had some dirt or water. Hey, spill some blood or something my way!"

"I'd help you if I could," Su-In said in a sincere tone. "But you'll just have to manage something. If you're really *his* hand, I find it hard to believe you'd be so stupid or good for nothing."

"Couldn't you phrase that a little more gently?" the hand said indignantly. "If I just had one drink of water, I could melt this damn thing or freeze it solid. Shit! I'm useless like this! Doesn't anyone ever come out here?"

"Not a chance. This is pretty far off the beaten path, so folks rarely pass this way."

"There'll be big trouble if we don't do something. We'd be better off if the thief came back," the hand remarked. "I hope he gets back before sundown . . ."

"What do you mean by that?" asked the woman.

"He didn't notice it, but something dangerous is sleeping near the temple. I can tell. I can smell it. When the sun goes down, they'll get up and they'll come here."

Su-In's mind became ten times more focused. "When the sun goes down . . . You mean Nobles or their servants?"

"Yes, damn it! And not fifteen feet from here. It might take all night for that drug to wear off you. While for my part, I'm malnourished."

"You've gotta do something!" Su-In said in a deadly serious tone. She realized she sounded pathetic. But that's how strongly humans feared the Nobility.

The hand twisted again, but it didn't look like it would work itself free in ten years' time, let alone before sundown.

II

D arrived at the Black Lagoon at the appointed time. It was an untamed spot about three miles west of the woods where the festival was being held. As the word "lagoon" implied, in days of old it'd been filled with crystal-clear water, but now the land eight inches lower than the road only showed a slight slope down to a circular area about three hundred feet in diameter, and at the very center it looked like a muddy bog. Of course, that was only a trick of the mind—the lagoon's waters had dried up more than a century ago, and its bottom was now covered with summer grass. Almost in the center of the lagoon there was a small island-like rise about fifteen or twenty feet in diameter, the remains of what must've been an actual island long ago. Now it was completely overrun with trees and high grass.

Stepping off the road, the Hunter's mount took seven or eight steps around the edge of the former lagoon before a voice called out, "Hold it!"

A figure suddenly appeared from the trees that had grown up to swallow the road on the opposite side of the lagoon.

Turning in that direction, D squinted. "King Egbert" had a scarf wrapped around his neck, and he gazed at D with a kind of dazed sadness in his eyes. The summer days were long.

"Glad you could make it. I suppose you thought you could come here and take all of us down at once, did you?"

Not replying to that remark, D asked, "Where's Su-In?"

"Before we get to that, you got the bead?"

When Egbert spoke, D knew that his foe wasn't working with Shin on this. "One of your colleagues has the bead," the Hunter replied. "Shin, I believe the name was."

"He's dead. Are you the one that arranged that?"

"At any rate, I don't have the bead. Where is Su-In?" D inquired.

"You know a guy by the name of Professor Krolock?" Egbert said. Not waiting for a reply, he continued, "Well, it would seem he's the one that killed Shin. So you mean to tell me he's got the bead, then?"

D was silent.

"The woman's right here," a voice could be heard to say from the island in the center of the lagoon.

Su-In and Gyohki stepped out from between the trees. Of course, the young performer who'd assumed Su-In's shape didn't have the right clothes, so to prevent that from giving away their deception, she was dressed only in her underwear.

"As you can see, we have Su-In. But if you don't have the bead, there's no reason for us to let her go. Or were you going to ask us to give her up in exchange for something else?" Grinning, Gyohki added, "Come on out here. I'm sure we can manage something. This used to be a lagoon, but now it's dry as a bone. Nothing for even a dhampir to worry about."

He beckoned to the Hunter.

Nothing to worry about? It was obviously a trap.

Seeing that D hadn't made a move, Gyohki pressed his right hand against Su-In's throat. Black claws that resembled scythes stretched from his fingers.

"Don't you care what happens to your employer? You're a disgrace to Hunters everywhere," said Gyohki.

Although Su-In grew pale, it was all just part of the act. The girl was doing this for the ample reward she'd been offered, and because she'd been assured it was all just an illusion. It never occurred to her that Gyohki would be more than happy to kill her if the situation called for it.

While it wasn't clear if he took the transformed girl for Su-In, D then calmly rode his horse down off the path and onto the dry lagoon. The ground under his horse's hooves felt like parched soil. Not seeming to be in any hurry, the Hunter advanced slowly, and high above his head, clouds streamed by sedately. Knowing nothing of the killing lust that was coagulating in this wild patch of land, they were simply part of nature's great bounty in the blue summer sky. But the question now was whether or not D had noticed the black ditch that'd been made all the way around lagoon.

Just another fifteen feet to the island.

Gyohki shouted, "Now! Do it, Egbert!"

At the same time, the girl screamed and dropped to her knees where she was. In the stand of trees, branches snapped off at the trunk, and one struck the barely standing Gyohki in the shoulder. Even D's horse planted its feet, trying to brace itself against the amorphous pressure that suddenly assailed it.

Egbert had altered the gravity in his "kingdom."

The girl cried out as her torso snapped forward.

With a heavy *whooosh!*, the whole bottom of the lagoon collapsed. Obviously the foundation had been weak from the very beginning. Deep black cracks appeared on the surface, and in no time at all they swallowed the earth, claiming the entire lagoon. A split second later, D and his horse were unfortunate enough to find themselves sinking up to their necks. Black spray shot up around them. Water.

It was true that the water in the lagoon had dried up centuries earlier. Dirt and dust had accumulated on top of it to form the present surface, and people had forgotten all about the water. However, subterranean sources continued to trickle in, saturating the ground beneath it and displacing a massive amount of dirt and sand to form an underground swamp. And having been born in the area, Gyohki had no doubt discovered this somehow.

Egbert had lifted his gravity attack from the little island, and now Gyohki stripped off his shirt. Naked to the waist, he then dove straight into the depths. As soon as his body broke through the water's surface, it underwent a transformation. The water seemed to take hold of his hair and stretch it as it streamed down his back. His skin became gorgeous and white, and his powerful chest swelled into full breasts. Still clad in a pair of trousers, his lower body was covered with countless scales, and the end of his tail split in two to splash violently from the water. The figure that was now closing on D with over-arm strokes was clearly a woman—a mermaid!—that once had been Gyohki.

D waited silently in the black water for the product of Meinster's accursed experiments. However, the Hunter's body was most definitely sinking in this bottomless abyss. Bubbles rose from the corner of his mouth.

Gyohki zipped closer. His burst of speed was incredible. The second he passed D's right side, his right hand shot out. Having gone right by, he turned around. A cloud blacker than the water trailed from the woman's hand, and as if in response, a thick stream of blood rose like smoke from D's right hip.

"My, but you're good," the woman said, but being who he was, D heard it differently—he heard it as Gyohki's voice.

The woman pressed her left hand to the opposite hip. It was an instant later that little explosions of blood rose in gouts from the same spot. Gyohki stared at the blade in D's right hand with terror and malice.

"I underestimated you because we're underwater. But this time I won't let you get away," the mermaid muttered with a deadly determination.

Slowly, she/he began to circle D, and a mighty cloud of bubbles spilled from D's mouth. Following them as they rose, D kicked his way through the water. Beyond the black depths, there lay a muted light. The surface was fifteen feet away.

Looking up at his foe from the depths, Gyohki donned a thin smile as he thrashed through the water. He was closing with the speed of a fish.

When D's head started to cause ripples on the surface, a woman's hands seized the Hunter's ankles and gave them a pull. D was dragged back underwater with incredible force. His foe moved with a speed and strength that was absolutely unbelievable for such a lithe female form.

D's face was twisted with pain. The store of oxygen in his lungs had reached its limits.

"I'll let you go soon," Gyohki laughed as he towed the Hunter toward the bottom. "But you can't have any air. Drink in the water. Fill your lungs with it. I'll pull you back down before you can get your face out."

There was no need to do that. Before Gyohki had even let go of him, D opened his mouth. His throat moved. He was taking in the water. A few seconds passed—and then he clutched at his jugular. Spasms ran through his body. Then they stopped sharply—Gyohki released the Hunter, and D's body began to slowly sink to the bottom.

"Three and a half minutes," Gyohki said to himself. "That's how long the average dhampir can last underwater."

Keeping his distance, Gyohki drifted down along with D. Then he brought his hand up to his mouth. Along with some bubbles, his mouth disgorged a wooden stake that was nearly a foot and a half long.

"Those of Noble blood don't drown," he said. "I'll have to put this through you to finish you off."

Just to be on the safe side, Gyohki watched for another minute as D drifted toward the bottom, then wriggled the fish tail sensuously. Going over to D, the mermaid turned him so his back was to the bottom. Staring at the gorgeous countenance that seemed to sparkle in the black water, he said, "How beautiful you are—and now, as a woman, I only feel it all the more. But if I were to do nothing, you'd destroy us all. So here you must die."

Raising her right hand, the mermaid prepared to drive the stake home. But surely she couldn't believe what happened then. The

hand the drowned man used to hold his sword tried to grab her wrist in mid-motion.

"Why, you—?!" she cried in amazement, but a second later her body began to be dragged upward with incredible force. "Just toying with me, were you?!" she screamed, and although she willed every muscle in her body to bring her back down, the rate of her ascent didn't diminish in the least. In fact, Gyohki rose with such speed there was no time to try anything else before he/she broke the surface, shooting up into the air along with D.

Then the mermaid saw the stern beauty staring down at him/her, and the black sphere above the Hunter's head that even now continued to ascend. The balloon was connected to D by a pair of leather straps. Designed to hoist people thrown into the icy sea safely into the air before they froze to death, the balloon was filled with a gas that was lighter than air. D had put on this piece of indispensable lifesaving equipment back in Su-In's barn. Ever since they'd met under Meinster's castle, he must've known Gyohki would try fighting him in the water. The Hunter may have even known that Gyohki was actually the mermaid.

More than the blade he raised, more than the distant blue sky behind him, it was D himself that mesmerized Gyohki as the Hunter brought his weapon down on the mermaid. What was it that Gyohki saw in that instant?

"Such skill—and that face—" he/she cried out absentmindedly. "Could it be that you are *his*—" A heartbeat later, as he watched the blade with all the colors of the spectrum streaming behind it slash his/her torso two, Gyohki reached a violent peak, the female upper body and fish-like lower body separating as he/she fell back toward the black surface of the water. Spray shot up.

Using his right hand to pull on a leather strap and slowly release the gas, D gradually sank back to earth. He landed on the road, about thirty feet away from Egbert.

"Not too shabby," Egbert said in a low voice, his iron staff in one hand.

Using his sword to cut himself free of the balloon from Su-In's barn, D took a quick glance at the rejuvenated lagoon. Although the woman's beautiful torso had at some point turned back into that of a man, the lower body remained that of a fish, and even now it writhed and splashed in the water. A hue darker than the black water began to spread through the lagoon like a blossoming flower . . .

Egbert said, "One thing you might want to know—the girl on the island ain't the real thing. Of course, I'm more curious as to whether or not you already knew that."

The girl's transformation probably wasn't good enough to fool D. But had the Hunter walked right into Gyohki's hands because he saw his foe was about to kill some girl he'd never even met before? Or because he knew what Gyohki's secret was?

"Just as I thought—you're no ordinary dhampir. What are you?"

Not replying to Egbert's question, D focused a look that was both vacant and sad on the scarf around the man's neck as he quietly said, "You've been bitten, haven't you?"

Tiny ripples of agitation spread through Egbert's face. They then became a look of agony as he reeled backward. He didn't actually fall over, and as he barely managed to turn around, there was a sharp dagger buried to the hilt in the middle of his back.

"You traitor!" a ferocious voice laden with indignation could be heard to say from a distant stand of bushes. Twin's voice. "You were acting strangely all morning, so Gyohki pretended to have me look for the professor while he actually had me keep an eye on you. On the slim chance D did make it to the surface, the plan was that you'd pump up the gravity to send him right under again, but you betrayed us. So now you'll get what you've got coming. I don't know where Samon disappeared to, but we'll take care of her and the other guy later." And to the Hunter he called out, "D, we'll meet again!"

Though a wooden stake flew from D's right hand in pursuit of the voice, only a few verdant stalks rustled before nothing more could be heard.

"He's not your real concern," Egbert said as he twisted his left hand around to his back. "Someone else is. A man you already know. I'm heading back to see him."

"Is he your new master?"

"Call it what you will."

"Where is he?" asked D.

"Well, let me see. If I told you I didn't know, would you cut me down?"

"Why didn't you attack me?"

"Because a certain lady asked me not to. Go ahead and laugh if you like. If you don't cut me down now, the Nobility will just gain another member," said Egbert, his words tinged with a hint of distress.

Of course, this young man wasn't the kind who could let something like that pass. The fact that Egbert was wounded and that he'd held back from attacking the Hunter were both irrelevant.

D strode forward.

Egbert held his iron staff at the ready.

A flash of light in all the colors of the spectrum sketched an arc between the two of them. With a shower of sparks, D's blade was stopped by the iron staff Egbert held braced over his head.

But look at what was happening! The blade had bitten halfway through the staff. D was using one hand, while Egbert was using both. And yet, the warrior who'd stopped the Hunter's blow was slowly being overpowered, and he'd already been forced to his knees. Was it because Egbert, in his present condition, was at a disadvantage in the abundant sunlight? No, there was simply too great a difference in the power of the two figures from the very start.

As the blade sliced steadily into his iron staff, Egbert actually gazed at it and the gorgeous young man behind it with a deathlike rapture. Perhaps that was the very last bit of humanity remaining in him. Without a doubt, Egbert's head was going to be split in two in a matter of seconds.

There was a splash in the water on the opposite side of the lagoon. D's concentration was disturbed ever so slightly.

A massive burst of strength shot up from below, and the two forms sprang away to different locations.

But both of them saw the splash. A blackish figure had just leapt out of the lagoon and was running off into the woods. Without a moment's hesitation, it vanished among the trees.

"It seems the ruler of Hell has decided to give me a little longer to live," Egbert called out, but as his voice faded in the distance, D didn't even glance in his direction.

The Hunter's interest had been caught by something the diminutive figure had held in its hands a split second before it vanished. The dazzling outline that'd glittered in the sunlight had been that of the bead.

III

As he raced down the forest trail at full speed, Toto coolly considered his next move. He'd gotten the bead. At that very moment, it sat in his right pocket as surely as he drew breath. Naturally, he'd have to take it to a trustworthy expert and have it appraised. Though a number of names popped into his head, and any of them would've been fine if he were just out for some pocket money, none of them would be suitable for a major score like this. It looked like he'd have to head into the Capital after all and be introduced to someone he could trust. Fortunately, he had plenty of acquaintances who could arrange that.

But first, what would he do about Su-In?

His greed-tinged expression suddenly clouded.

If he just let things run their course, the drug he'd given her would probably wear off around 6:00 Night. He couldn't guarantee that she wouldn't be attacked by one of the supernatural creatures infesting the area around the ruined temple, though—that would be determined more or less by the woman's own luck.

That look of complete faith she'd had in her eye when she'd taken him for a traveling holy man and asked him to perform a funeral knifed into his heart. Once more he heard the same voice as the night before, when she'd tried to persuade him to get out of thievery and settle down in the village. Both were just dreams. Giving his head a shake, Toto tried to dislodge the face of a woman that shone like the sun.

His horse was tethered by the exit from the woods. Once on it, he could be out of this foul-smelling little coastal village in less than an hour.

Even D and Egbert hadn't noticed him as he went into the water, swam out to the island, got the bead out of the girl's clothes where they'd been left behind a tree, and swam back again. In fact, things had gone so well, he'd gotten sloppy and made some noise getting back out of the water. But if he was good enough to swipe something without even a Vampire Hunter noticing, he figured he'd be able to stay in the game another thirty years at least.

Untying the reins from a tree, Toto straddled his horse.

Just be one of us—

"Dammit," Toto muttered as he wheeled his mount around, toward the ruined temple where he'd imprisoned Su-In.

Just then, a wrinkled old voice echoed through Toto's head.

"Get off the horse, and get the bead out."

Before he could even begin to wonder what the hell was going on, his thoughts faded like sparks. Toto's brain now heard nothing but directions given by a bizarre voice.

Oh no!, reason cried from the dark corner of his mind where it'd been shoved.

Toto took out the bead.

"Throw it straight ahead."

The bead limned an arc and vanished into the bushes in front of him. A scrawny figure quickly stood up. Professor Krolock. But although the thief knew who it was, his consciousness couldn't make his body do anything at all.

Bringing his face up to the papery object in his hands, the professor whispered something: "Die. Stab yourself through the heart." This time, his voice was low and husky—and overwhelming.

Toto felt his own right hand going for the belt around his waist. His burglary tools were stuck in the belt. His hand chose an awl.

Don't! a distant voice inside him shouted.

Toto brought the tool to the right side of his chest with a fluid movement.

"No. The left side."

The tip of the tool hovering over his chest finally came to rest against his left nipple.

You can't! The voice inside him was practically a scream.

As the cold steel ripped through his flesh, Toto screamed and collapsed against a nearby tree. The strength left the thief's ankles, knees, and waist in turn, causing him to slide down the trunk.

As Toto lay there, the professor looked down at him with surpassing cruelty, and then quickly turned to peer into the depths of the forest.

"Watching D since last night certainly paid off. Now I'll be able to make Nobles of whomever I please. Let the fools who don't know the true use of the bead keep killing each other if they wish. I still have the final preparations to make!"

His tattered cloak fluttering abnormally, the professor ran off toward where he'd tethered his own horse.

After a short while, the thick scent of blood began to hang over the area. And as if it were an invitation, unsettling cries and chirps and rustling started to come from the bushes and the trees.

The summer woods were brimming with life. Dangerous life.

In the darkness formed by the leaves of the bushes, countless lights winked on, then became eyes set in hideous faces as the creatures slid out through the green grass. "Pan-eyes"—bugs with giant compound eyes on their ash-gray heads. Flesh-eating worms with black spots on their ocher skin. Bristling caterpillars with dozens of glittering fangs. Hopping, crawling, and slithering vilely, they closed on the prone Toto. If the ravenous forest denizens sank their teeth into him, not even a fragment of bone would be left within an hour—he'd utterly vanish from the face of the earth.

The first thing the flesh-eating worms did was make a beeline for Toto's ear. There was nothing they liked better than to enter through the ear canal and munch their way through someone's brain.

But they never would've thought the corpse would move. Toto's right hand flashed out, bisecting several of the worms in midair. No sooner had those pieces hit the ground than the remaining worms pounced on them without a sound.

A "pan-eye" wasted no time in launching itself at Toto's throat, but a slash from the thief's sharp tool ripped open the bug's lizard-like torso.

But that was all the resistance the dying man gave them. Matting the verdant grass as it flopped to the ground, his arm would move no more.

"Dammit . . . So I end up . . . food for the worms . . . ," he cursed, his hatred and mortification made into words so they might roll across the ground.

Having finished devouring their bloodied compatriots, it took these insects with no concerns aside from their own instinctive hunger less than ten seconds to recall the other, larger meal.

Was this the end of the corpse's unexpected resistance?

As the supernatural beasts prepared to descend en masse, something seemed to billow over them. The blood-crazed creatures then retreated without a sound.

A figure in black appeared from the grove across from the thief. The ghastly aura that'd frightened the monsters emanated from D. Quite a way off, there was a young girl. She no longer wore Su-In's face. And the spot where she remained must've been where the stench of blood ended.

D went right over to Toto and took his left hand. The awl in the thief's right hand didn't even warrant a glance. To the Hunter, it was something he could take care of with his little finger.

"Hate to tell you . . . but . . . I'm still alive," the thief said, his bloodless lips twisting into a smile. "Stupid bastard . . . had his chance . . . and had to go and miss the spot . . . My heart . . . ," he chuckled, "is on the *right* side . . ."

"Who did this to you?" D asked, not sounding at all concerned.

"Professor Krolock . . . whispered something . . . to this weird paper . . . and got me to do whatever he wanted . . . Watch out . . . The bead . . ." The expression slipped from Toto's face. "He's gonna . . ." All the strength then drained from the thief's body.

Taking the man's pulse, D then pulled out some emergency sheets with his right hand. Made of a highly porous cellophane, they were eight inches square. Even when the bandages came in bundles of a hundred, they weren't bulky at all. The medicated layer could serve as a styptic and an antiseptic, provide nutrients, and act as a heating pad or a cold compress. Out on the road, they were indispensable for dealing with everything from minor colds to major lacerations.

Applying one of the bandages to the left side of Toto's chest, the Hunter then lay the thief over his shoulder using just his right hand. Seeing how the Hunter easily rose again with this new burden, the girl's eyes went wide. It was almost as if he were carrying a hollow doll.

"Come here," D called to the girl as he stood by Toto's horse.

As she tottered toward him like a marionette, the expression that came to her face was so rapt it was almost obscene. After all, she'd been right by D's side ever since he left the lagoon.

"Is he, you know . . . dead?" she asked.

"He has a pulse. I'm going to bring him to the hospital, but you can get off wherever you like. And I'll thank you not to mention what happened today to anyone."

The girl nodded. The beauty and mysterious charm of the young man extended to the very words he spoke. There was no way she'd be able to refuse him.

With Toto over one shoulder and the girl sitting behind him, D gave a stern kick to the horse's flank.

†

Before a desolate expanse of rubble, Professor Krolock dismounted from his cyborg horse. He also unloaded some baggage from his mount—a blanket and a leather bag.

Looking up at the sky, which had begun to take a vague bluish tint, he said, "The sun will be going down soon. What a fitting time for my wish to be granted."

As twilight descended, the professor began cautiously picking a path through the rubble. Six hundred feet ahead of him loomed the remains of what looked like a castle wall. He knew that beyond it lay a gaping chasm of incredible proportions. His sole concern now was whether or not the coil of wire he'd brought in his bag would be long enough to reach the bottom.

"This is *not* good," a voice that sounded both relaxed and tense said from the wooden floor of the room.

"What is it?" Su-In asked disagreeably.

There was good reason for her mood—that cryptic remark was all the hand had to say when it broke two hours of silence, and because the light that filled the room had begun to dwindle perceptibly in the last few minutes. The outline of the hand impaled by the metal wedge had also begun to dissolve into deepening blue.

"I told you before, didn't I? There's something in this temple. Or rather, someone."

"Well," Su-In said, "that guy did spray some odorless monster repellent around the place."

"Hasn't that drug worn off yet?"

"It's still no use. I've got a little feeling back . . . but I can't move at all."

"By the feel of it, how long do you think it'll take?" asked the hand.

"Another hour. I wonder if we'll be okay for that long."

The hand was silent. After pausing for a beat, it then asked, "Would you mind if I deviated from the subject for a moment?" Its tone was so lascivious, it made Su-In's eyes go wide.

"What is it?" she asked sharply.

"You said you'd got a little feeling back, right?"

"Yes," Su-In replied, her tone cautious. There was a look of suspicion in her eyes.

"Hmm."

"What do you mean, 'Hmm'?"

"Well, the truth is, I'm starving. At least, that's how you'd put it in your terms. Basically, I need nourishment."

"What kind of nourishment?" Su-In asked, her curiosity piqued.

"Well . . ."

"Don't be such a tease!" Su-In scolded him, and then her ears suddenly perked up.

Off in the distance—if memory served, it was in the direction of the entrance—she'd heard a sound. Had someone come? Just at that moment, the light coming in through the window began to rapidly fade. It couldn't be that Noble . . . After all, there was no way he could know she was out here of all places. No, it wasn't him. It would be someone from the village. But even thinking that, Su-In couldn't bring herself to cry out for help.

"Hey," she called out to the hand. "Hurry up and say what you're gonna say. What should I do?"

"When did you eat last?" the hand asked her, oddly enough.

"Sometime before noon yesterday."

"Did you have some water then, too?"

"Of course."

There was a pregnant pause from the left hand.

"Oh," Su-In cried. As she flushed all the way to her ears, she glared at the talking hand.

"Well . . ."

"What do you mean, 'Well'?! That's disgusting!"

"It's just a minor inconvenience."

"I don't see what's so minor about it! You're talking to a lady!"

"I think it'd have to be less objectionable than becoming a servant of the Nobility."

The color drained right out of Su-In's face at that moment partly because of the left hand's words, but also because she'd just heard a number of footsteps behind her. The feeble footsteps she could hear somewhere out there were slowly drawing closer.

The world had passed through the blue and was surrendering itself now to an inky black.

"That can't be—"

"Oh, yes it can. It feels just like them," the hand said, its tone hard. "Getting back to what I said—can you do it?"

"Well, this is all pretty sudden."

"Your life—no, your very soul—depends on it. You've gotta do it somehow."

"I don't want to. How disgusting!"

Su-In held her breath. The footsteps stopped. Stopped right at the door. They were looking for her. Su-In could tell. But why didn't they come in? Why didn't they call out to see if there was anyone there? And why weren't they even talking among themselves, for that matter? Cold sweat rolled down her cheek.

"Haven't you gone yet?" the hand asked her.

"Wait—just a second now."

"Hey, we don't have any time here."

The door creaked.

Don't open it, Su-In thought.

The sound continued for a long time, flowing into the room. It was probably for the best that Su-In couldn't turn to look. The figures that stepped from the shallow murkiness like ghosts numbered three in all—two women and a man with blood staining the base of their necks.

"Here?" a girl with a round face asked. Her complexion was like paraffin.

"Yes, here," a girl with red hair replied. She sounded so happy she could weep.

"It's cold. And I'm hungry," the third figure—a young man—said sorrowfully. "I want to warm up. But it's supposed to be summer."

The trio exchanged glances. And as their gazes intertwined, they fell on Su-In, too.

"Here!"

"She's here!"

"Let's go!"

The three of them started walking again. Their eyes were vacant, and they seemed glazed with the colors of hell. There was no circulation in their lips. And yet they looked red. But that was only due to the color of their skin. Their hearts beat out the rhythm of the night, and the blood in their veins was the hue of darkness. Their breath held the odor of dirt from a grave.

"Don't look behind you, okay?" the hand told the woman.

"I couldn't look if I wanted to!" Su-In said, but she could barely work her tongue now.

"Have you gone yet?"

Groaning with exasperation, Su-In said, "Hold on. I just need a little longer."

"We can't wait any more. I hate to tell you this, but the leader of the pack is only about ten feet from you!"

Su-In was speechless.

"Oh, I see you stretched yourself out some. Keep at it. You've almost got it!"

Three shadowy figures clustered around Su-In's body. Su-In could sense them bending over her. Icicles were pressed against the nape of her neck. They were fingers. Fingers pale and cold as ice itself.

"She's warm," the young man said. "So warm! Hot blood runs through her veins!"

"Do you think she looks tasty?" asked the girl with red hair.

"I'm sure she's delicious," the young man replied. "Unlike us."

"I need to drink. A *lot*," said the girl with the round face, almost singing the words.

"It won't be easy drinking from her like that."

"We can flip her over."

"Yes, let's do that."

Six hands reached out and rolled Su-In over onto her back. For the first time, she could see their faces.

"Hannah? Clem? Ricardo?!" she cried out in astonishment. "But you're—Why?!"

"Su-In," said the young man—Ricardo. Only the slightest surprise could be felt in his hollow voice. However, his youthful face was quickly covered by the lewd smile of a sinful centenarian as he said, "So it was you in here, was it? Your blood is bound to be so very—"

"Delicious!" the girl with the round face—Hannah—moaned.

"When did this happen? When was it? When were you bitten?" Su-In inquired in desperation as she watched Ricardo's hand drawing closer to her throat.

"Last night . . . The three of us . . . were out picking moonlight grass together, you see," said Clementine. In the darkness, her red hair looked like a filthy vermilion rag. As her thin lips moved, a number of strands of hair stuck to them, pulled to and fro by their movements. "And then the two of them came . . . They stared at us with those red eyes . . . and we couldn't move . . . But I see now, Su-In, and you will, too . . . You'll see just how wonderful this can be. And then all of us went to sleep under the temple's porch."

Su-In's breath had been taken away. Ricardo's hand grabbed the neck of her shirt and tore it open. Though the rich swells that her white brassiere could barely contain were exposed to the eyes of all three of them, this was no time for embarrassment.

"You smell good, Su-In. Warm. Now there's a nice human chest! Surely it's pumping with the freshest of blood. That's the only regard in which your kind surpasses ours." Saliva dripped from

Ricardo's lips, splattering between Su-In's breasts. "I'll go first. No one has any complaints, I take it?"

"That's fine," said one of the others. "Just hurry."

Ricardo opened his mouth. Fangs peeked from his gums.

Seeing that they were coming down toward her throat, Su-In shut her eyes.

"Just a second," said a hoarse voice that made the three vampires turn around.

As his glittering eyes bored through the darkness, Ricardo said, "What a strange creature. A hand that can talk! But from the look of things, you can't move. Well, nothing ventured, nothing gained—so once we're done drinking Su-In's blood, it'll be your turn."

"Hell, take me first!" the hand shouted.

No longer looking at the hand, Ricardo turned back toward Su-In. White fangs bared all the way to the gums, he pressed his teeth to her trembling flesh for a split second before unleashing a cry of surprise and jumping back up. As his crazed eyes fell to the woman's feet, they found a steaming puddle of liquid coursing in the hand's direction.

Soaring Cliffs

CHAPTER 7

I

"W hat the hell?!" Ricardo cried as he jumped aside, but he grinned just as quickly. "Are you scared?" he asked Su-In. "I'm not surprised. But you won't be for long. Just between you and me, I've always sort of had a thing for you. Once you're one of us, I'll give you a nice long poke," the boy said in the tone of a veritable fiend.

However, Ricardo's last remark brought Su-In back to her senses. His crude suggestion stirred an explosion of womanly ire.

"Who the hell would ever wanna be with you?!" Su-In shouted as her right hand whined through the air. The drug that'd kept her paralyzed had worn off—her fury had swept away the last of its effects.

As a well-practiced punch made his cheekbone creak, Ricardo reeled backward. But that was all it did. In the blink of an eye, his face was right back in the same position, and wearing a smirk. While the servants might not be as powerful as the true Nobility, their musculature still had five times the strength of an ordinary person. Now Ricardo—or Hannah and Clementine, for that matter—could weather a blow from a professional boxer without any problem.

"You bitch!" Ricardo snarled, fangs bared in his evil countenance. But just as he was lunging for Su-In's throat, he staggered backward once again. A gleaming wedge had burst through his chest from behind.

"Oh, my, that was a close one. But now you clowns have to deal with *me*."

Ricardo's blood-spattered eyes reflected the hand crouching on the floor like a pale spider. Beside it ran the dark stain that flowed from Su-In's lower half. With a low groan, Ricardo fell flat on his face. A knife had gone right through his heart.

"You bastard!"

"You won't get away with that!" the women cried as they got up. They leapt toward the hand. Su-In had been entirely forgotten.

Suddenly Clem, who was at the fore, began to glow. Her form was enveloped by pale blue chemical flames. Every bit of color on her was rendered a luminous white, and before the girl could even scream, she fell across the floor as a pile of stark white ash.

Hannah stopped dead in her tracks, and the pale hand raced right between the vampire's feet.

"We're getting out of here, Su-In," said the hand.

"But there's still one more to deal with."

"Sorry, I just went through the last of my juice."

"Oh, you really are completely useless," said the woman.

The two of them made excellent time as they headed for the door in the far wall. There was another room beyond it.

Her hesitation lasting only seconds, Hannah pursued them at a furious pace.

Turning around just in front of the door, Su-In hurled the knife she'd pulled out of Ricardo's corpse. The weapon flew fast and hard enough to penetrate the skull of a giant killer whale, but Hannah simply clapped the palms of her hands together to stop it right in front of her face.

"This is *not* good!" the hand cried at the same moment the door opened.

The two of them made a mad dash into the next room, bolting through it without a backward glance.

"This way!" shouted the woman.

They took a right in the corridor—and it brought them straight to the main entrance. Hearing Hannah's footsteps behind them, Su-In began to tremble. The front door was falling off its hinges.

They burst outside. Gasping, Su-In halted sharply. Thanks to her incredible momentum, she barely managed to keep herself from falling over.

A pale moon floated in the heavens. It was a crystal-clear summer night.

In a moonlit garden where even the weeds that had grown to their hearts' content looked gorgeous, there stood two figures. Samon and Glen. Even before it could dawn on her that they were both foes of D and herself, Su-In simply recognized them as fellow humans.

"Help me—the girl behind me is a vampire!" she shouted as she pulled up alongside Glen.

Hannah stood in front of the entrance to the temple. Her pearly fangs gnashed together, thirsting for Su-In's lifeblood in a way that was more detestable than words could convey. "Out of my way," she growled. "Let me drink the girl's blood!"

Looking first at Su-In and then at Hannah, Samon asked, "What should we do?" Naturally, her query was directed at Glen.

Not replying to the question, the seeker of knowledge took a step forward. Free of even the smallest injury, his handsome face was immaculate in the moonlight.

Hannah charged at him.

The flash of white light that shot up from the young man's waist mowed right through the girl's neck. It was just like being in town and watching Old Man Krakow expertly take the head off a salmon with one swipe. After the flash had passed through her effortlessly, Hannah ran about ten feet more with black blood spraying from her body—from the headless torso her legs carried.

When the girl's body fell at length, Su-In finally noticed Glen and Samon's complexions. "You . . . both of you, too . . . ," the woman mumbled.

"Stupid children," Samon said as she coldly surveyed the decapitated remains. "They should've restrained themselves until we arrived . . . I suppose you killed the other two, did you? After we went to the trouble of showing them a whole new world."

Su-In felt like all of the blood had drained from her body.

Sword still lowered, Glen spoke at last, saying, "When you came out . . . you had something odd with you, didn't you?"

His voice was as hollow as the abyss. It was the voice of the night.

"It's hidden itself in the grass—what is it, some pet of yours?"

With the two of them staring at her, Su-In couldn't move a muscle.

"In a manner of speaking," a hoarse voice replied from somewhere in the bushes. It sounded like it had its cheeks filled with something or other. Though Samon looked all around them, she couldn't determine where the voice had originated.

Su-In felt an incongruity. While it was the same voice, it was as different in tone from the one she'd heard in the temple as day and night. The words were filled with immeasurable confidence.

"My, my. It seems I vastly underestimated you," Glen said as he brought his blade up to his lips. "I sense a frightful power in you. If we were to fight now, even the woman might be in jeopardy."

Samon's expression changed. She'd just realized she was the one to whom the swordsman was referring.

"As *the old me* would've been," Glen continued. "But not anymore. The killing lust I get from you feels almost the same—you're on D's side, aren't you?"

"Well, I certainly spend enough time *by his side*," the voice responded.

"In that case, give him a message. We're taking the woman. If he wants her back, he's to come to Cape Nobility tomorrow just as the sun sets. Until that time, we won't do anything to her."

There was a brief silence.

"Understood," the voice said stoically.

Glen's sword was tilted against his lips. His tongue was touching the blade, licking the blood that clung to it.

"Come," he said.

With that one word alone, Su-In followed along after Glen like a marionette when he walked off. Samon was pulling up the rear, and once the three of them had vanished into the far reaches of the temple grounds, a protracted sigh could finally be heard from the grass.

"I'll be damned if we don't have one serious pain in the ass to deal with now," said the hand. "I thought about trying to get the girl back, but that probably would've got me killed in the bargain. He could even tell where I was hiding. Before, he wasn't much of a problem, but I have to wonder if you'll really be able to take him now, D."

It was twenty minutes later that the left hand finally met up with D—beneath the dilapidated main gate to the temple. After the Hunter brought Toto to the hospital, the thief had regained consciousness and told him where he could find Su-In.

"It really was too bad," the left hand told D, going on to explain everything that had transpired. It was already neatly reattached to the Hunter's wrist.

"Cape Nobility, eh?" said D. But that was all he had to say.

"It's finally coming down to that time," the left hand remarked. "It looks like you would've been better off leaving the village when you had the chance earlier. A lot more blood's gonna be spilled. Are you sure you don't know what that bead really is?"

D was silent.

"And the Noble—what's he?" the hand continued. "Then there's the story we heard at the museum. Are you sure there isn't a link between him and the warrior we heard stayed at Su-In's house? I've already found one. How are you doing on that?"

Giving no reply, D looked off to the left. The horse and rider were halfway up the side of a hill overlooking the sea. There were no trees. White waves shattered against the jet black world, and the undying roar of the surf sang a paean to the north. Summer had come from out beyond the glittering ice floes, as a Noble in blue raiment. And it held a final paintbrush that was now stained with a vermilion hue. But it would be neither D nor the seeker of knowledge who would wield said brush.

"Why did you come here?" the voice asked. "Was it because of the girl murdered in Gilligan's basement? Because the last word she said was your name? Oh, you just keep getting softer and softer. Can't break your promise to the dead? Even though it's the living who get angry, while the dead never say a thing."

D remained silent as he gazed out at the sea, as if the movements of his heart that the hand described were something about which he knew nothing at all. Perhaps he'd never have a heart of his own for all eternity.

Presently, the Hunter gave a single kick to his mount's flanks and raced off on the steep, narrow path up the incline like an ominous black wind.

Su-In lay on the floor of the mud room. She was in Glen and Samon's hideout in a shack by the sea. Although she hadn't been tied up, she didn't move. If she got the urge, she could've stood up or even run. But she wouldn't get the urge. Desire, aspirations, competitive spirit— all the positive aspects of consciousness seemed to have been drained from her eyes when she met her foes' gaze.

"Girl, there's something I'd like to ask you," the sorceress Samon said after a while. Glen sat to one side of the hut and was seeing to his blade. The warrior woman's eyes gave off a vermilion glow every bit as evil as Glen's, and as she gazed at Su-In, she made no attempt to conceal the hunger and greed in her gaze and on her lips.

"What would that be?" Su-In replied, seeming to make an effort to somehow rouse her own will.

"You were under my spell once, back in the sheriff's office and at the temple gate. When you were, you showed me a certain man. A man you want to see more than anyone in the whole world, someone you simply can't forget."

"A man?" Su-In said, knitting her brow. She remembered the incident. But what did this woman mean, it was a man? It was Wu-Lin. Wasn't it?

Knowing nothing of Su-In's own doubts, Samon continued, asking, "How does he fit into this? What's his connection to the Noble who comes from the sea?"

Despite her semiconscious state, Su-In's whole body tightened with a terrible shock, and it wasn't simply because of the completely unexpected suggestion that there was some connection between the Noble and herself. But for an instant, she'd caught a glimpse of the answer through countless overlapping layers of gossamer. She'd seen it with a geometrical, geological precision.

"What are you talking about?" asked Su-In.

"Don't play stupid with me," Samon snarled, baring her fangs. "He's the man whose loss you mourn more than anyone or anything else. But why was it *him*? That's what I want to know. Answer me."

Su-In shook her head. "It was Wu-Lin! Wu-Lin!" she insisted.

"Don't give me any more of that!"

"It's no lie," Su-In retorted. "*You* should stop lying to *me*."

Samon's features twisted into an atrocious expression, but it quickly vanished and the sorceress stared intently into the woman's eyes. Points of light like rubies drilled through Su-In's eyes and tried to drain the dregs of her soul through them.

Before two seconds had passed, Samon muttered, "Oh . . . So, you're under hypnosis, I see. And a very powerful kind at that . . . erasing memories and clearing up feelings of guilt . . . But not perfectly, I'd say. Wait just a moment. I'll see what I can find now."

The rubies became flaming crystals. Su-In's eyes grew more dazed, while Samon's face glittered with jewel-like beads of sweat.

Several seconds passed—

Closing her eyes, Samon swayed on her feet. Clinging to a pillar strung with nets to steady herself, she rubbed her eyelids with one hand. When her eyes opened again, they were ablaze with the most malicious delight the world had ever seen.

But what did Su-In have locked away in her heart that would please Samon of all people?

"I saw everything," said the sorceress. "So that's what happened, is it? Dear me. I can see why you'd want to hide that. And now, I'll show it to you, too."

"Don't!" Su-In cried, frightened without even knowing why. A ghastly fear beyond comprehension was rearing its head from the darkest depths.

"Look into my eyes," said Samon, holding Su-In by the chin as she brought the woman's face closer.

"Stop it!" Su-In cried, but her voice faded feebly. Samon's hands had a grip on her chin, and a blurry white mass immediately began to take shape between them. "Samon of Remembrances"—the name may have had a romantic ring to it, but Su-In was learning now just how terrible the woman's spell could be.

An outline formed. The eyes took shape. A nose was added. And it wasn't Wu-Lin. While the face was still far from defined, it clearly was that of a man.

Su-In shut her eyes tightly. But Samon pried the woman's lids open again.

"Take a good look," the sorceress told her. "Peer into your own soul. And see exactly what you did."

There was a powerful tug on Samon's shoulder. Her surprised gasp brought a disruption to her spell, and the image that'd been formed by Su-In's heart vanished.

"Just what do you think you're doing?!" the sorceress cried, her shout of shock and anger being absorbed by Glen's powerful chest.

"Knock it off," the swordsman told Samon.

"What's the matter? I was simply showing the girl her own true nature. Is there some problem with that?"

Glen swung his left arm in a rough arc.

Easily knocked head over heels, Samon hit the wall boards back-first. A wooden box fell from above and landed at her feet.

"Of all the nerve," Samon snarled. "Have you forgotten who it was that kept you here in this world?"

"Yes, I have," Glen said, his face completely emotionless. A ghastly aura gusted from every inch of his frame, knocking the wind out of Samon.

"Why, you . . . ," the sorceress groaned fearfully. She'd just realized the young man she'd risked her life and soul to save had, at some point, become something completely beyond her reach. Fear changing to rage, Samon wore a demonic visage as she crept along the wall and made her way back toward Su-In. "You would defend this woman and treat me this way? That's unpardonable," she said. "See how you like it when I do *this*!"

Samon's mouth snapped open. Her face twisting with the supple speed of a whip, she drove her pair of fangs toward Su-In's throat as the woman lay on the floor in a stupor.

A flash of white zipped between the two women.

In a spectacular move, Samon flew through the air, but as she landed again, a blade pressed right against her chest.

"You traitor!" she cried. "You want the woman's blood . . . You'd have it all for yourself, wouldn't you?"

Glen responded in a low voice that sounded like he was spitting up his own blood. "I promised I wouldn't lay a hand on the woman until sunset tomorrow. And having given my word, I intend to keep it."

"How stupid of you to make such a promise . . ."

"To you it may be stupid, but to me, it's more important than life itself! You're not to lay so much as a finger on this woman until tomorrow," Glen said, and his blade slid forward.

A rich vermilion flower blossomed on the breast of Samon's blue dress.

"If it's blood you crave," the man continued, "you can drink your own. But wait—I have something even better to show you."

His blade danced through the air, and Samon's clothes fluttered down to the floor like the wings of a butterfly.

This was how the seeker of knowledge rewarded the woman who'd risked her life and soul for his own sake, a woman whose full bosom was now stained with blood?

As the woman stood stock still, the swordsman pressed his lips fiercely to her throat. A stream of crimson instantly began to spill from the space between her skin and his lips. Samon's face was pointed skyward, and as her expression changed from one of excruciating pain to extreme pleasure, the woman cradled Glen's head in her arms.

"I am yours," she fairly sobbed. "But you are mine, too."

The face that'd been turned toward the heavens fell against the nape of Glen's neck. So cruel, yet so erotic.

Su-In lay on the floor, unable to do anything but watch as a man and woman who'd both received the kiss of the Nobility began to feed on each other's blood.

II

Night was over. The sea breeze bore the scent of summer to the northern village and made the white flowers and the green grass glisten. Performers pulled three-eyed monsters and robots out of thin air while the villagers danced an unfamiliar waltz to music that played in a clearing edged by a pond and fields of flora. Although the bodies of the three missing young people had been discovered in the ruined temple on a hill some distance from the village, everyone involved had been gagged by the mayor's orders. The patrols along the shore had also been increased. Above all else, the one week of summer had to be gently and secretly protected. Children's pleas to go to Su-In's school were met with reproach from stern-faced members of the town council, who informed them that Su-In wasn't a good woman. A better teacher would come to the school, and they no longer needed such a disreputable person.

Just four more days, they all thought. Summer couldn't be tarnished. For it was a hopeful season brimming with light. However, even this season had its inescapable consequences. The coming of night was still a certainty.

D opened his eyes.

He was out in Su-In's barn. Getting up, he went outside and got on Toto's cyborg horse. There was nothing stilted about his movements. They were as precise as a machine, as beautiful as nature, and as orderly as the universe.

Leaving the road, D turned right. Today, the watch fires flickered on the beach once more. The Noble was almost sure to come. What did he seek? Three years. And this summer, he'd come in search of Su-In. Why in the summer? Perhaps listening to the song of the northern sea had made even the Noble long for the blue season once more.

"Hey there! Hey!" the Hunter heard someone shout in the distance. D stopped his steed.

Dwight was racing toward him on a single-seater hydro-bike. A compact two-wheeled vehicle powered by amplified hydroelectric energy, it was a popular form of transportation in areas near rivers or the sea. Although its top speed was less than thirty miles per hour, it was more than sufficient for traveling short distances.

"Wait up. Where are you going?" the fisherman asked, spinning the handlebars around for no particular reason. "At this hour, would you be going out for Su-In? You're gonna go rescue her, aren't you?"

Not addressing Dwight's question, D asked, "What brings you out here?"

"It's that goddamn Toto. Sorry, but he ran off on us."

When the thief was brought to the hospital for the wound to the left side of his chest, Dwight had been there having his own injuries treated, and D had asked the fisherman to keep an eye on Toto's condition. After the Hunter told Dwight that this man knew about the bead, he'd agreed to do it without any argument.

"I had one of my men keeping an eye on him, but when I heard the way he was tossing around in bed, I went to have a look for myself. Seems he slammed my guy up against the wall at some point and knocked him out cold. Hurt as bad as he is, he couldn't have got very far, but we checked everywhere and came up empty. He must be tough as hell. Anyhow, I came out to tell you that."

"Go home," D told him. "I'll bring Su-In back."

Riding alongside the Hunter for a short time on his bike, Dwight then gave a determined nod. "Those sound like words I can put my faith in," the fisherman said. Then he added, "You better come back alive, too, you hear me? I don't care if you've got Noble blood in you or any of that. So long as you're still living, something good's bound to come your way."

Up until that point, D had been facing straight ahead, but then he turned and gazed quietly at Dwight. "That's right," he said. "As long as I'm still living. And Su-In will make it out of this alive, too."

"I'm counting on you," Dwight said, extending one hand. But he quickly pulled it back. Even *he* knew a Hunter didn't like to use his sword arm for anything else.

Dwight's vehicle stopped. D alone would go, illuminated by the moonlight.

Turning off the narrow road, the Hunter advanced down a side path leading into the hills until a wide road appeared. Light could be seen leaking out from beneath its dirt covering. It was the Nobles' road. The soil that covered it must've dried out and been worn away over the years, allowing the surface below to peek out.

Continuing down the road for thirty minutes, D came to the resort area. The shadows of the horse and rider fell on the ground. Only the rider's shadow was faint. Such was the destiny of those of Noble blood.

A black carriage raced by D's side. By the blue glow of an electric light, men and woman dressed in formal wear laughed and chatted. The lights were on in every house. Fireworks blazed on their front lawns, and pure spring water spread like the wings of birds in marble fountains. Surely there must be a ball tonight. A nocturnal bird with bones of silver and wings of crystal passed over D's head. Perhaps the letter it carried was a message of love from some gentleman to a lady.

The wind gusted across the street. A shower of white petals blew from the gardens of all the houses, striking D in the face. He caught one in his hand. It was a grimy scrap of wallpaper.

There was no sign of anyone moving on the road. All of the houses lay in utter darkness, and as the wind blew through their weedy, eroded gardens, they joined it in singing a song of abandonment and decay. It was all just a dream.

Silently D advanced down the white path, and before long the sounds of the sea grew closer—he'd arrived at the cape. Off in the darkness, he could see three figures about a hundred feet away.

Massive stone sculptures of people's faces lined either side of the road. Since these effigies had been coated to resist the elements, they still retained the same color and form that they'd been given thousands of years earlier.

Once D closed to within forty feet of them, he got off his horse. His hair and the hem of his coat fluttered with the sea breeze.

The central figure was Su-In, while Glen was to her right and Samon to her left. The paleness of their skin couldn't be attributed to the moonlight alone, and from this D could see for himself the true nature of her captors.

Glen opened his mouth and said, "Not at all surprised, are you? Oh, that's right—your left hand probably told you all about us. But this is the road I've chosen in order to beat you."

Although Samon then shot a quick glance at the swordsman, she said nothing.

Seemingly under a spell, Su-In wore an expression that showed no signs of any will of her own.

"I don't have the bead," said D.

"That is of little consequence. I simply want to settle things with you. And this woman no longer has need of it, either," Glen said, his voice quivering with jubilation.

"Let the girl go."

"Just as soon as you and I have settled this. Relax. We haven't laid a finger on her, and we won't after this is done, either."

And saying that, Glen suddenly looked up at the sky. The moon was out. It was so perfectly clear, it seemed like it could reflect all the activity taking place on the world below. Glen smiled.

"Lovely moon, isn't it? It's a pity we have to fight on a night like this." With a light shake of his head, he then turned to D again. "But my blood just won't wait. Even though I've been made a servant of the Nobility, my blood alone remains unchanged. What's more, you can't very well let me live in my new form."

"Are you the only one I'll be facing?" D asked.

Although the Hunter didn't so much as glance at Samon, her whole body stiffened with fear. D seemed to be saying he'd destroy them both at the same time if necessary.

"No, both of us," she snarled with bared fangs, but Glen raised a hand to silence her.

"It'll just be me. There's not a chance in a million you'll survive, but should that somehow come to pass, let the woman go on her way."

"I can't do that," D replied.

"I thought you might say that," Glen said with a smile that was actually rather refreshing. Had this man ever looked up at the moon and smiled in all his life?

Samon, on the other hand, was utterly exasperated. "If you die," she said, "I'll fill your heart again with the blood of the girl and the Hunter. I won't allow you to die and leave me here alone. I'll bring you back time and again if need be!"

"Let the woman go," said Glen of all people.

Amazed, Samon was about to say something, but she quickly nodded her consent. Although anyone could plainly see she had something in mind, no one could tell exactly what it was. Su-In was given a shove against her shoulder, and as the woman staggered forward, a flash of white came before her face. Samon's dagger.

While it wasn't clear exactly what effect it had on the woman, it was only a second later that intelligence returned to her round face. Shaking her head two or three times, Su-In may have still been under the effects of the hypnotism, because she started to walk toward D without any hesitation.

"Go home," D said succinctly.

"No," Su-In replied. "I can't leave you here all alone. I'm staying."

"Do what you like. Stay if you want to watch how the Hunter dies," Glen said, his right hand rising from the sheath to the hum of steel. He'd quickly drawn his blade.

Su-In swiftly ran over to one of the stone carvings. No longer even watching the woman, D drew his blade, too. Samon ran to one side like a gust of wind.

Two gorgeous men—and neither of them moving. If Glen was the epitome of deadly determination without affectation as he held his sword out straight at eye level, then the breathtaking sight of D assuming a "figure eight" stance with his blade by the side of his head was just as much the picture of a warrior whose beauty transcended life . . . or death. Most likely, anyone would stand there astonished and accept their fate if it were this young man delivering their end.

However, Glen's eyes glowed with crimson—the color of the Nobility. As he took a step forward, his sword's thrust had something behind it that hadn't been there before, and the instant D parried the blade in a shower of sparks, the impact jarred both the Hunter's arms. Perhaps feeling more than just a ferocious blow, D blocked a quick follow-up strike without ever getting off an attack of his own. In Su-In's eyes, it looked as if D were entirely surrounded by showers of sparks.

The two combatants moved around, tracing a tight circle. Glints of light flew madly in the space between them, then the two handsome figures leapt away—one to the right, the other to the left. The sea was to D's back. Su-In was behind Glen's.

The moonlight revealed dripping streams of black. From D's right eye. Down Glen's left wrist. The figures of beauty were frozen in place. The place was so still, even the sound of the wind and the crash of the waves breaking at the foot of the cliff seemed to have been transformed into pure moonlight.

One working with one eye, the other with one arm—the real question was, who would be at an advantage, and who at a disadvantage? D already had his right eye shut, and Glen was managing his blade solely with his left hand.

D kicked off the ground. As he brought his sword down, it was aimed precisely at the right side of Glen's neck, but the attack was parried by a horizontal slash from the left of his foe's blade—a blow that knocked both the Hunter's sword and his arm back against his own chest and left him reeling. Without time to right himself properly, D made a horizontal swipe of his sword at his opponent's temple. The only thing that allowed Glen to dive to one side and avoid the slash was the new level of power his blood so kindly supplied. D glided closer without making a sound.

A refreshing melody rang in the Hunter's ears.

D's sword became a white flash of light flowing toward Glen's chest. Glen's sword did likewise. Before the Vampire Hunter's flash could pierce his chest, the seeker of knowledge drove his silvery streak through D's heart.

"D?!" Su-In cried, and she was about to race over to him when Samon spread her arms to bar the woman's path. "Out of my way!" Su-In shouted as she launched a fierce and certainly unladylike jump kick she'd learned from a warrior. But Samon suddenly vanished from before her, and the woman took a sharp blow to the neck as she landed on the rocks.

Ahead of her, D had already fallen to the ground.

"D!" she yelled once more, but as her hair was seized and jerked backward, Su-In's words became a cry of pain.

"Take a good look," Samon told her. "He's dead. My man has killed him. My love promised to let you go unharmed, but I didn't. You can go right after the Hunter. And once you comprehend what I'm about to show you, you'll beg for death."

Although it felt like her neck was about to snap, the agonized Su-In stared at the end of the promontory.

D had been slain. The blade jutting from his chest was proof of that.

However, wasn't Glen also on his knees by the Hunter's feet? His sword had pierced D's chest. And D's blade had done the same to him. The only difference between the two had been a slight twist of the body that'd kept one from being hit in a vital spot.

"Glen?! Has he slain you?!" Samon asked when she finally managed to wring the mournful tone from her throat.

Su-In heard the words through her pain and horror.

"Don't worry," the swordsman quickly replied. "It seems that I've won. Samon, let the girl go."

"Don't be ridiculous! I just won't be right with all this if I don't send her right after him. Oh, that's right," she laughed, "you still don't know, either. Well, have a good look at what our chaste little maiden is truly like."

"Stop it," said Glen.

But there was no further reply from Samon. Putting her hands to Su-In's head, she peered down at the woman's face from behind.

The figure that took shape before Su-In's eyes was the same one as the night before. He was every bit as tall and muscular as D or Glen. And when fully formed, his vaguely cruel features bore a resemblance to someone.

"Who's he? Who is this man?" Su-In moaned, while above the woman's head Samon bent backward with laughter.

"Don't you recognize him? Then I shall have to show you something else—with the power my new blood has given me. Look!"

The air before Su-In stirred, and an image of a second person came into being. Su-In stared at it in a daze, and Glen forgot all about his pain and one other matter as he watched her.

Indeed, everybody makes mistakes. Near D's waist, there was a muffled noise that sounded like dirt being eaten.

"But that's—" Su-In cried out in astonishment when she stood face-to-face with the completed image. She recognized it. There was no way she couldn't. After all, it was Su-In herself.

"Now, go to it," Samon told her. "Just as you did back then. Re-enact the scene that's been purged from your memory."

The tableau that unfolded before her eyes at Samon's command seemed as if it could only be some nightmarish bacchanal. Su-In's other self—the one that'd appeared from her mind—drew a knife, then came up behind a man who seemed to be mulling something over and drove the blade straight into his heart with breathtaking ease. The two Su-Ins screamed. So did the young man. Truth and fiction were in perfect accord. Clutching at thin air, the young man fell forward. But before he could hit the ground, he vanished. The phantom Su-In disappeared, too. All that was left was the woman pinned by Samon, staring absentmindedly into space. Tears rolled from her eyes. Su-In realized she would never again be the same person. The memories her grandfather's hypnotism had sealed deep within her heart were tainted with sorrow and fresh blood.

That was the warrior who came to my house four summers ago. And I murdered him. Stabbed him in the back . . . So Grampa Han used his skill on me to keep me from losing my mind . . .

Su-In's personality was imploding. Cracks formed with surprising ease in the ego of the rugged, honest woman, branching out through her entire psyche like the veins of some ill-fated and disturbing circulatory system.

"Stop it!" Su-In shouted. As if mere screams would be enough to check her own collapse.

And as if to keep that from happening, Samon's laughter split the darkness.

But then both Su-In's sobs and Samon's malicious laughter stopped. Glen got up. Before his very eyes, a figure darker than the darkness was eerily rising to his feet, like an immense and gorgeous mountain.

III

"You broke your word," said the voice of the night. Glen had sworn that Su-In would be released, and that nothing would be done to her.

Two points of light burned into Glen's eyes—D's eyes as he got to his feet again. They were ablaze with a vermilion hue. Bits of black rained down at the Hunter's feet, and pieces of earth that spilled from the palm of his left hand.

"Yes indeed, nothing beats good solid food. It takes more than wind to fill your belly."

When Glen realized the second voice had come from the Hunter's left hand, his lips unleashed his deadly whistle.

The wind snarled with the sound of something slashing through the air.

The instant the glittering moonlit wave touched Glen's neck, it became a bloody streak of black. The line raced diagonally to the left, splitting him open all the way to his left lung when D pulled his blade away. Simultaneous streams of blood spread from Glen's chest and back like the wings of a black butterfly.

As the seeker of knowledge fell to the ground without a word, D prepared to bring his blade down on him.

There was nothing Samon could do, but she howled like a beast. Perhaps that was what stopped D's blade.

Just then, the Hunter felt gravity slam down on every inch of his body. It felt like the darkness itself was sinking. Glen was splayed across the ground. He couldn't move a muscle.

"Oh, here comes another one," D's left hand said with amazement, drawing a fifth person out from behind one of the carved stone faces. There was no need for him to name this man who had gravity at his beck and call.

"Egbert, kill him! Kill the Hunter!" shouted Samon. Unbeknownst to Glen, she'd called the giant here and kept him in hiding. And the line across the tip of the cape marking the boundary of his "kingdom" was so faint, even D wouldn't notice it.

"So, we meet again," Egbert said in a ghostly voice. "But this time will be the last. Although I had hoped for a proper fight . . ."

"And here I thought you had more character than this," D's left hand barked scornfully as the Hunter barely managed to stand erect. "You don't even know what it means to have a serious one-on-one duel—which makes me wonder what the hell country are you king of?!"

"Laugh if you like. But I'm in love with her. I want to defend those whom she'd defend."

Those whom she'd defend—wasn't that the very man Egbert had tried to kill?

The whole reason Glen had received his Noble blood was because the giant had used his power on the seeker of knowledge and knocked him off of the other cliff. Out of that whole quintet of warriors who would exploit any advantage or use whatever treacherous means they could, Egbert alone had shown a unique character that'd come as a refreshing change. Even when he'd attacked Glen, it had only been to save the woman he loved from being a mere pawn in the hands of the seeker of knowledge. And although he'd agreed to gang up on D, he was surely the only one who'd felt any reservations about doing so. And now, he was ambushing D to protect a man he'd once tried to kill.

"Make sure you don't kill Glen," Samon commanded in a tone steeped in bloodlust. "Just get *him*. Kill the Hunter alone."

"I know," Egbert said. Slipping his hand into his breast pocket, he pulled out a number of tiny shapes and tossed them on the ground not far from where D stood. Everyone but Su-In could see that they were little mud figurines. Egbert then threw something else. Even upon seeing that they were twigs and nails, there was no telling how he intended to use them.

At that point, D said something strange: "Aren't you going to call in the other two?"

Egbert got an odd look on his face, but he said nothing.

A few seconds later, D was surrounded by bizarre soldiers there in the moonlight. A tree of some unknown form sprang from the ground at his feet, like smoke given substance. Roughly spitting up mud, the soldiers then charged forward. Their swords and spears flashed out like dazzling blossoms. Although the kingdom was under five Gs, the soldiers could move about freely. This alone would've been difficult for anyone to believe.

The shadowy figures overlapped as they made a beeline for D, but a split second later, they all turned to dust as every head was severed and every torso split. The wind carried away the remnants of the soldiers, and D alone remained standing in solitude. His eyes were gleaming with crimson.

"It's no use," the Hunter said. Samon was directly ahead of him. Up until now, the young man had never said anything about his own victory or his enemy's defeat, no matter how weak his opponent was. Perhaps it was some animosity toward the woman who'd laid Su-In's heart bare that made him say it now.

D looked at Glen. The swordsman was in retreat. A pair of soldiers were dragging away his unconscious form.

D's left hand let loose a howling gale. As needles of rough wood pierced both soldiers through the base of the neck, they were instantly reduced to dust.

Seeing D walking calmly toward where Glen lay on the ground, Samon shouted, "Oh no! Egbert! You must do something!"

As if in answer to Samon's cries, a bizarre form burst from the soil near Glen's feet. At first glance, it looked like an ordinary bush. But from the way it threw twisted, tapering thorns out into the darkness in all directions, the vegetation was clearly meant to bar D's path and to shield Glen. By the light of the moon, the sharp branches had a metallic luster. It was doubtful that even D could've imagined the nails Egbert had scattered earlier taking on such a form to hinder his foes.

Whistling through the wind, another branch sprang from the bush. In a manner reminiscent of someone holding a rose rather than seizing a razor-sharp thorn, D caught it with his left hand. A thin black stream quickly rained down onto the ground. The rate at which lifeblood dripped from the Hunter was far greater than normal.

"Impossible!" cried Samon. Having received the kiss of the Nobility, she now understood something she might not have known before. She knew now what fresh blood meant to a dhampir.

A number of branches besieged the Hunter like whips, but each was slashed away to rain back down to earth in a wild dance. Making a single swipe of his sword, D then rushed forward toward the steely bush with incredible speed.

There was a flash. With a single burst, and the bush was split in half down the middle.

Glen was motionless.

As D tried to get through the split, a flash of black lightning shot by his side. Deflected with an earsplitting sound, it was an iron rod. Changing his position, D looked over at the ruler who'd just entered his own kingdom.

"Hurry up! Take him and get out of here!" Egbert said in a forceful tone to Samon, who was behind him. It was not because he was acting on Samon's orders. Rather, he was risking his life because he knew this was the hated enemy of the woman he loved. Even though he'd become something inhuman, this man of the ancient warrior code hadn't entirely forsaken his former self.

And D, for his part, took up a position directly opposite the man.

"Strange, isn't it?" Egbert said flatly. "I'm not doing this just to play hero. I mean it from the bottom of my heart. D, is that how a Noble's mind works?"

His only answer was the wind.

As a human, Samon had risked her own life to save Glen's, as had Egbert when he received the kiss of blood. Humans and Nobles—how did they differ?

"I'm ready to pay for my ambush with my own flesh," the giant said. "I know I can't win, D, but I'm gonna have at you!"

D readied his blade in a low position. To this man who was facing him fair and square, he didn't say, "It's no use."

The gravity suddenly eased away. Egbert had relinquished his kingdom.

"Hyaaah!"

Backed by his new Noble blood, the giant's blow was harder and faster and more precise than ever, but D's eyes glowed crimson and the blade he swung up from below deflected the iron staff, executed an elegant turn in the air, and slid right through the heart of the king who'd cast off his crown. Even after D had drawn his blade back out again, Egbert stood stock still.

"So . . . death is true peace? Now I see," the giant muttered, his words following him as he fell to the ground.

Letting his eyes drop to the warrior's remains momentarily, D then turned his gaze toward the road. With Glen over her shoulder, Samon was closing on Su-In.

The Hunter's left hand flicked out.

Having accepted the blood of the Nobility, the sorceress would get no mercy merely because she was a woman. A needle of unfinished wood pierced the left side of the temptress' neck, poking out again on the right side. Samon staggered for a few steps, her knees buckling. And yet she still wouldn't let go of Glen.

"Come," she said, bloody bubbles spilling from her pale lips along with that challenge. D's needle had gone through the carotid artery. Naturally, it wasn't a fatal injury for a vampire. Samon drew her dagger. "Come, Hunter . . . I'll never allow you to kill him. I'll never let anyone lay a hand on my man . . . I'm still alive. Come . . . Come to me . . ."

Though her chin and breasts were drenched with fresh blood, Samon still showed incredible tenacity.

"That sure is something," D's left hand remarked with admiration.

However, as D stalked forward, there wasn't the faintest hint of emotion in his eyes. Three villagers had been bitten, and he was a Vampire Hunter.

Just then, the whole world shifted with a rumbling from below. There was a roar as if some subterranean demon had discharged all the world's evil and hatred at once. And rather than stop, the rumbling kept spreading, baring colossal fangs at the land mass.

To say the least, it was extremely unfortunate D was standing at a spot about ten feet from where the part of the cliff that jutted out over the sea connected to the rest of the land. Strength surged into his legs so he could make a leap, but the ground beneath him had already crumbled. Along with several hundred tons of stone, D plunged headlong toward the dark crests of the waves.

†

Although the earthquake that struck the Nobles' resort area destroyed half of that vast territory, it had almost no effect at all on the village. Musical performances at the festival continued to ring out, and the people soon erased the anxious looks from their own faces as they tried to convince themselves that nothing could possibly go wrong on a summer night. Tidal waves weren't even a concern. The water level merely rose a few inches, but the young men standing guard were in no danger, and nothing happened aside from four or five of the watch fires being knocked flat.

A point of light glowed in the midst of the darkness. The shape it took was not a cone, but rather closer to a globe. It was the illumination cord.

The scene that emerged was one of pure destruction. Heaps of stone and building materials had formed, yet the fact that the waves beating against the piles of wreckage hadn't changed their flow or location seemed to indicate that no severe damage had been done to the underlying structure.

It was the area deep below Meinster's castle.

"This place sure as hell got hit hard," said a hoarse voice. "This was the center of the devastation, but it looks like the shock waves were all set up to emanate outward. Isn't it strange that someone would know how to do that?"

Climbing over the rubble, D moved further into the subterranean chamber—to where the bizarre tanks stood in a veritable glass forest. Water still dripped from the hem of his coat. Less than two hours had passed since he'd fallen from the cliff at the cape.

Though he'd gone back to the cape, there was obviously no sign of the two vampires, nor was there the faintest trace of Su-In. Surely they'd taken her with them. So long as Glen still lived, he was sure to contact the Hunter again. D had no choice but to wait until he did so. Any emotions he might've harbored regarding Su-In's fate couldn't be discerned from his handsome features beneath the interplay of pale light and shadows.

As the Hunter ventured in further, the devastation took on a sharper tone. All the tanks had been shattered, and shards of glass continued to drop from their sides. At what seemed to be the center of the tanks, D halted. This was where an incredible energy had gone wild.

Aside from D, there were only two people who'd have any business down here. But if either of them had been down there, it didn't seem like they could've possibly survived.

D looked far off to the left. There'd just been a sound of metal grinding on metal. Perhaps it was responding to his light.

Something heavy rolled down a slope. Probably a chunk of masonry.

Pulling out a wooden needle, D tied the illumination cord around the middle of it and hurled it right at the source of the sound.

In the circle of light, something that looked like a black leg could be seen wriggling. It must've been about forty feet away.

"Oh, him, is it?" said a voice down by D's left hip.

Slowly extricating itself from a pile of rubble was a familiar aquatic machine—Gilligan's giant crab.

D didn't even draw his blade, and the reason for this quickly became evident.

In the process of extricating itself, the giant crab seemed to have run out of power. Toppling forward, it clumsily rolled over once, and then fell heavily against the slope. A great scythe of a claw struck the ground by D's feet, and then stopped. It didn't move another inch.

Catching the feeble hum of a motor, D approached the crab's body.

"Wow, this is something else! The arms and legs have been ripped right off," said the voice.

But the pitiful image of that gigantic crab robbed of all its limbs save one was already burned into D's retinas. However, its legs hadn't been carelessly torn free. Each stub sparkled with a nice smooth cut, as if the limbs had been severed by some trenchant blade. The whir of the motor swelled, and the glass dome on the crab's body circled around to the front. The bubble was much more clouded than it'd been during its battles with D due to the cracks it now bore.

"Is that you, D?" a feeble voice called out to the Hunter. "I'm finished. I managed to hold out against you . . . but this time, I just didn't have what it took."

"Who did this to you?" D asked when he finally spoke.

"Professor Krolock . . . He's given himself the power . . . of a Noble . . ."

"With the bead?"

"That's right . . . He continued the experiment down here . . . just like I wanted to do . . ."

"How did you get here?" asked D.

"I was trying to fix the parts you'd damaged . . . while underwater," Gilligan replied. "As chance would have it, I sank deep to the bottom of the sea . . . And down there, I found the opening that leads back into here . . . That bastard Krolock . . . When I found him, he was floating in one of those glass tanks . . . and on the bottom was the bead . . . half-dissolved . . ."

"What was the bead?"

"You mean to tell me you don't know?" Gilligan laughed. "Here we were, risking our lives . . . and the whole time, the biggest threat to us . . . didn't even know what it was for . . . Ah, that's life for you," Gilligan said, cackling. "A long time ago . . . I saw a laser recording in the Capital's archives that'd been made by a certain Noble . . . In it, there was information on Nobility who could live underwater . . . Now, Nobility in their natural form couldn't do so . . . but if they used a human body, they could then live underwater or even in broad daylight. But if they did that . . . then once a year, all the impurities that collected in their body . . . had to be expelled . . . And that's what the bead was . . . In other words, all you had to do was analyze that . . . and the secrets of human and Noble genetics would be yours. That was as much as I knew . . . But that damned Krolock . . . he even knew about this research facility. Let me tell you something else . . . If the human psyche is resilient . . . the personalities compete with one another . . . Two minds in one body . . ."

His voice was stretched terribly thin.

"I wanted to have the power . . . of a genuine Noble. I read all the literature I knew of and tried every conceivable means . . . and thanks to that, I survived even after you cut my head off . . . But now I'm done for . . . When I shattered the tank . . . that skinny bastard pulled out this scrap of cloth . . . The next thing I knew . . . I was having the crab cut off its own legs . . . After he finished me off . . . he blew up the damned lab . . . Hurry . . . He must've gone to the village . . . He's hungry . . . wants blood . . . But watch yourself . . . He's stronger than you are . . . And another thing . . ."

The last thing the kingpin said was like a final breath he squeezed from himself.

"He's . . . crazy . . ."

And after that, Gilligan was silent. It was a pitiful end for him. Twice he'd fought D in that mechanical monster, and both times he'd managed to escape with his life. What did that say about the old artist if he could defeat such a machine?

"This isn't good. We'd better get right on this—because if we don't find Krolock before he gets back to the village, there'll be hell to pay!"

Without even waiting for the hoarse voice's words, D had already turned to leave.

When Winter Comes Again

CHAPTER 8

I

Samon chose a dilapidated house for their hideout—it was on the complete opposite edge of the village from the fisherman's hut they'd used previously. True to her cautious nature, she'd abandoned the other building just in case anyone had already found out about it. Needless to say, the half-dead Glen and the nearly demented Su-In were there, but there was also someone new. Twin.

The same man who'd thrown a dagger at Egbert's back at the Black Lagoon knew he was the only one of the whole quintet that was still human, but that realization only served to make him all the more eager to stay in the fight. No matter what it took, he was going to get that bead.

However, it remained a mystery to Twin who even had the bead now. The only information he had was that Shin and Egbert had gone after D in a bid to take the bead from him, but Egbert alone had returned, and he'd said that Shin had been slain. That being the case, it should've been in D's possession as always, but at the Black Lagoon, the Vampire Hunter had told them he didn't have the bead—and it was neither a lie nor a bluff on his part. Twin's instincts told him D wasn't lying.

But if D didn't have it, who did?

What Twin had elected to do was follow Egbert and see what the giant did. Back at the Black Lagoon, Twin hadn't run off right away, but rather he'd stayed to watch Egbert's every move. Although he'd tried to get in contact with his partner who'd hidden in Su-In's home, he hadn't received any reply at all, and Twin decided that meant his brother had been killed. By following Egbert to a rendezvous with Samon and Glen, he'd also learned the location of their fishing hut. And he saw with his own two eyes the horrible fate that had befallen all three of them. Stealthily trailing after them, he'd even watched the confrontation at the cape from afar.

All of this had been possible because of Twin's abilities. Erasing all trace of his presence, he also remained downwind at all times. The only reason Samon had become aware of him was because, while following them, he'd stepped on some rubble thrown to the ground by the earthquake. Noticing the sound, Samon had done nothing, but continued walking back to her hideout. There she laid in wait for Twin, pouncing on him without a word and marking him with her fiendish kiss.

"Perfect timing," Samon said. As she licked up the blood that dripped from her lips, she gave Twin a smile that would've frozen whatever remained in his veins. "Since Egbert was slain, I was just thinking how I could use someone else to carry our bags. And your abilities could still prove useful in our battle."

And then the sorceress shifted her gaze between Su-In and Glen where they lay on the floor as an expression of indescribable evil took shape on her face.

"Is the Hunter dead? No, he can't be. A man like him could come through something like that without as much as a scratch. We're sure to face him again." Chuckling, she added, "And I'll have this woman in a shape we can use when we do."

The only reason Su-In had been safe in Samon's custody up until now was that the seductress had been too worried about Glen to even think about drinking the woman's blood. But there was nothing to stop her now. Did the "Noble psyche" that Egbert had mentioned mean nothing to her? Her blazing eyes dyed with the bloody hue of hatred, Samon began slowly walking over to Su-In like some pale serpent slithering toward a gorgeous and paralyzed insect.

"Stop . . ."

Even when she realized the vapid voice that seemed to creep across the floor was that of Glen, Samon didn't turn around.

"You can't . . . ," the swordsman groaned. "Don't touch the woman."

"I've had about enough of that," Samon spat. "Don't you want to triumph over the Hunter? Twice you've fought him, and twice you've lost. Even after you got the blood of the Nobility. However, the third time shall be different. I'll see to it you win. But to do so, it is essential that I make this woman into our puppet."

"Don't," Glen told Samon. "I still haven't forgotten . . . what I promised him."

"You still have the nerve to say that?" she said with a haughty laugh. "Even if you recover completely, do you actually believe you'll win next time?"

"I'll win."

Perhaps sensing something in his voice, Samon finally turned to look at the man. In his pale corpse face, his eyes alone gave off blood light.

At that point, the strangest thing happened. Samon smiled. And it wasn't the spiteful grin of a demon like she usually wore, but rather a smile that would grace the face of the purest maid. She glided over to Glen as if Su-In, who lay on the floor, had been completely forgotten.

"And can I put my trust in you?" she asked in a soft tone, her gaze equally gentle.

"When all this is over—" Glen began to say to the woman, a faraway look in his eye.

"Yes?"

"Why don't we head down south?"

"That would be nice," Samon said with a nod.

But what would they do when they went south? Even if Glen managed to slay D, nowhere in the world would be safe for these two who'd received the kiss of the Nobility. They had joined a family whose day had long since passed.

Samon gazed at Glen's chest—the bleeding had stopped. All he had to do was drink some fresh human blood, and he'd quickly make a full recovery. As she looked at Twin standing there by the doorway, her accustomed cruelty returned to her gaze with lightning speed. "Come here," she commanded him in a low tone. Her voice had the ring of blood to it.

Twin moved. But so did something else.

Glen sat straight up, as if he'd been pulled up on a string.

The door to their dilapidated house had slowly opened.

When Samon realized just who the figure standing in the rectangular frame was, she squeaked, "Professor Krolock!"

"Oh, you remember me?" the cloaked figure laughed.

It certainly was the professor. But what in the world had happened? His wiry gray hair had become jet black, his wrinkles were gone, and the scraggly beard around his mouth had become smooth and luxuriant. Beside his incredibly pale skin, his lips were like a vivid crimson stain, and seeing the pair of pearly fangs that jutted from the corners of his mouth, Samon drew her dagger.

"You've been changed, too?" asked the sorceress.

"So it would appear, wouldn't it?" laughed the elderly professor—or rather, the professor who'd been returned to his manly prime. Every inch of him seemed to radiate an intense vitality, and even Samon couldn't look him squarely in the eye. "However," he continued, "I'm not one of your ilk. I have no master. I became this way through my own efforts."

Entering the room, the professor surveyed his surroundings with glittering eyes. A mere look from him was enough to give Samon goose bumps.

He's not like us, she thought. *Has he become something else entirely?!*

"What do you want?" Glen asked as he got to his feet. "If it's the bead you're after, it's not here."

"The bead is within me," the professor said. Something white dribbled from the corner of his mouth. Saliva. "I have no more need of it," he continued. "My wish has been granted. However—I'm famished!"

His tone was such that even Su-In leapt up off the floor.

"Do you know why I've come here?" asked the professor. "Initially, I intended to descend on the village. But as I was leaving the castle, I caught the scent of blood. A warm, sweet aroma that would be simply perfect to slake my thirst. I am not like you. One alone will not suffice. I'll need the blood of all of you. You shall fill my belly well!"

"How interesting," Samon said, baring her fangs. "We were just getting ready to do the same thing. You're like a moth to the flame. Know now that this shall be your last night!"

Wearing a demonic scowl, Samon was about to advance when a tall figure stepped in front of her.

"Take the woman and go," he said.

"Glen?!"

"Hurry up and go," the swordsman told her. "I'll be right behind you."

"But . . . ," Samon stammered, inky black anxiety gushing into her eyes.

Glen's voice was crystal clear—heart-wrenchingly clear. The eyes of the seeker of knowledge gave off a crimson glow, and he drew his sword.

The professor had his right hand in the breast of his clothes.

Light raced out in every color of the spectrum. A heartbeat later, the sound of harshly severed bone could be heard. A black line zipped through the professor's right wrist, and then everything from there to his fingertips started to slide off. Although Glen was injured, his draw and strike had been flawless.

The severed limb stopped before it hit the floor. The professor had caught it with his left hand. Pressing it back to the spot where it had originally been attached, he then took his left hand away and used it to wipe off the black line. No wound remained from the blade.

Samon groaned in a low voice. That was the sort of thing that would usually happen if a human were to turn a blade against a Noble. But Glen was one of the Nobility!

"Go," Glen commanded her sharply.

As she dashed over to where Su-In was, Samon heard another voice that was practically a whisper.

"I am not the one who should be tasting your steel. You are. Take your sword and jab it into your throat," said the professor as he held a roll of parchment open in front of his chest. The portrait of Glen he'd drawn in his own blood was so detailed, it looked as if someone could feel the heat of the swordsman's skin or his very breathing just by touching the picture.

Fear lanced through Samon. "Stop, Glen! You mustn't listen to what he says!"

But as Samon shouted, she saw Glen's sword move from where he had it poised at eye level, slowly but steadily approaching his throat. Glen's cheek twitched. Deep within him, a fierce psychic struggle was taking place.

The tip of the blade reached his throat. Then sank into his flesh.

Glen's lips puckered. Would his deadly whistle be able to outdo the devilish whisper?

"Glen?!" Samon cried.

At the same time, a melody of unearthly beauty streamed from Glen's lips—a melody, and then blood. The blade pierced the base of his throat in the front, and all but jutted out from the back of his neck. Crimson foam splattered against the floor, sending up a tiny spray.

Pursing his lips once more, Glen struggled to whistle. Out it came. But it was only a prolonged breath and a stream of blood.

"A neck wound won't kill you, will it?" the professor said, smiling as if he'd just remembered that. There was no trace of the contemplative scholar in him now. "Stab yourself in the chest," he said.

"Stop it!" Samon's body became a bolt of lighting as she shot toward the professor.

The professor's neck split open—and quickly closed again.

A second later, the blade Glen had pulled from his own throat sank deep into its owner's heart like a pin being driven through an insect. As his knees buckled, one last sound sprang from his lips.

"D . . ."

For a brief instant, the swordsman's eyes were flooded with a tragic persistence, but it was quickly replaced by nothingness.

Silence descended. And it was not that of death alone. It was formed from the soundless grief of one woman.

Before long, Samon said flatly, "This can't be right! It can't be!"

"You've seen for yourself," the professor said as he pulled out another piece of vellum. "It only stands to reason, given the mere fraction of a Noble's power someone in your position receives. I won't kill you. A woman's blood burns when she despises you, and that hot blood is something this new Noble looks forward to tasting. You should consider yourself honored."

And then he began to whisper to a new piece of vellum—one that was etched with Samon's face.

"Come. Into my arms."

Though the woman was crazed with hatred and fear, those emotions drained swiftly from her eyes. As if in a dream, the woman began to walk toward the professor. Not only had he ensnared Glen, but now he had Samon as well. Just what sort of transformation had the professor been through?

It was at precisely that moment that the professor's eyes made a rapid movement. He gnashed his pointed teeth with an ineffable malice and resentment. With that almost metallic sound, he spat, "An interloper at this of all times?"

And then the professor shoved Samon aside and headed to the door with powerful strides.

He went outside. A cyborg horse that'd been racing like the wind stopped right in front of him, and a figure in black got off it without a sound. His eyes were like the glittering darkness made solid as they coldly reflected the new Nobility.

"There's one thing I don't understand," the professor said as his right hand slipped into the breast of his clothes. "How did you manage to follow me?"

"Is Su-In inside?" was the first thing D asked. His soft tone suited the night perfectly, but there must've been something else in it that forced the professor to respond.

"Yes, she's here." And saying that, the professor smiled with complete confidence. "However, you won't be going inside. You must die right here. Die just as the other man did."

D watched silently as the man unrolled the vellum he'd pulled out. The Hunter's right hand went to his sword hilt with lightning speed, there was another flash, and the weapon fell in a perfectly straight line from the tip of the professor's unprotected head down to his crotch. Anyone who knew of D's skill with a blade could well imagine the professor dropping to either side like a split log while viscera flew everywhere.

The professor grinned. An inky black line remained in the same spot where the silvery flash had passed. He then ran one hand along it—no slice remained in his cloak, nor was there any scar on his skin. He lapped noisily at the blood that clung to the palm of his hand.

"How do you wish to die?" Professor Krolock asked through blood-stained lips. "Shall I have you do what the last man did and stab yourself in the throat before gouging yourself through the heart? No, I must see to it yours is a much more painful death, as punishment for interfering with my feeding. Now, take that sword and put it to your neck. You're going to slowly saw into it. You're not to stop even when you hit bone. Keep going until you've cut your own head off completely."

Even before the professor underwent this eerie transformation in Meinster's subterranean lab, his power had made Samon his plaything, and after the change he'd gone on to slay Glen. He gazed raptly at the bizarre canvas. A portrait of D the artist had drawn in his own blood lay there in all its glory.

"Exquisite," said Professor Krolock. "What a lovely countenance. That's why I had to labor underground until this morning to finish drawing you. I put my heart and soul into this masterpiece, and now there's no escape for you. Cut away. Once you've finished taking your head off, I'll preserve it in salt and keep it with me for all eternity."

D's sword went into action. The Hunter brought it to the nape of his own neck, exactly as the professor had instructed.

As the professor watched the silvery line move across the pale, nigh-translucent skin, his whole body trembled. Something red welled up at the point of contact. At the scent of fresh blood in the air on a summer night, Professor Krolock closed his eyes in rapture.

And that was why he missed something crucial. He didn't see the crimson flames burning in D's eyes.

Even when the cold steel pierced his heart, the professor didn't so much as scream.

Opening his eyes, he said, "How did you escape my power?"

The thin piece of animal hide dropped from his hand.

"It was a crappy picture," a hoarse voice said with a scornful laugh. "The rougher the picture, the weaker the effect of your power. There's no way you'd snag him with the likes of that."

"Is that so? I guess you were just too beautiful after all," the professor muttered pensively before taking a step back. The blade came out of him.

D didn't give chase.

"Shall we try this again some other time?" Professor Krolock said as he slowly retreated.

"You have no tomorrow," said D.

Watching the Hunter quietly sheathe his sword, the professor laughed scornfully. The wound on his chest had vanished without a trace. But a second later, a hellish agony seared through his heart. From the center of his chest—the same spot where the wound had vanished—black blood gushed from him and rained down noisily on the earth.

"Impossible!" the professor said as he gazed at D in utter disbelief. He realized something for the first time—the young man before him was an entirely different form of life from himself. "This . . . this just can't be," he stammered. "I used the Nobles' secret . . . to make a new race . . ."

"You failed," the voice said. "There's only ever been one success."

As the professor fell forward, D swung his blade at the man's neck. The wizened head that flew into the air had a horribly wrinkled face. When it thudded back to earth, D then opened the door to the dilapidated house.

The first thing to greet the Hunter's eyes was Glen's corpse, which lay on the floor. But that's all there was. There wasn't a single person left in the room.

II

D went into one of the back chambers. The window on the far wall was open—that must've been how they'd fled. There was no sign of anyone still being there.

The Hunter went back to the front entrance.

A figure stood by the Hunter's horse. He wore a brown shirt with blue stripes, and where the garment was open, bandages were visible on his chest. Regardless of the fact he said his heart was on the right side, he'd still punctured the lung on the opposite side, and it was incredible he'd been able to escape from the hospital.

"By the look on your face, I take it things didn't go well," Toto wheezed. "And after I nearly killed myself getting that info to you."

When D had returned to the surface from the subterranean region below Meinster's castle, it was the thief who'd informed him of the strange happening out at this shanty. Although his meeting with D had been a coincidence, his discovery of Samon and Su-In's location had been quite intentional.

During his confrontation with Egbert on the cape, D had asked, "Aren't you going to send in the other two?" One of the people to whom he was referring was Twin, while the other was Toto. Twin had trailed Egbert, while Toto had escaped from the hospital to follow along after D when he was called up to the cape. When the massive quake ensued and D was swallowed by the waves, the thief had then followed after Samon and the others. The temptress thus had two pursuers on her tail—Twin and Toto. While it was understandable that Samon might miss him, the reason even Twin didn't notice Toto was because, even gravely wounded, he was still the greatest burglar in the northern Frontier.

Toto's sole aim was still the bead. Although Professor Krolock had made off with it, he had a feeling that if he followed Samon and company, they were bound to come into contact with the professor sooner or later. In a manner of speaking, his hunch had proved correct. While keeping watch over the vampire pair in the ruined house, Toto was horribly surprised when he learned that the professor had come.

The tragedy that followed was like something out of a nightmare. Deciding that this was far more than he could handle, Toto could think of only one person with the skill to undertake the task, and he went back to the cape in search of D. And there, he'd met the Hunter. Giving D his own horse, Toto had continued on foot, arriving at the dilapidated house just now.

"Is Su-In okay?"

"Are you worried about her?" asked D.

"Well, sort of," Toto replied nonchalantly.

"There's no bead anymore. Time for you to exit the stage."

"Do you expect me to just go, 'Anything you say, sir!'?"

"Do as you like," D said as he straddled his horse. With the darkness for a backdrop, his face alone seemed to glow.

"That's my horse!" Toto exclaimed.

"It's the hospital's horse."

"And you'd just leave an injured man stranded?"

"Su-In's in mortal danger," D replied.

"Where is she?"

"I don't know."

"And the night's just begun," said Toto. "Tell me something—if the bead's gone, why is everyone still so worked up about it?"

"I suppose they think they might get back whatever it is they lost."

"In that case, folks would be better off not having anything they could lose in the first place. Well," the thief added, "I suppose that wouldn't work either. Humans sure are dumb, aren't they?"

"The same is probably true of the Nobility."

"They're not dumb, but they *are* monsters. Which do you suppose would be worse?"

D said nothing, but wheeled his horse around.

He came to the road that led back to the village, then raised his left hand and said, "Not too long has passed yet."

The wind groaned across the palm of D's left hand. But anyone who felt it on their skin certainly would've bugged their eyes in surprise. A ferocious gale of over a hundred miles per hour was being sucked into a tiny yet unmistakably human mouth that'd opened in the palm of the Hunter's hand.

"Well?" asked D.

"I'm barely getting something. I don't know what they're doing, but somehow they're keeping the blood scent to a bare minimum. Another minute and it'd be so faint even I couldn't catch it. Go straight down this road. But . . ."

"But what?" asked the Hunter.

"I'm sure you've already noticed. The air is strangely cold. Looks like it's going to be a hell of a summer."

D gave a kick to his horse's flanks.

After galloping along for about a minute, a horizontal ribbon of silver could be seen ahead and the sound of water was audible. A river. A little bridge of logs and packed earth spanned it. On it stood a figure bathed in moonlight. It was Twin. Surely he was there to buy time for Samon to escape.

Rather than pull back on the reins, D charged forward.

Twin didn't move.

As he galloped by the stock-still man on the right side, D swung his sword at him. Twin made no move to protect himself. Most likely, he'd never had any intention of doing so. The young villain's head sailed into the air.

But at just that instant, the Hunter's mount came to a sudden stop—or rather, it got stuck. The horse found itself in the most unnatural of poses, as if all four of its legs had suddenly sunk into deep holes.

Not surprisingly, D couldn't help but go tumbling forward. Flying off at a speed and angle that would've undoubtedly been bone-shattering for an ordinary person, D would be able to give an easy twist and land gracefully. But he didn't. He hit the ground shoulder-first, sending a dull rumble into the air. Still, he quickly tried to get up again, but then staggered in a strange manner.

A semitransparent gelatinous substance clung to D's arms and legs. Although D realized that it had gushed from Twin's gaping neck wound, he couldn't be sure exactly what it was. Like the substance Twin had produced before, it was supple as jelly when it gushed from him, but mere seconds later it congealed with the strength of steel. This same substance that restrained D's muscles had been spread across the road to snare the legs of the cyborg horse, had sealed the windows and doors at Su-In's house, and had clung to the Hunter's blade during his first duel with Glen. What's more, it'd become obvious that the substance became hard as steel or a sticky slime in accordance with its master's will. The unyielding nature of the substance was made clear by the portion that'd spilled into the river—it'd formed a solid sheet that blocked the flow of the water.

"This stuff is a pain—give me a second," the voice said.

All five fingers were open on D's left hand. As the Hunter moved it along his leg from the knee to the thigh, the hardened substance began giving off a whitish smoke and dissolving.

It was two minutes later that D got to his feet.

"This jelly stuff looks disgusting, but it's pretty tasty. Wonder if I should keep some aside in my belly for later? Anyhow, that was a tough break."

Not reacting to the voice that sounded both blasé and disappointed at the same time, D turned around.

In the middle of the road sat Twin's severed head. The thoroughly corpse-like lips moved, and he said, "I have Su-In." The sound of his voice was enough to make anyone want to plug their ears. "But don't worry," the head continued. "In accordance with Glen's wishes, I won't do a thing to her. Tomorrow evening, come to the beach in front of Su-In's house at 11:00 Night. But if you try to find us before then or if you fail to show up, I'll feed the woman to the fish."

Once Twin had finished speaking, his features twisted into an unsettling death smile and his head fell over.

"It's that woman, isn't it?" the left hand said in an appreciative tone. "We've got no choice but to wait another day. That's our deadline for destroying the Noble, right?"

D was gazing in the direction of the village.

The distant melody played on eternally. Young men and women danced, trampling the shadows they cast by the moonlight. Tin goblets clanked together in toasts, and fireworks exploded in all the colors of the rainbow. Summer would never end.

Before the night gave way to dawn, people noticed that something had changed. The wind was cold. Unlike the bitter sting of winter, it felt like a gentle summer breeze on their skin. Anyone who wasn't from the village probably would've said it was too cool. But it was cold—and not merely in regard to the sense of touch.

When the very first gust raced through the woods and village, the people stopped in their tracks, dazed—as if something breathing deep within them had suddenly stopped. On realizing that their blissful days were a mere dream, the adults were sadder than the children, but they also recovered more quickly than the little ones. Before long, people started walking around and talking again, or stepping in time to the music. Though the wind remained just as cold, they acted as if it couldn't touch them.

That night, there were more victims. A young man who'd been standing watch on the beach and his girlfriend. Guard duty was done in groups of five. If they spotted a Noble, they were supposed to blow the whistle they carried. The young man had vanished behind the nearby rocks with his girlfriend when she brought him a snack. It was just before daybreak that the two of them were found with bloody blossoms left on the napes of their pallid necks.

A messenger from the mayor was dispatched to Su-In's house in total secrecy.

D had returned. After hearing news of the victims, he'd first sped to the scene of the crime with the messenger, and after looking into the situation, he'd then called on the mayor.

"May I remind you, you only have until tomorrow to destroy the Noble," the mayor said as a wind that carried the same message gusted from his gloomy eyes.

"I know," was all D said.

"Is Su-In doing all right?"

"Are you worried about her?"

"I've known her since she was a toddler," the mayor replied.

"Four years ago, a warrior came to stay at her house. You remember that, don't you?"

The mayor grabbed the back of a chair and used it to support his own weight. "So, Su-In's figured it out, has she?" he said in a voice choked with heartbreak as he stared at D.

Why he decided then it was okay to tell the Hunter the rest was anybody's guess.

"Well, he did stay at their house," the mayor explained, "but only for two days. The man in question was someone we'd called in to organize us so we could prevent attacks by bands of pirates. Since the inn was being remodeled at the time, he wound up staying at Su-In's place. But we moved him to my house right away. That's why I figure none of her neighbors would've told you about him."

What had happened during those two days?

It was in the woods one night that the forms of Su-In and the young warrior had caught the eye of the museum curator. By the light of the moon, the young man's naked muscularity and the woman's supple form had moved together in a fevered frenzy. After being informed of this incident by the curator, Su-In's grandfather and the mayor had decided to turn a blind eye to it. The young warrior was most likely capricious, the time the village had to receive his tutelage was short, and there was no substitute available. And if he'd become attached to Su-In, that was essentially the same as his forming a bond with the village. With the couple's quietly blooming romance remaining a secret, the warrior provided the necessary instruction to the villagers and the day of his departure arrived without incident. The last day of summer.

That evening, the mayor received a visit from Su-In and her grandfather in the utmost secrecy. Su-In couldn't stop crying.

"You see," the mayor continued, "the warrior had suggested to her that they steal the money from the town offices and run off together. But with her grandfather and sister dependent on her, there was no way Su-In would ever agree to such a thing. Still, the warrior wasn't about to give up. He threatened to let the whole village know what'd been going on between the two of them. Sadly, our village isn't the sort of place that'd be very forgiving of that kind of behavior from a woman. Not only would Su-In no longer be able to live here, but her grandfather and sister probably would've been finished as well. If she wouldn't leave her family behind, the man said he'd name her as his accomplice in the theft of the village funds. And so—"

Su-In had stabbed the man. Up on Cape Nobility.

As for what happened next, D already knew. Whether her grandfather's ability had proved fortunate or not for Su-In was the real question. Perhaps when she'd invited D to stay at her house where she was now a woman living alone, it was her way of subconsciously resisting the spell her grandfather had used to make her forget that tragedy.

"Tell me something," the mayor said, his gaze clinging desperately to D. "The Noble that comes from the sea—we've been calling him Baron Meinster all this time, but is that really who he is? Did someone who vanished a thousand years ago suddenly rise again from the sea three years ago? If I were to tell you Su-In's grandfather and I didn't have our suspicions, I'd be lying. He's that guy, isn't he?"

D turned to the mayor. There was a window behind the old man. The black sea was visible. And that was where it had all started.

During the legendary battle, Meinster had been sent to the bottom of the sea, coffin and all. Or rather, Meinster had escaped, but a final attack by the baron's foe ruptured his coffin. Nevertheless, it seemed that he'd survived. It seemed wholly unrealistic to believe Meinster wouldn't have taken advantage of the knowledge he'd gained from the numerous examples of human/monster fusion that remained beneath his castle. And for an interminable time, the baron remained in that place, oh so deep and dark and cold.

What happened later was a happy coincidence that bordered on the impossible. The corpse of a man who'd been stabbed drifted down to the bottom of the abyss, where it made contact with the psyche of the sleeping fiend. Unfeasible. But this flesh housed two minds—controlled by both the Noble and the human, it would subject itself to the command of each at different times. However, when that fateful season came, it was bound to follow the heart of the unnamed warrior alone. Impossible. Yet in light of the facts, there was no point in denying it.

In D's ears, the roar of the sea may have sounded like the scream of the young man who'd vanished there. Softly he said, "Tomorrow it should all come to an end. And there's no head to worry about anymore. Don't say anything; just accept Su-In back."

"We'll hold up our end, I'm sure," said the mayor. "She's a good girl. Everybody likes her. But I suppose we should keep what I told you a secret from Dwight, eh?"

"Do whatever you like," the Hunter replied.

As D headed for the door aloofly, the mayor called out to him in an exhausted tone, "This summer's almost over. At least, that's what it feels like. Don't you think so?"

D went outside without ever answering him.

III

That day, those who walked along the beach found their eyes riveted to the figure in black who stood by the shore. His longcoat called to mind the darkness of night as its hem billowed in the salty breeze. People's hearts raced at the beauty of him standing there with his back to them, framed by the white sand and the blue of the sea. And yet, they couldn't bring themselves to stop, but rather walked away as quickly as they could. But oddly enough, when they would turn again after having gone a little further, the figure dressed in the hue of darkness would be nowhere to be seen. Adults would rub their eyes as if they'd just wakened from a dream, while children would instantly decide that someday they'd grow up to look just as tough, sad, and beautiful so they could stare out at the sea.

The festival continued. The villagers remained as boisterous as ever, yet a strange resignation seemed to hang in the air. *Four more days to go*, the people said. Summer wouldn't end before then. But they had to wonder why the boats loaded with fireworks had headed out toward the ice floes. The fireworks had always been the crowning glory on the last night of summer.

Darkness fell. Another world was about to begin.

The faint buzz of an engine could be heard offshore. D's face turned. Just how long had he been staring out at that one spot in the sea?

The moon shone high in the sky again this evening. By its light, D could distinctly see Samon and Su-In in the small boat that was approaching. Forty or fifty feet from shore, the boat pulled parallel to the land and the growl of the engine died out.

Leaning out of the steering room back by the stern, Samon cupped one hand by her mouth and shouted, "Glad you could make it, Hunter. Su-In's right here. As promised, she's come to no harm."

Mixing with the sound of the waves, her voice rolled high and low by turns. Back on the rocking vessel, Samon quickly moved over to Su-In's location at the stern and brought her right hand to the woman's neck.

"However," the sorceress continued, "that promise was made to you by a man called Glen. And it was to last until the woman had been returned to you. I'm giving her back, here and now. Therefore, said promise is now null and void."

There was a metallic glint in Samon's right hand, and as soon as it became visible, fresh blood spouted from Su-In's neck. Even then, the woman still didn't notice. Her stuporous expression was as blank as that of a doll.

"Here, I'm giving her back to you. Come and get her, my two foes!" said Samon. "If you die, Hunter, Glen can rest in peace. And if the Noble is destroyed, this woman will never be herself again. I want you all to feel pain," she laughed. "If my man's no longer in this world, I'd just as soon destroy it all!"

And then, giving off a booming laugh that drowned out even the roar of the ocean, Samon pulled Su-In upright and hurled her headlong into the sea.

It was a heartbeat later that flashes of white light became needles that pierced the sorceress through the chest and the base of the neck. Knocked across the boat by the impact, Samon's body slammed against the opposite gunwale, bent backward, and followed right after Su-In in a spray of bloody droplets.

D had already thrown himself into the sea. Knifing through the water in a way that was unbelievable for a dhampir, he then pressed his hand against the neck of the bobbing Su-In. The sea around her looked flooded with black paint. When the Hunter pressed his left hand to the wound, the blood ceased to pour from her.

D was just about to swim back to shore with her, but at that instant he twisted his torso and looked directly off to his right. A head had bobbed to the surface about ten feet away. And it wore the Noble's face. Or rather, it wore a fearsome face where the young warrior Su-In had killed was intermingled with the psyche of Baron Meinster.

Slowly, D began moving toward shore. The Noble was following along right behind him at exactly the same speed.

A wave swept over the Hunter's shoulder, and then tugged at his waist. The two of them stopped right where they were. Su-In's weight was being supported by her buoyancy in the water, and if D went any further, there was a danger of her being choked by the hand he had pressed against her throat. On the other hand, if he took his hand away, Su-In would surely bleed to death. He couldn't possibly have been in a worse position. Particularly against a Noble who'd lived on the sea floor, and who'd be faster and stronger than D here.

"I'll take the girl," said the Noble in a voice that seemed to bubble up from the very bottom of the sea. It wasn't the voice of Meinster, nor was it that of the warrior.

"Do you remember her? Do you know this girl?" D asked softly. His words came in time with the sound of the waves.

"I don't know," said the Noble, shaking his head. "I just don't know. Who is she? Why do I come back here every summer looking for her?"

"You don't need to know," D said in a tone every bit as callous as the moonlight. "Simply accept your fate."

A split second later, three silvery flashes knifed through the top of the approaching waves. In an impossible spray of sparks, the wooden needles were struck down right before the Noble. It almost seemed as if that made a beautiful sound, too.

D saw that the Noble gripped a steel short spear in his right hand. When used properly, it could stretch yards longer and totally dominate the space between two combatants. But the weapon suddenly vanished, and the surface of the water churned. The sea eddied like a whirlpool because the spear had been spun at a ferocious speed beneath the surface.

Still holding onto Su-In, D leapt into the air and brought his blade down in the center of the vortex. The next spray that went up was from D and Su-In landing again. Only the sound of the waves circled around D. Focusing every nerve, he looked out at the expanse of waves where black and silver danced together.

The waves said, "Is that the fastest and the furthest you can leap? You'll never reach me here."

As D twisted to face that direction, a pair of pale serpents whined toward his torso. Silvery light flashed out to slice one of them apart, while the other pierced the left side of the Hunter's chest clean through to his back, where it became a bloody jet of water that dropped back into the sea.

"Water spears," said a voice that came from the same direction as the serpents. The water rose with those words, and was then instantly replaced by the Noble. "While you are a man to be feared, I have the edge on you in the water," he said. "And though I don't know why, I'll take the girl."

Once more, the sea churned in front of the Noble. The water then surged forward. Twisting like pale serpents, three blasts of water the Noble had rendered hard as steel ripped through the waves. D cut down one of the three, but the others were true to their aim and pierced his abdomen. Tough as D was, he couldn't take much more of that punishment.

Never letting go of Su-In, the figure in black sank into the water up to his chest. Something inky drifted out around him like a cloud. Yet D gazed straight ahead—his foe was fifteen feet away. If he were to make a leap carrying Su-In, certain death would await him.

"Farewell, Hunter. There will not be another summer," the Noble said, throwing back his right shoulder.

As the moonlight poured down on D and the sea roared around him, the black hands of Death prepared to close in on the Hunter.

But it was at that very instant that another voice was heard.

"Don't, my darling!"

The question was, did D realize that the cry came from Su-In, who only regained consciousness for a brief instant?

Like a gorgeous mystic bird, D sailed through the air. Su-In wasn't with him.

The fifteen feet separating the men ceased to have any meaning, and as the tip of the Noble's spear stretched up into the air, it was knocked aside all too quickly. With the force of D's full weight added to his unholy skill, the silvery blade came straight down on the Noble's head and split it in half. But it didn't end with his head—he was effortlessly sliced in two right down to the crotch. The naked blade glittered again, taking off the Noble's head and penetrating his heart before the figure in the blue cape slowly fell over like some colossal tree split by lightning, then sank into the sea.

Watching as the deep blue shape was carried out to sea by the waves, D then went back over to Su-In. Her eyes were closed. As for the wound on her neck—it was covered by a lump of semitransparent slime, and it didn't appear to be losing blood. At the last second, D's left hand had spit up some of Twin's mucus.

"Carry her back while she's still asleep," the voice from his left hand said in a consoling tone. "You think he heard what she said?"

D didn't answer. But apparently his left hand had heard it, too. The second D's blade caught him, the Noble had said, "Su-In." And he'd worn a youthful and sad face they hadn't seen before. Yet he'd left with the waves. The Noble was dead, and D had kept his promise.

"The vision we saw in the tunnel—I think maybe it was called up by a combination of memories of a girl he didn't know anymore and a reaction to the Noble blood that flows in your veins," said the left hand. "He didn't forget her completely. In the end, it looks like he was human after all. So, which are you, then?"

The Hunter's five fingers curled.

Just then, the night sky lit up. The heavens shone like melted black crystal, but gigantic blossoms then opened, with the roar of their explosions only coming later.

D glanced down at the ground by his feet. There was one heavy shadow, and a lighter shadow carrying it on its back.

The fireworks boomed again. Between those thunderclaps, there was a sad, cold sound. The racing wind.

"Has their weather controller finally given up the ghost?" the voice said listlessly. "Looks like that's the end of summer for this year. And I don't know whether they'll be having another one or not."

No one answered.

The night sky was still being lit up. In the distance, the music played on eternally. Summer hadn't ended yet.

Her gaze focused on nothing in particular, Su-In watched the bits of white fly by on the other side of the glass. The snow that'd started falling that morning was growing heavier and heavier—it would probably only take a few hours more for the entire village to be blanketed in the same silvery white.

Three days had passed since their shorter than usual summer had ended. The performers had already gone. Power boats were zipping to and fro out on the sea. As the villagers busily set to their winter preparations, their shoes trampled the wilted and faded remains of the summer's flowers.

No one had changed at all. The village and its inhabitants had long existed by the blustery North Sea, with its snow and ice.

Bracing both arms against the lectern, Su-In looked out at the classroom where not even a single child sat. With a bandage still wrapped around her neck, she was a pitiful sight. She seemed devoid of any deeper emotion. Even when she looked at the face of Dwight, who stood over by the windows to the right, all her blanched consciousness could do was dig his name out of her memory.

Su-In's future was now blocked by her past.

I killed a man who meant something to me, she thought. *A man I loved for a summer.*

The shock had been so great Su-In had even forgotten how to cry, and the woman felt like there was a big gray opening where her heart should've been.

What am I even doing here? No one's gonna come. Everyone knows I'm a murderer. There's nothing left for me now.

The haggard look on the face of the dazed woman only served to make shadows of anger and anxiety flicker by turns in Dwight's heart. *Who the hell was responsible for this? Who said I should bring Su-In here?* he asked himself. *She's been thrown back into her miserable past all alone, and this is only hurting her more. What a lousy thing to do. I'm gonna find him and beat the hell out of him!*

"Su-In," he said despite himself. "Su-In, let's go already. No matter how long we stay here—"

A crisp, clear sound made Dwight stop.

There it was again. A sound that a traveler lost on a winter's night could hear six miles away; it could make him get back up with hope in his eyes and spring in his legs again. The school bell.

Glancing up at the ceiling, Su-In then looked at the fisherman as if seeking his aid. Dwight backed away. In all his life, he'd never been more sure of what he should do. Going back over to his previous spot at the window, he said in a soft but powerful tone, "Over there."

Su-In stared straight ahead. Dwight looked, too. At the door.

At some point, the bell had stopped tolling.

Neither the man nor the woman moved.

Little footsteps. And they were drawing closer.

The door opened quietly. A tiny face peered in. Eyes that were big and round glittered with anxiety and expectation. But finding Su-In there, one of those emotions faded from them.

It was the same boy who'd asked D for the flute. Snow was piled on top of his hood, and in his hands he held a little package. Moving up between the rows of desks with a bashful smile, he took a seat at the very front of the class. After all, school was about to begin. And this was obviously a seat of honor.

The boy put the package down on his desk and opened it. Wrapped in the rough fabric were a textbook, a notebook, and a few writing implements. His father had told him he wasn't to go anywhere near Su-In. But why would he say that? After all, school was starting today. Wasn't the tolling of the bell proof enough of that?

More footsteps became audible. This time there were many of them. The door creaked open, and a number of faces appeared. Hope and relief spreading through their eyes, they faced a future that was small but also incredibly vast at the same time.

The boy at the head of the class turned around and puffed his chest with pride. *Look at me*, he seemed to say. *I was the first one here!*

Su-In shut her eyes tightly. And though she was sure she had them closed, something hot began to seep from them. Wiping it away with her hand, she turned to Dwight and nodded.

Just watch me.

Taking a deep breath, Su-In turned to the rosy faces crowding the doorway and said in a gentle and dignified tone, "Please come in. The lesson's about to begin."

Quietly slipping out of the classroom a few minutes later and proceeding to the bell tower, Dwight furrowed his brow when he saw the face of the person who stood beneath the bell rope.

"Pleasure to meet you," the man said with an affable expression before bowing. "Toto is the name. I met a Ms. Wu-Lin in the town of Cronenberg. She asked me to come help with the classes at your school. Naturally, I have experience as a teacher, as well as working in a number of other fields. Ah, yes—here's my letter of introduction."

Re-folding a letter that certainly looked like Wu-Lin's handwriting and returning it to the man, Dwight clapped him on the shoulder. "Great!" he exclaimed. "You're just what we needed. But are you sure I haven't seen you somewhere before?"

"Don't be ridiculous," the scowling Toto said as he shook his head. "It's this way."

As they walked side by side down the hall, Toto suddenly stopped in his tracks and looked out the window.

"What is it?" asked Dwight.

"It's nothing. I just heard a horse whinny."

"A horse?"

"Yeah. Probably belongs to the same young fellow who told me to ring the bell."

Dwight followed Toto's gaze, but there was no one moving out in the world of white.

"What'd this young fellow look like?" asked the fisherman.

"He was all dressed in black, and so good-looking it'd give a corpse the chills. I was hanging around out by the gate wondering how to go about getting someone's attention when I happened to run into him. Oh, that's right—as he was leaving, he took a peek in through that window there. A little while after the children went in, he left without a word. Wearing a smile."

"A smile?"

"Yes, I do believe that's what it was," Toto replied with confidence. "I don't suppose I'll ever see a smile that fine again. I have to wonder who put it on his face. I envy them, you know. You could take pride in that for the rest of your days."

Dwight was silent for a bit, and then he said, "You don't say? So he ended leaving after all, just like I figured. All alone."

"Absolutely."

Catching in that brief reply an even deeper sentiment than his own, Dwight stared at the new instructor for a moment. But he quickly dismissed those thoughts and said, "On the other side of that door is the classroom. You head on in. I suddenly remembered something I need to take care of. I've gotta go thank someone," he said.

Just a few minutes shy of hitting the Nobles' road, D halted his horse on the crest of a hill.

Beyond the veil of lightly falling snow stood a figure in blue mixed with red. Still some fifteen feet away, it was Samon. Though D's wooden needle had pierced her through a vital point, something had kept this woman alive. But her face had already taken the color of a corpse, and the bloody blossom that'd flowered on her chest was mysteriously damp. For three days, the woman had survived while the blood continued to seep from her body.

"We meet again at last," she said in a ghostly tone as D got off his horse. "Only you and the girl remain now," said Samon, her whole body trembling. "You'll get yours first. Then I'll head back into the village and dispose of the girl. You should thank me. It's only right that you be with the one you love when you die. Show yourself!"

As she said that, something white that wasn't snow began to crystallize before D's eyes. This was the spell of "Samon of Remembrances"—nostalgia. If a person's lost love requested his or her death, that person would have no choice but to comply while under the seductress' spell.

But who would D summon?

Black hair swayed modestly. Gently turning her long, narrow eyes to the ground, a matronly woman in a white dress stood before D. Samon's lips moved. As did those of the woman.

But how did the seductress' voice sound to D?

"Die, D."

Samon raised her right hand to her own throat. In it, she held a dagger.

To D, it should've appeared that the mature woman was indeed performing the action.

The Hunter's hand drew the sword from his back.

"Die. Just like that," she said. Taking care not to let the blade touch her throat, Samon made a powerful jerk from one side to the other.

D's sword moved as well. Vertically.

Slicing the image of the graceful matron in half, the blade then spun around and stabbed deep into the heart of the sorceress Samon.

"Impossible!" the staggering Samon moaned in amazement. "I can't believe you'd do that . . . to your own . . ."

No bloody spray shot from the last of the warriors as she fell to the ground.

D's exquisite skill somehow kept his blade clean of even a single drop of blood, and he'd returned the weapon to its sheath and was walking toward his horse when an unknown voice said, "She died with a peaceful look on her face. But only humans have remembrances," it added. "Still, the way you cut that vision down without a second thought—boy, you sure are all business!"

D got back on his horse as if nothing had happened.

"You're leaving their village covered with blood right to the very end, without anyone to even see you off. Hell, sometimes you even give me chills. Where are you headed next?" the left hand asked.

Of course, there was no reply.

After the Hunter's mount had taken a few steps, a crisp sound came to D from the village.

"That's the school bell, isn't it?" the voice said.

D turned around.

The snow had stopped. A faint light shone on the village below him—winter sunlight slipping through a gap in the clouds.

Once more the bell sounded, as if bidding him farewell.

D faced forward again. Ash-gray clouds hung heavily over the road he'd be taking next. His cold gaze trained ever forward and his incredibly placid face devoid of all sadness and fear, the young man in black suddenly vanished over the top of a hill like some gorgeous mirage.

Postscript

I n the last volume, I wrote that I'm not a big fan of anime, and the first thing I don't like about it is the art. Now, this kind of like or dislike is a sensory problem, and there's not much that can be done about it. But when I think about having a character I created drawn in a style I don't care for, my anger starts to rise even before the chills can set in. Fortunately, I was quite pleased with the way the second D turned out.

Another problem I have is the voices. I believe my dislike of anime can be attributed to the endless volleys of shrill, squeaky voices I endured during the countless kid-oriented anime programs I saw on TV as a child. As you are probably well aware, the voice duties for all anime heroes seem to be handled by women. In other words, the better part of kid-oriented anime is packed with thin, girlish voices, and for someone like myself—who can't handle anything but the sweetest female whisper—that whole world has left me exasperated since childhood.

What's more, the way anime characters deliver their lines, they sound so pretentious. I mean, I realize it's intended for children and everything, but it's simply too much. I always ended up wondering if what I was watching was supposed to be some kind of opera. And the stories are naturally geared toward children—or as we say in Japan, "so simple they could only fool a child." Why a program intended for children would want to fool them is something

I could never understand—and that must be why I can't stand them [*laughs*].

Now, think for a moment about the technology back then—this was about fifty years ago. Movies weren't too bad, but TV anime was positively wretched. And things only got worse once I became acquainted with American animation like Disney's Mickey Mouse, Woody Woodpecker, Hanna-Barbera's Huckleberry Hound, Felix the Cat, and others at the movie theater. While *Tetsuwan Atomu* (*Astro Boy*) was the product of the blood, sweat, and tears of the genius comics creator Osamu Tezuka, when you stripped away the nationalistic cries of "Japan's first serialized TV anime," the difference between it and the foreign product was like night and day.

Well, let's just leave it at that. The quality of our homegrown product has improved greatly in recent years. As I've stated before, I'm extremely satisfied with the two animated versions of D. The same director and staff who have expressed an interest in doing an animated version of *Demon Journey to the North Sea* also made the second D anime (which I particularly enjoyed), so that's practically a guarantee of high quality right there. The problem is, the president of the production company the director belongs to doesn't care too much for the project [*laughs*]. *Demon Journey to the North Sea* is a work that I'm quite fond of, and I have high hopes for an anime adaptation of it. And I'd be overjoyed if all the readers of the English edition would join us in our support of such a feature.

Hideyuki Kikuchi
February 19, 2007
While watching *Dracula A.D. 1972*

And now, a preview of the next novel in the
Vampire Hunter D series

VAMPIRE HUNTER D

VOLUME 9
THE ROSE PRINCESS

Written by
Hideyuki Kikuchi

Illustrations by
Yoshitaka Amano

English translation by
Kevin Leahy

Coming in November 2007
from Dark Horse Books and Digital Manga Publishing

Prologue

O nce the sweet perfume began to waft through the crystal clear darkness, the villagers hurried off the cobblestone streets and hid themselves in nearby homes.

The fragrance had always been part of the history of this village. On the evening of the village's centennial celebration, the night the new female teacher arrived from the Capital, the evening when a daughter was born to the mayor, a silent night when winter's white storms blustered—the fragrance that swept so sweetly over the road made the people avert their gaze from the castle on the outskirts of the village as the pain of eternal damnation left their eyes bloodshot.

Why did the wind have to blow through town?

People prayed in earnest for the aroma to be gone and waited expectantly for the dawn. However, the sun that rose would eventually have to set again, and night would cover the world like the wings of a crow. And every time the perfume returned, the people's suffering carved deep wrinkles in their faces, and the community's only watering hole set new sales records.

The shades were drawn on every window, leaving only the streetlights to dimly illuminate the road where the fragrance alone still lingered. The aroma of flowers.

As befitted an evening of this warmth-filled season, the wind seemed to request the poetry of the night.

A castle gate studded with hobnails rumbled like thunder in a sea of clouds as it closed, but before it had even started to move, the black-lacquered carriage went racing through the arched gate to the central courtyard. The wheels creaked to a halt, and the door opened.

Inside the carriage sat a girl who was scared to death. Although her ample breasts betrayed the wild racing of her heart, her plump face had all the color of a corpse. Even when the sweet aroma and dazzling colors crushed in through the open door, the girl didn't move a muscle.

How old am I again? the girl thought. *Seventeen years and one month. Is this the end? Can't I live a little longer? And just three days ago, I was talking with my friends about going to the trade school in town. Who decided this has to happen? Who chose me?*

"Get out," said a voice like steel from beyond the door. It must've been one of those that'd been sent to get her.

At the urging of a will that would brook no resistance and an eerie aura, the girl headed toward the door. The carriage steps had already been extended. As her nostrils filled with the fragrance and her eyes were met by a brilliant wash of colors, the girl suddenly felt as if she'd been swallowed by an abyss.

"Go straight that way," a voice told her, the speaker apparently pointing directly ahead of her.

As the girl tottered forward, her mind was already half blank. She just kept walking. Although she felt something prick at her cheeks and her exposed arms, it didn't bother her. When the girl finally halted, her breathing was terribly ragged. And not merely because of the distance she'd walked.

Her almost nonexistent consciousness had detected a faint figure standing directly ahead of her. It approached her like a beautiful mirage. The sight of the woman in a dress left the girl frozen with fear—but much to her own surprise, the girl also felt a vague fascination. She knew what was going to happen. When she saw that the dress was white and she hazily made out the woman's face, the girl then shut her eyes.

What would she do if the woman who'd come to suck her blood was some hideous Noble? She knew them from the masks she'd seen at village celebrations. They were monsters, mentally and physically warped.

The girl was seized by both shoulders. A chill spread through her like ice. That, and a sweet perfume. But before she could notice that the latter was actually the breath spilling from the woman, the girl lost consciousness completely.

Even as pale fangs punctured her tragically thin carotid artery she remained completely still.

As the girl's head fell back and she went limp, the woman gently laid her body down on the stone road, then turned around. When she'd taken a few silent steps, there were suddenly footfalls behind her and she detected a presence thoroughly unsuited to this place.

"You goddamned monster!"

Perhaps two seconds passed from the time the woman turned until the powerful man pounced on her. Although the man weighed nearly twice as much as she did and had the momentum of his dash behind him, the woman wasn't knocked back at all. Instead, black iron went through the center of her chest and came out her back.

When the man let go of the blade, the woman finally fell back a step.

"I did it," the man—actually a kid of fifteen or sixteen—muttered like a death rattle. "I did it . . . I really did it! Nagi!"

Judging by the way he then raced over to the girl and hugged her close, his last cry must've been her name. His movements carrying both the despair of having lost a loved one and also the faintest hope, the young man shook the lifeless form.

"Get up, Nagi," he said. "I took care of the one who bit you. Now you'll be okay, right? You should be back to normal."

"Absolutely," said a voice that poured ice water down the young man's back.

He looked up. A figure in white stood quietly in the moonlight.

"However," the woman continued, "in order to destroy me, you must pierce my heart. And you were a bit wide of the mark."

The young man got goose bumps as he rose to his feet. The girl's lifeless husk was still clutched to his chest. Dead or not, he wasn't going to let her go. That was the resolve that seemed to radiate from every inch of him.

"Will you not run?" the woman asked. "If you don't, you shall end up exactly like that young lady. Although if you loved her, that may be for the best. Now—come to me," she said. "Or would you prefer that your young lady feed on you instead of me?"

Before the young man even had time to comprehend the full meaning of the woman's words, a pale arm had wrapped around his neck.

"Nagi?!"

There could be no more heartrending cry than his in the entire world.

Cradled against the young man's chest, the girl opened her eyelids.

The young man knew her eyes had always brimmed with hopes for the future. He'd seen them sparkle with the dreams of a seventeen-year-old. And he knew that it was not his face but rather that of another young man that her eyes often reflected.

But now her eyes reflected him. In shape and in color, they were no different than before. However, the normally sharp black pupils were clouded and dark, and where the memories of a seventeen-year-old had been there was now a despicable vortex of hunger and lust.

"I'm so hungry," the young man heard the girl say, though it seemed like her voice was something out of a nightmare. "You came to save me, didn't you? I'm so glad. Let me give you a kiss as thanks . . ."

"Stop, Nagi—don't do it!" he shouted. Pulling free of the arms she wrapped around him, the young man knocked her cold body to the road.

The girl didn't even cry out.

"My, but you are a cold-hearted paramour."

As if triggered by the woman's voice, the young man started to run. Though panic gripped him, at least part of his thought processes remained wide awake.

In one spot in the dazzling mix of colors the young man saw a glimmer of a different material. Leaping into the riot of color, he left the whole mass of flowers trembling.

It only took the young man about a minute to strap on what he found there. As he fastened the last belt around his left thigh, he heard footsteps closing on him from all four points of the compass. They didn't sound like those of the woman he'd just encountered—they had a foreboding tone to them. As the ground seemed to tremble beneath his feet, the young man felt his stomach tighten. The next thing he knew, he was shaking, too.

The second the wild mix of colored blossoms to his right was pushed aside, the young man kicked off the ground. A heartbeat before his airborne form was due to sink, wings opened on his back.

Just in time—and as relief swelled in the young man, he gazed into the darkness ahead of him. Nothing could've possibly felt better than to be gaining altitude like this.

He looked down. Far below him were scattered pinpricks of twinkling light.

In contrast to that, a heavy shadow fell across the young man's heart. He'd never be safe here now. But where could he go?

Impacts to either side of him were transmitted to the center of his back. His body dipped seriously. Clearly his wings had been slashed.

Craning his neck, he looked up above.

Although it was pitch black out, the crimson armor he saw there was branded into his retinas.

Don't tell me he can fly, too?!

Although the young man madly attempted to pull back on the lever he gripped, the wire that relayed the movements to his wings seemed to have been severed, and his descent didn't stop.

"Do you have any idea what you've done?" a voice called out from above him.

Was it following him down?

"Your life alone will not be enough to atone for the crime of raising your blade against our princess," the voice continued. "Look back from the hereafter and watch what results from your reckless actions!"

Suddenly, the young man felt the base of the wings tear free from his back. Without a peep, he plummeted straight down, dropping into an endless abyss.

Unable to lose consciousness as the wind howled in his ears, he found a dull band of silver growing in his field of view. It was a river that stretched like a ribbon far below him.

The Road of Stakes

1

The road was just wide enough to allow two farm vehicles—which were relatively rare in these parts—to pass each other. Going east, it led to the village of Sacri, while to the west it hit the dusty highway.

Verdant waves flowed to either side of the road. Prairies and wind.

As the high stalks of grass bowed in succession, they seemed to be passing something along. The name of the distant rulers of this world. Their lost legends. Or perhaps the tale of the current dictator whose manor stood on the outskirts of the village. And the situation in the trio of wagons racing madly out of town. And the reason the horse-lashing farmer and everyone in his family had fear burned into their tense faces.

"Halfway left to go!" cried the farmer working the reins on the lead wagon. "If we reach the highway, they won't give chase, since that's outside their domain. Hannah, what's it look like back there?"

"The Tumaks' and Jarays' wagons are both doing well," replied his wife, who'd leaned out from where she was riding shotgun. Drawing the little boy and girl she held closer with her plump arms, she added, "At this rate, we'll be fine, dear."

"It's too early to say. We've still got half to go—this is where we brave the fires of hell. I don't know if the horses will make it or not," he said, the words coming out like a groan.

But any further comment was cut short by a shriek from the farmer's wife.

Thirty feet ahead, a horse and rider so crimson they seemed to brand their image into the couple's retinas had just bounded onto the road from the high grass on the left.

The farmer didn't even manage to pull back on the reins.

In an attempt to avoid the horse and rider that seemed to be ablaze, the team of two steeds made a sudden turn to the right.

Packed with all the family's worldly possessions, the wagon couldn't follow the animals around that sharp curve. The wooden tongue that connected the wagon to the team twisted, and the body of the wagon tilted as it did. The tongue snapped in midair, and the vehicle threw up a cloud of dust as it rolled.

Without so much as a glance back at the rumbling of the ground and the tableware that was being thrown everywhere, the horses kept galloping toward the promised land of freedom.

The Tumak and Jaray families narrowly avoided crashing their own wagons. Desperately whipping the hindquarters of the halted animals and tugging on the reins, they tried to turn back the way they'd come. It didn't look like they would even try to help their friends who still lay on the road with their toppled wagon.

"It's the Blue Knight!" Jaray's son exclaimed, his cry of despair rising to the fair sky.

The road they needed to take home was now blocked by the blue horse and rider that stood about fifteen feet from them. However, the rider's hue was not that of the pristine heavens, but rather the dark blue shade of the depths that led to the unsettling floor of the sea—the blue of freezing cold water.

With the sun still high in the sky, an air of deathly silence and immobility was thrown over the three families there on the stark white road.

"Where do you think you're going?" said the one in front of them—the crimson rider on a horse of the same color. The people had called his compatriot a knight, and he, too, was sheathed in armor from the top of his head to the tips of his toes. His breastplate was wide, the pauldrons and vambraces were thick as a tree trunk, and he was so tall people would have to look up at him whether he was on horseback or not. If he were to ride out onto the battlefield on his similarly armored mount, he'd be such an imposing sight it seemed likely the very demons of hell would recoil in horror. On his back were two pairs of crossed longswords—four blades in all. Gleaming in the sunlight, the weapons looked so large and heavy they'd leave even a giant of a man exhausted after a single swing.

"I believe we made it quite clear that it's been decreed no one is to leave this domain," said the Blue Knight. He was such a deep, dark shade of blue, he seemed to drain the heat from the rays of the midday sun and make the light drift away in vain like soap bubbles. "Not a single soul will be allowed to flee from the village where that little bastard wounded our princess," he continued. "You should consider yourselves fortunate we didn't slaughter the whole community out of hand. But then, there's no need for any of you to concern yourselves with that business any longer. The stakes await you."

A thin sound like a note from a broken flute split the air and a short, fat old woman clutched at her chest as she fell—Mr. Jaray's elderly mother. The rest of the family consisted of Jaray and his wife, their nineteen-year-old son, a sixteen-year-old daughter, and another daughter aged twelve.

As for the Tumaks, there were six of them—the husband and wife, Mr. Tumak's mother and father, and a five-year-old son and three-year-old daughter.

No one seemed to be paying any attention to the old woman, who'd suffered a heart attack out of sheer fright. Their eyes were trained instead on death as it stood barring the way before them and behind them in the form of knights of flame and water.

Their fate was inescapable.

The two armored knights turned to the sides of the road. Toward the fifteen-foot stakes that were driven into either side of the road at roughly three-foot intervals. Oh, they ran on endlessly, too numerous to count, and on their sharpened tips shook the stark white bones of the impaled. Apparently the stakes were quite old, and perhaps less than one in ten still had skeletal remains hanging from it. And in most cases those were just the spine and rib cage, while the arms, legs, pelvis, and skulls lay sadly at the base of the stake as part of a fairly large mound of bones.

However, while the families stood there as if their lives had already been lost, the corpses staked to either side of them were almost completely intact, their rags dancing in the wind and the eye sockets in their skulls aimed at the road like soul-swallowing caverns in the land of the dead as they cast a spell of silence.

The two knights closed the gap.

"Help!" someone shouted.

A flash of crimson cut off the cry.

The grass swayed in waves. It seemed to speak of shock and destiny.

Mr. Tumak's aged father looked down at his chest. Blue steel ran right through him. Tumak's wife looked down at hers as well. The bloodstained tip of a weapon stretched from it. The weapon that'd impaled the two people as they stood back to back had to be more than eight inches long, but it wasn't the blade of a sword. It stretched more than three feet from the old man's chest before coming to a guard that was twice as big around as a man's fist. The hilt then sloped upward for another six feet before disappearing into a blue gauntlet, and it extended another three feet beyond the knight's little finger.

Though the gigantic warrior was over six and a half feet tall, how could he wield a fifteen-foot lance with such skill? Both the weapon's tip and its metallic hilt were etched with elaborate designs, and altogether it must've weighed at least two hundred pounds, and probably more than four hundred.

The weapon bent supplely. The blue lance flexed upward, and the two victims were launched into the air like they were on springs and came right down on the stakes as if they'd been aimed. The old bones turned to powder and flew in all directions as new victims were run through the heart.

"Although our princess instructed us to wait before meting out any additional punishments, we, the Four Knights of the Diane Rose, cannot allow this to pass. We were just beginning to get frustrated when you were good enough to try and escape. Although this is only for fun, you should provide a slight diversion."

As if driven by the Blue Knight's words, the people started to run. But the Red Knight was in front of them. A crimson wind gusted between the fleeing people. Still, they ran right by the sides of the Red Knight. Even though their heads had fallen off five or ten feet back, they didn't stop running. Another gust of even redder wind shot up from the ground to the sky, blocking the people and knights from the rest of the road.

"Ungrateful insects. This is the price you pay for your foolish actions."

Before the knights bellowing with laughter, Jaray's wife and Tumak's son had fallen to the blood-soaked road. The pair hugged each other tightly.

"So, which of you shall I—" the Red Knight was saying when there was suddenly the shrill sound of engines approaching from the village at a frantic pace.

More than a few.

"Looks like we have company," the Blue Knight said, gleefully rolling his head from side to side.

Less than two seconds later, gasoline-powered motorcycles with high horsepower engines arrived at the scene of the cruel butchery.

While their engines remained running, a white-haired figure hopped off the back rack of the lead bike. He was an old man with a cane.

"Mayor Torsk is my name and . . ."

The reason his voice died as he was making his introduction was because he'd just seen the grotesque piles of corpses that littered the road.

The riders of the roughly ten motorbikes were speechless as well.

"What the hell is this?!" said the rider of the bike that'd carried the mayor, spitting the words one by one.

Although he was more than fifteen feet away, the Blue Knight must've had unnaturally keen ears, because he then looked at the rider and muttered, "A woman?"

"So what if I am?!"

Stripping off an apparently homemade cloth helmet along with her goggles, the rider revealed the face of a beautiful young woman with a slight pinkish flush. Her hair was cut shockingly short, and her eyes were ablaze with anger.

"What the hell . . . ," she groaned once more, the words sounding crushed and lifeless as she turned the nose of her bike toward the Blue Knight.

Two steel pipes pointed forward from either side of the vehicle—four in total. If the pressurized gas in the tank to the rear were to launch the steel arrows within, they were certain to fly straight and true into the heart of the knight.

"Ah, more prey to amuse us? And this one looks to have a little fight in her," the Blue Knight replied, his mere words freezing the atmosphere again.

"Knock it off, Elena," the mayor of the village said, breaking the silence. Turning to the two butchers, he said, "I'll make no complaint about those already dead. But could you at least be so kind as to show mercy on the last two?" he pleaded in a hoarse voice as the wind stroked his profile.

The grass was singing,

Stop, I say, stop,

For they will never spare you.

"These people disobeyed an order from our princess," said the Blue Knight. "Until the one who attempted to take her life is captured, no one whatsoever is to leave the village. Nor is anyone to enter. Anyone attempting to leave without her permission will be considered to be in league with the culprit and be promptly executed. And it is our duty to see to it her word is upheld."

"The only reason they tried to leave was because you enjoy killing everyone just for the fun of it!" Elena shouted. "That hag of yours ordered more than just that. If the guilty party hasn't been caught within ten days of her decree, ten villagers are to be impaled on stakes. And every day after that, five more are to be drawn and quartered. It's only natural for some people to try and get away!"

"Only natural?"

The two knights looked at each other and laughed.

"And we could say to you and your whole village that what *we* do is only natural. Take a good look around you at this verdant land and its bountiful fields of grain—just who do you think made all this possible? Lowly humans scratching away at the untamed wilderness with rusty hoes like stupid beasts? Do you recall what it was you said to the princess back then?"

Elena gnawed her lip. Agitation swept like a wave through the group behind her—and judging from the way they were all dressed alike, she was undoubtedly part of the same group. However, Elena quickly looked up at the knight and shouted, "That was a long time ago!"

"What?" the Blue Knight growled, his lance rattling slightly in his right hand.

"Now, hold on a minute," the Red Knight interjected. "There's no point arguing all that here and now. We've disposed of those who disregarded the rules. Take those other two back with you."

Joy suffusing his countenance, the mayor stammered, "May I— may I really?"

"You may. Be quick about it."

"Very well—Come along now, you two," Torsk said, extending his arms toward the exhausted woman and child.

But neither of them said a word, and foam spilled from their lips. It wasn't the world around them that filled their eyes, but rather death itself.

"Oh, this isn't going to work. Come now, let's be quick about this," the mayor seemed to tell himself with new resolve as he advanced across the bloody road.

One more step and the two of them would be within reach—but at that instant, the wind snarled.

Even before the geysers of blood went up chasing the two heads that flew into the air, the grass was already singing,

Stop it, just stop it,
For they shall never spare you.

Just as the Red Knight's blade returned to its sheath in a gust of bloody wind, the Blue Knight's lance danced out.

The fluid of life gushing so vainly from the stumps became a thousand droplets in the wind, forming a crimson curtain that slapped against the people's faces.

From behind it, the Red Knight called out, "The rules are the rules, and we make no exceptions. And now to deal with the little monkey bitch who called our princess a hag."

Although Elena tried to aim her gas-powered launcher purely out of reflex, the dark red stain across her field of view wouldn't allow her to do so. She had to wonder which would come for her instead, the steely blade or the bloody lance? The face of the girl was stained with the hues of blood and death.

Just then, the vermilion curtain was torn in two, as if to announce the beginning of a new tale.

Even the deadly knights and their mounts averted their gaze and backed away from the wind that gusted down the road.

But the bizarre phenomenon ended quickly.

And everyone who looked up then saw it—an inky black horse and rider advancing eerily through the corpses and the stakes. For some reason, it would've seemed a terribly appropriate image in anyone's eyes.

The teeth of skulls still impaled on the stakes chattered in the wind. The green grass bowed, and the sun—ever generous with its light—ducked behind a cloud at that very moment.

Everyone had forgotten all else as they gazed intently at the new arrival.

About ten feet from the Red Knight the rider came to a halt. The face below the traveler's hat was not of this world. Unearthly in its beauty.

Even the wind died out. Probably because it, too, was awestruck.

"Clear the way," said the traveler.

"And just who are you?" asked the Red Knight. "This is our mistress' domain. No one may enter. Leave at once."

However, didn't the knights currently have orders to kill any intruders on the spot? What did these merciless killers sense in the young man before them?

"The village of Sacri lies ahead, doesn't it? I have business there," the young man said, not seeming the least bit hesitant. His long hair fluttered in the breeze.

"Oh, so you want to die, do you?" the Blue Knight said to him. "What's the matter, Red Knight?" he then asked his comrade. "Have this man's good looks got the better of you? If that's the case, I'll handle this."

Needless to say, he was joking. The Blue Knight knew better than anyone the skill of his crimson compatriot, as well as his cruelty and his valor.

And that was why it was only natural he was dumbstruck when the Red Knight told him, "You're welcome to try."

"What?" the Blue Knight asked in return, but that was only after the space of two breaths had passed.

"I leave him to you. Give it a try."

The reply had certainly come from the Red Knight. And the crimson rider had even fallen back to the edge of the road.

The mayor, Elena, and the bikers all just stared, dumbstruck. One of the Four Knights of the Diane Rose was backing down— was this some sort of waking nightmare?

As if nothing at all had happened, the young man gave a kick to his mount's flanks. He advanced without a glance at the headless corpses still locked in an embrace or the mayor that stood beside them—but the Blue Knight was waiting up ahead.

II

As they watched the distance dwindle between the two figures, the mayor and the others wore strangely calm expressions. Finally, normalcy had returned to the world. Finally, the Blue Knight would fight. That was what they honestly believed. That's how unnatural it had been for the Red Knight to let the young man in black pass.

The Blue Knight adjusted his grip on his lance.

There was fifteen feet between them.

The green grass twisted plaintively, singing a song.

Halt, I say, halt,
Or one of you shall die!

Ten feet.

The Blue Knight's horse whinnied loudly, as if trying to repress its urge to bolt.

There were dark clouds in the sky.

Five feet—now.

The Red Knight suddenly looked over his shoulder—out at the grassy plains. "Hold," he cried. "His honor the Black Knight is on the way."

Another figure on horseback was galloping toward them from the farthest reaches of the emerald expanse. As his name implied, the knight on the horse's back was encased in black armor. Even if the Red Knight hadn't referred to him as "his honor," the sight of him streaking through the sea of grass with thundering hoofbeats and bounding onto the road certainly would've had all the impact of an iron spike of immeasurable weight.

The young man had halted his horse, too.

Tilting his onyx helm to survey the carnage, the knight spat, "How callous. Are you idiots responsible for this?" His voice was also as heavy as iron.

"I resent that remark, sir," the Blue Knight declared.

"Silence!" the Black Knight roared like the crashing of the distant sea, and with that single word the other two fell silent. "I have no objection to you killing those who flee," he went on to say. "Such is in keeping with the wishes of our princess. But you've gone and taken the lives of even the youngest of children. We are not soulless demons! Mr. Mayor, our princess is sure to make reparations for the children at a later date. See to it that no one else discards their life in such a manner again."

The old man bowed his head without saying a word.

Then the sound of hoofbeats reached the ears of all present. Incredibly enough, the young man in black had continued riding on. Bold, perhaps even impudent, the move was so far from expected norms, the Blue Knight and Red Knight could only watch mutely as he went.

"Wait," the Black Knight called out.

But the traveler in black just kept going.

Perhaps expecting as much, the knight in the jet-black armor didn't have a mote of wrath in his voice as he said, "I would have your name."

"D."

At that point, a single ray of sunlight poked through the clouds to illuminate the young man's face. His fairly bloodless complexion was given a rosy hue—that was how beautiful he seemed.

Gasps arose from those on the road, and a murmur rumbled through them like the tide. Elena was the first to make a sound, with her compatriots following suit after.

"I'll remember that name," the Black Knight called out.

The young man who'd given his name as D rode off calmly. As if he hadn't been witness to this tragedy in broad daylight.

At some point, the knights had disappeared, too.

"We'll bring the bodies back," said Torsk. "Give me a hand with them."

Seemingly oblivious to the way the other bikers scrambled forward at the mayor's request, Elena alone kept a dumbfounded gaze turned toward town—the direction the gorgeous young man had gone. "You see that?" she asked.

Another biker who was about to walk by her stopped in his tracks and replied, "See what?"

"They didn't make a move against that guy," Elena said as if she were still dreaming. Perhaps she was. "Three of the Diane Rose knights—and they were practically cowering, and couldn't even draw on him. He might be the guy to do it. He could save us all," the girl muttered, her tightly clenched fist making her resolve abundantly clear.

Beside her, the grass whispered,

What's that you say?

The young man's visit couldn't help but cause a great sensation in the tiny village. People stopped in their tracks and stared as D rode down the street. Dazed, they continued to stare off in the same direction for a long time after he'd gone. And every single person with a scarf around their neck pressed down on it with terrible embarrassment, then hung their head.

"I wonder which inn he'll be staying at?" women muttered, irrespective of age.

"Did you see that sword, or the look in his eye? There's nothing ordinary about him," the men said to each other.

Contrary to the women's expectations, D didn't end up registering at any of the village inns. Halting in front of a house on the outskirts of town, he got off his horse and rapped on the door with a knocker fashioned from animal bones. The sign next to the door had the words *Mama Kipsch—Witch Doctor* burnt into it.

After a moment, an elderly woman's voice from behind the door asked, "Who is it?"

"A traveler," D replied. "Are you Mama Kipsch?"

"Just ask anyone."

"I have a message from your grandson."

In the middle of her heavily wrinkled face, her eyes opened as wide as they'd go. Then she said, "That good-for-nothing brat—I don't see how he could do this. Where is he at, anyway?"

"He passed away."

"What?!" the old woman exclaimed, her body growing stiff as a mannequin. Her blue eyes said the young man before her was some beautiful grim reaper. "Now wait just one second," she stammered. "What do you mean by that? Tell me more."

"He was hung up on the riverbank about six miles south of your village. He told me his name as well as your own and where you lived, then asked me to tell you, 'Take care,' before he passed away. And now I've done that."

"Yup," the old woman said with a nod, and by the time she'd returned to her senses, the man in the black coat was back on his horse.

"Wait just one minute. Hey!" she wheezed as she raced out the front door and grabbed hold of one of his saddlebags. "Aren't you the inhospitable one. My, but you are a looker, though." Feeling the pulse in her right hand, she added, "Look, you've gone and got me up over a hundred fifty beats per minute. I've gone through two artificial hearts already, you know. Putting in a third would probably be the death of me. If I die, it'll all be your fault," she told the traveler. "I'll haunt you till the end of your days!"

"I'm used to it."

At D's reply, Mama Kipsch looked up at him as if just coming back to reality. It seemed that while she'd been gazing at him so intently, she'd even forgotten how short of breath she was. Nodding, she said, "Is that a fact? I suppose you would be, at that. You've got an unbelievable aura. I didn't think I should've been that winded after running just a tad. But now I see you scare the hell out of me. How many people have you killed with that sword, anyway?"

"If you have no business with me, I'll be going."

"I said wait, blast it! If you're always that cold to folks, you won't meet a pretty end." Mama Kipsch then added, "Though I suppose even if you aren't cold, you still won't have a peaceful death. Wait, already! Whatever became of my grandson's remains?"

"I let them float down the river," D replied. "Those were his instructions."

"That's a lie," the old woman said, stomping her foot angrily. "Who in the world would ask someone to chuck their body in a river? For starters, if it was only six miles from here, that wouldn't have been very far to bring him back. I think you're trying to hide something."

"He said he didn't want you to see the body. By the look of it, he'd hit quite a few rocks on his way down the river. Do you want to hear all the gory details?"

"No, spare me."

"I'll be on the edge of town," D told her. "Come find me if there's anything else you want to know."

As the horse began to move, Mama Kipsch let go of it.

Once the rider had gone so far he wouldn't have seen her if he'd turned and looked, a hoarse voice said, "That's one hell of an old girl!" The amused tone issued from D's left hand, which was wrapped around the reins. "Of course, if she wasn't such a tough old bird, there's no way her grandson would've been able to do what he did, either." Chuckling, it added, "Floated him down the river, did you?"

The voice was then choked out in an anguished cry.

Although D had clenched his left hand tightly, not the least bit of that strength was conveyed to the reins.

Heading straight for the edge of the village, D arrived at some mysterious ruins after twisting and turning down several narrow paths.

Rising from the center of a clearing covered by a wild green carpet of grass, the walls of stone and metal looked like they'd been melted by extreme heat in places or had crumbled in others.

Although the structures no longer retained their original shapes, a concerted gaze would reveal the remains of stonework foundations, paved corridors, and the partitions that had delineated each individual room. Amid grass and white flowers that swayed in the breeze, the remains were more than six hundred feet in diameter, spreading in a way that perfectly illustrated the vain nature of mortal existence and the callousness of the winds of time.

Passing through what little remained of the bronze gates and stone pillars, D entered the ruins. The wind snarled above him. Perhaps due to the legacy of some ancient architectural technique, when the wind blew through the gate it took on a strangely morose whistle before it blustered against the traveler in black.

Tethering his cyborg horse to a wooden pole that looked to have been part of a fence and taking the saddle and bags from it, D gazed off to the west.

Green hills rolled on and on like something out of a picture. At the summit of the one farthest back there towered a solemn castle. This region could almost be considered mountainous, and while the Nobility's manors in such places had mostly doubled as fortresses, this was an exception. It had been constructed with a grace and refinement befitting the character of those who lived by night. Surely it had to be the castle of the princess the murderous knights had mentioned.

However, D returned his eyes to the ruins without any particular emotion, then began to walk around the barely extant roof and ramparts with a measured gait that made it seem like he was performing some sort of inspection. When he'd gone halfway around the perimeter, the ostentatious roar of engines could be heard growing closer from the same path that had brought him there.

Elena and her friends had stopped their motorcycles out in front of the ruins. The air carried the heavy scent of gasoline. Just as the bikers were about to enter the ruins, they froze in place as if they'd just taken a jolt of electricity, and then backed away as D appeared.

Even the sirens who lured captains to their doom with their lovely countenances and sweet songs would've undoubtedly fallen victim to his beauty in exactly the same way with just one glance. But far surpassing his good looks was the ghastly aura that knifed into the flesh of all who beheld him—something that gave Elena the feeling they were dealing with a fiend even more powerful than the four knights.

"I've come out here because I've got something talk over with you," the girl finally managed to say. The words seemed to catch in her throat, and her voice was terribly hoarse.

"What kind of talk would that be?"

As the young man spoke, his unearthly aura seemed to wane, and Elena let out an easy breath. A slight spell of dizziness came over her, but she was able to stand her ground. Her friends were watching. She couldn't make a fool of herself.

Coughing once, she said, "You impressed the hell out of us. So we were thinking we'd let you hook up with our outfit."

Seeing D turn his back on them, the members of the group looked at each other. There was neither turmoil nor anger on their faces. All of them had seen with their own eyes the true power of the traveler in black.

A young man straddling a bike a bit larger than the rest rose from the seat. In keeping with the size of his vehicle, he was about six and a half feet tall. "I told you he wouldn't go for it, Elena," he said. "Seriously, why would he ever join us? Any way you look at it, he's a lot tougher than we are. All we can do is try and get on his *good* side."

"I'm not about to bow and scrape to some drifter I don't know from a hole in the ground!" the girl exclaimed, vermilion rising in her cheeks. Pressing her lips into a hard, straight line, she continued, "Everyone, head on over to Grau's bar. I'm gonna stay here and hash this out."

"Hey now," the giant shot back.

"Just who's the leader here, Stahl?"

"You are. And I don't think anyone here questions that. It's just, this time—"

"This time I'm in over my head, so you thought you'd shoot your mouth off? So, I suppose you've just been watching out for me all this time, have you?"

The girl's eyes blazed with a fierce light that silenced the giant—Stahl.

"Okay," Stahl said after closing his eyes and persuading himself. Gripping the handlebars once more, he shouted, "You heard what she said, people. We're going to Grau's!"

Once she was sure the roar of their exhaust and all other signs of them had vanished, Elena glared at the ruins.

There was no sign of the traveler.

Putting one hand to the left side of her chest, the girl tried to get her breathing back under control. The weapon she had wound about her waist felt awfully unreliable. Still, Elena sent herself into the ruins with a gait that firmly planted one step after another on the paving stones.

Although she soon found the horse, D was nowhere to be seen. The ruins covered quite a large area, and there were plenty of places to hide. Having played here since childhood, Elena knew the area like her own backyard, but finding the traveler on the first try would be difficult.

"Just you wait and see. I'll show you what you get for ignoring me!"

And as she said that, the right hand that'd rested on her hip came up, a streak of black shot out and wrapped around one of the ruin's stone beams. A second later, Elena was swinging easily into the air.

From the top of the highest beam—some thirty feet up—she commanded a view of the whole ruins. But as much as she strained her eyes, all she could find was scant spots of green between the ruins and the ground below. Although she was supposed to be searching for D, Elena then turned her gaze to the west. Even before her eyes had focused on the manor, her lips twisted and her teeth ground together.

Just as her anger was approaching its peak, a voice called out behind her, "Don't even think about it."

The fact that it took Elena a full second to turn in amazement showed just how angry she was.

A metallic clatter resounded from her right hand, and out of her fist spilled a long, thin chain. With a weight the size of a small stone at one end, it was this same chain that had allowed her to swing up there.

The young man of unearthly beauty who stood behind her was met by a razor-sharp gaze.

"These ruins haven't done you any harm," said D.

"Well, I'll take it out on you, then," Elena replied as she toyed with the chain in her hand. She must've had nearly fifty feet of it wrapped around her trim waist. That wasn't the sort of thing they taught girls at finishing school.

If D hadn't come out when he did, she probably would've broken some of the beams or knocked a hole in the ceiling.

"You've been a real jerk," the girl continued. "And just to clear something up—if you think we're afraid of those lousy knights, you couldn't be more wrong."

"What do you want?" asked D.

The wind fluttered the hem of his black coat. Some of its threads were loose, and the lining was visible. The edge of the garment was badly frayed.

"To do this!" the girl cried.

A whirring flash of black ripped through the wind to coil around D's arm and torso.

"Ah!" Elena gasped, but the wind devoured her cry. Stunned, she stared at the tree branch her weapon was wrapped around. D must've had it ready all along. No doubt he'd figured out earlier what kind of weapon she carried. He still stood in exactly the same spot as before.

"You're good," Elena remarked.

Her second shot made a beeline for D's chest.

D turned one shoulder toward her and avoided the endlessly stretching links.

Behind him, the chain whipped around without slowing down at all, headed back in the opposite direction, and wrapped around D's neck.

"Sucker! That's like the first trick you learn to do with a weighted chain. Where are all your tricks now?" she asked. "Or were you just lucky last time?"

"Not really."

Elena looked all around despite herself. Because she didn't think the hoarse voice she'd just heard belonged to D.

A second later, the inky black form leapt into the air. The move was so unexpected that Elena was left without any options.

Light shot out above her head.

With a shriek, the girl extended both arms. Even given the outstanding reflexes with which she'd been blessed, the girl still found her own reaction miraculous.

Her chain stopped the steel with a *cha-chink!*

But Elena couldn't move. D held his sword with one hand. Elena, however, was using both hands. Even taking the strength difference of their respective sexes into consideration, she should've at least been able to jump out of the way. Yet she couldn't move at all, as if her body had been turned to lead.

But that wasn't entirely true, either—her hands alone continued to sink, slowly but surely.

When the edge of the chain finally touched her forehead, Elena exclaimed, "I give up!"

The way she said the words, it seemed like she was spitting up blood.

III

To be completely honest, she wasn't even sure that was going to save her. *He'll just cut me down here and now*—that was her strongest feeling. Somewhere in her heart, she thought it would be inevitable coming from that young man. And that was why she was left so stunned when the pressure she felt was gone so suddenly.

But the surprises didn't end there.

D had turned his gaze toward the manor as if he'd lost all interest in her, but she saw his right hand.

"Where's the sword!" the girl exclaimed.

It was at that point every inch of Elena's flesh rose with goose bumps. She'd seen a flash of steel, felt it strike her chain, and even heard the sound of it. Although each of these had the earmarks of a fierce blow from a skilled blade, she had to wonder if it'd all been an illusion. Could it be the blow she'd barely managed to stop, and then struggled with all her might to deflect with absolutely no success, had been nothing more than a barehanded chop?

"Is there anyone in the manor aside from the four knights?"

It was only several seconds later that the girl understood D was asking her a question. And she didn't answer until several seconds more had passed.

"I don't know. No one's been inside."

And that was all she said before she hung her head. She'd realized that if D was holding his sword, she'd never be able to stop it and would inevitably be cut in two. Then she suddenly thought of something. Looking up again with desperation on her face, she asked, "Do you want something up there? Say, could it be—you're a Vampire Hunter, aren't you?"

"Ever been outside it?" asked D.

"Sure I have. Plenty of times," Elena replied, feeling the center of her chest grow hot. In dribs and drabs, blood began to work its way through her frozen heart once more. "There are no defense systems right up to the castle walls. There used to be all kinds of stuff set up in the old days, but if there's any now they'll only be on the inside."

"How about entrances?"

"Nothing but the castle gate—I was going to say, but there's one more. Again, this was a long time ago, but when some folks from the village were preparing for guerrilla warfare, they made a hole in the wall the day before. Not long ago—maybe three days back—I was out that way and it's still there. Don't worry," she added, "it's more than big enough for you to get through. So, you going up there?"

"If you don't have any business with me, go home."

"No way. Take me with you," Elena said as she felt power surging through her body.

All her despair was banished. The young man who'd bested her like she was a mere infant was going to fight the Noble up in the manor. The mere thought of it was enough to make her body tremble with excitement.

"I've got some serious ill will toward those clowns," Elena said. "The princess, in particular. Come on, you've gotta let me help you. I take back what I said earlier. I've got no problem with you running the show."

"It takes more than ill will to destroy a Noble," D said frostily as he looked up at the sky.

Elena imagined he was calculating how long he had until sunset.

The figure in black leaned forward casually. Without a sound, he drifted down from a height of fifty feet. The way his coat spread out reminded the girl of a certain creature. It looked just like a—

As the traveler was heading for his horse, the girl called out to him, "I'm going, too!"

And with that cry Elena tightened her grip on her chain and raced after D.

Less than five minutes after leaving the ruins, Elena found herself mired in a new sense of surprise. Although her bike was supposed to be twice as fast as the average cyborg horse, she could barely keep up with the galloping rider. Since it didn't look like he was riding a custom model, the only conclusion she could draw was that it was due to his horsemanship.

276 | HIDEYUKI KIKUCHI • VAMPIRE HUNTER D

When they reached the foot of the hill, D looked back at the girl and said, "Wait here."

"Not a chance," Elena replied, shaking her head. "After all, I haven't even told you where the hole is yet. I don't care how good you are, you'll still be looking for it when the sun goes down. And once that happens, much as you may hate it, the princess will be in her element. Even if that doesn't happen, the four knights still move around by day, too. You could use all the friends you can get."

Saying nothing, D rode up to the bike and leaned over. His left hand reached out and took hold of the handlebars. A second later he let go and wheeled his horse around. He didn't lash his mount or give it the spurs; he just rode on with the reins in his hands.

"Of all the nerve," Elena spat. But as she gave the accelerator a twist, her eyes bulged in their sockets.

Her bike wouldn't budge. Although the engine was running, the transmission wasn't functioning.

"You've gotta be kidding me!" she grumbled. "I just tuned the damn thing this morning!"

Without so much as a backward glance at Elena as she wildly wrestled with the throttle, the black pair of rider and mount swiftly dwindled in the distance.

"You're gonna pay for that, buster!" Elena shouted with all the anger in her heart.

The layout of the grounds around the manor and the traps set there were things D had committed to memory.

Mazes, quicksand, flooding areas, spear-lined pits, swarms of monstrous insects—these were not the only death traps that might prove inescapable for invaders. The electronic brains that controlled everything surely maintained their constant vigil through the day, too. And even if someone made it through all of those defenses, the four knights would be waiting for him. This wasn't the sort of place anyone who valued his life would go.

D advanced in silence.

Suddenly the scenery changed. Greenery so dark it was nearly black seemed to have been utterly rooted out here, leaving the reddish brown soil exposed. Bereft of a single rock or tree or blade of grass, the tableau that stretched before him was one of relentless destruction and ruin.

Without even a moment's hesitation, D rode right through the area. Soon he heard the sound of running water growing closer. After continuing on for another five minutes, the horse and rider found their advance blocked by a powerful torrent of water.

Clear as glass, the river seemed to swerve away from the hill to the west—where the castle loomed—as it rushed along to provide water for this whole region. Further upstream—about sixty feet from the Hunter's present location—a rope bridge spanned the river. Thirty feet in the air, it stretched three times that length and ended at the base of a steep slope that led directly to the castle gate.

When he was just fifteen feet shy of the bridge, a voice that D alone heard said, "This sure is fishy." The words echoed from the vicinity of his left hand, which was wrapped around the reins. "The brush we came through earlier, this river, the bridge—they're all rigged with all kinds of traps. That's what my gut's telling me. What," the hand then exclaimed, "you've already started across it?! You just don't listen, do you?"

Yet for all the objections and dissatisfaction the voice had carried, D crossed the bridge without incident and came to a path that ran like a tunnel through rows of trees with interwoven branches. The sun was blotted out, and shadows and light began to form a vivid mosaic on the rider and his horse.

"See—it's starting already," the voice said.

At the round exit from the sheltered pathway stood a crimson horse and rider.

The air was tinged with omens of combat.

This was enemy territory—and D would be at a tremendous disadvantage. Yet the gorgeous huntsman advanced. As if that was the way he'd always gone, without hesitation or fear.

The Red Knight remained just as he was, too.

An irresistible force and an immovable object—what would happen when the two of them met? Even the leaves on the branches interlacing overhead seemed to listen intently and have their eyes wide open for that moment.

However, the Red Knight quickly stepped to one side.

D went right by him on the covered path as if it were completely natural. He didn't even glance at his formidable opponent.

"I've come to meet you and serve as your guide," the Red Knight said in a voice like grating metal after the Hunter had gone several steps past him.

"I don't need one," D replied.

"I'm afraid I can't allow that. We've known for some time now that you would come. I have orders from the princess to come meet you, but to do nothing else."

The sun was still high. Although this was the time when the Nobility should be slumbering, there were some who merely entered their coffins but remained awake.

Giving a kick to his mount's flanks, the Red Knight galloped over to D. "Regardless of your wishes," he continued, "I will serve as your guide. That is my duty to my liege."

Still facing forward, D asked, "What would you do if I came at you with my sword?"

Rarely did the Hunter pose a question like that.

"I would have no choice but to stand there and be cut down. I've not been told to fight."

Those were surprising words coming from the mouth of a knight whose ferocity was unrivaled.

"Then your lady must be quite important to you."

"Correct."

"And if you were ordered to do so, could you stand by and watch as I cut down your princess and the others?" asked D.

"In that case, I would take my own life after killing you," the Red Knight replied. "However, there's no need to worry on that account."

In a tone of unassailable confidence he continued, "If you think the princess could be killed by the likes of you—well, once you've met her, you'll understand."

Saying no more, he continued on for another five minutes, and the two of them came to the bottom of a wide slope. At the top of that nearly sixty-degree incline the manor and the walls that surrounded it were visible.

"This slope is the last line of defense," said the Red Knight.

His ordinary voice was enough to make children go pale, but now it had an even stranger ring to it. That of nostalgia.

"In times past," he continued, "we came down this to meet our foes in battle. Forces that vastly outnumbered us have pushed in this far. However, not even the mightiest of foes ever gained the top of this slope. We formed an iron wall where wave after wave of attackers broke until the enemy eventually retreated. Though that was all so very long ago."

His voice cut out. And when he quickly started speaking again, his tone had changed once more.

"What we did then and do now has always been prompted by the spirit of our princess, who defends this solitary outpost. In the world below, they are quick to speak of the end of the Nobility, but we recognize no such occurrence. We shall not allow that in the domain of our princess. For here the Nobility are still resplendent in their glory."

The crimson horse set one hoof on the steep slope. The way it climbed so easily seemed to defy the law of gravity.

After ascending roughly a hundred and fifty feet, the knight asked, "Having trouble keeping up?" But when he turned around, what he saw made his eyes go wide within his helmet.

D was less than three paces behind him.

The soil covering the slope would collapse with frightening ease—this was to prevent foes from advancing any further. Climbing it at a steady pace required equestrian skills far greater than most riders possessed.

As they sent black earth sliding downward, the pair finished their ascent of the slope and soon came to the gate. The towers that adorned all four corners of the manor, the passageways linking all the smaller buildings, and the very manor itself all had a stately air, but those who beheld this structure were bound to get a far different impression. Thousands of cracks formed spidery webs in the towering stone walls, the spires of the towers were on the point of collapse, and the masonry was riddled with little holes that gaped like vacant eye sockets. And while the crossed antennae for harnessing both the power of the wind and the electrical energy in the air continued to turn, that only served to make the rest of this place seem dead by comparison.

These were clearly ruins.

"Open the gate!" the Red Knight bellowed. His voice was so loud that it seemed like it could blast away the air before his mouth and create a vacuum. "On orders from the princess, I've brought D," he added. "Open the gate!"

Before the echoes of his voice had faded there was the sound of iron scraping iron and a black shadow dropped across them from above. Between the two of them and the gate lay a deep moat that was bone dry. And the door that barred the gate was actually a drawbridge.

While such an accessory was appropriate for a fortress, it hardly suited a manor of such simple but elegant taste. Two thick chains stretched from either side of the drawbridge to disappear into the castle.

After the bridge touched down with an earth-shaking thud, the pair crossed it and entered the castle.

A desolate sight greeted D. The front yard of the manor.

The mounds of brush and dead leaves that had accumulated called to mind the random peaks left by eroding soil. The roof of each and every bower had collapsed, and in part of the main manor all that remained were white pillars. When mercilessly exposed by the sunlight, the scene didn't have an iota of the grace the term "extinction" might imply, and the light only served to emphasize the lurid nature of the place to a spine-chilling degree.

"Don't let any of this mislead you. This is merely its daylight form," the Red Knight told the traveler as his horse advanced toward an outbuilding that was fairly undamaged by comparison. One room that D passed through seemed to have been maintained by someone, as it still retained the luxurious gold and crystal appointments from its construction long ago.

"As you are no doubt aware, you shall have to wait until night."

And with that final remark, the Red Knight headed toward the door. Then stopped in his tracks. When he spun around, D was standing right behind him.

"Why, you . . . ," the knight groaned as the most unearthly aura blasted his face—and for the first time he realized what the gorgeous young man actually was. "Only once in the past has anyone ever angered me so," said the knight. "Are you one of those, too—a Vampire Hunter?"

"Yes, I am," said D. "Where can I find the princess and everyone else?"

As D asked the question, both his arms hung idly by his sides. He didn't have a single muscle tensed. And that's what was scary. That was why he was someone to be feared.

"Do you actually think I would tell *you?*" the Red Knight finally replied with a mocking laugh. "Will you cut me down? So be it. I should love to fight you. However, my princess has ordered me not to raise a hand against you even if you take your blade to me. At the very least, you will not pass this way. D, I shall see you again in the next world."

The knight stood tall in front of the door, his chest thrown out with determination. A veritable Cerberus guarding the entrance to Hades.

"Aren't you going to run away?" asked D.

The Red Knight roared with laughter. "I don't believe I've ever even heard that expression before."

Even if it might mean his own death, he seemed intent on watching every last movement of D's blade. But as the knight's eyes were open wide, their depths reflected a sudden flash. A flash of black.

Seeing the giant lose consciousness from a thrust into the thinnest part of his armor—the gorget around his throat—D returned his sheath and the sword it still held to his back.

"My, but he was a patient fellow," a low voice said with admiration from the Hunter's left hand.

The Red Knight didn't fall. He'd lost consciousness still standing there like a wrathful temple guardian.

"Well, that's that. Mind if I ask you a question?" said the disembodied voice. "Are you gonna knock him over, or did you have something else in mind?" the voice cackled, but its laughter ended in a muffled cry.

Clenching his left hand tightly enough to nearly break his own fingers, D kicked off the floor. The hem of his coat fluttering like wings, he soared like a mystic bird to the skylight fifteen feet above him.

To be continued in

Vampire Hunter D

Volume 9
The Rose Princess

available November 2007

First came
the anime...

then the novels...

now the
MANGA!

HIDEYUKI KIKUCHI'S

Vampire Hunter D

In 12,090 A.D., a race of vampires called the Nobility have
spawned. Humanity cowers in fear, praying for a savior to rid
them of their undying nightmare. All they have to battle the
danger is a different kind of danger...

Visit the Website:
www.vampire-d.com

VOLUME 1 - ISBN# 978-1-56970-827-9 $12.95

DMP
DIGITAL MANGA
PUBLISHING

www.dmpbooks.com